TO SAVE A SAVAGE SCOT

A TIME-TRAVELER'S HIGHLAND LOVE, BOOK 2

TAMARA Gill

COPYRIGHT

ISBN: 978-0-6489050-4-2

PROLOGUE

1605 Highlands, Scotland

*B*en stormed up the stone stairs leading to his private room in the keep, the eerie quiet of the castle at odds with the clawing panic that coursed through his body. The servants looked away as he passed them, each of them not willing to meet their laird's eye. It was probably best that they did not, for at this very moment, Ben wasn't sure what he would do should he see fear, sadness...pity, even, in their gazes.

The long corridor toward his chamber was dark, the lanterns not yet lit for the evening, and he yelled out orders for the sconces to be lit. Muffled chatter sounded from behind his wife's door, along with her sweet voice that was broken with intermittent sobs.

He entered and read the room easily. The castle healer sat at the bedside, the old woman's brow furrowed in worry and compassion. The redness of Aline's eyes gave her despair away, and he joined her, pulling her tight against his chest. "What is wrong, lass?" She sobbed again, and he

1

looked to the healer for enlightenment. "Tell me what causes this distress?"

The healer sat back, folding her wrinkled hands within her lap. "The babe has been born and is now with a wet nurse. You have a son, Laird. A healthy babe who'll grow up and do you proud, I'm sure. But what we thought was a twin sibling is nothing more than a hardened mass that will never be born or heal with time."

Ben frowned, leaning back to gain Aline's attention. "What does that mean?"

"It means," the healer said, standing, "there is nothing further I can do here." The elder placed her hand gently on Aline's brow. "May God bless you, my child."

Shock tore through him at the implication of the woman's words and the finality of them. "There's no second child?" He took a calming breath, his heart too fast in his chest. The room spun, and he clasped the headboard for support. "Are ye sure?"

"Aye, I'm sure. 'Tis a miracle that you have a healthy child at all, but Lady Aline will unfortunately not recover from this birth. The birth of the boy has caused this mass to bleed—slowly—and it will not abate. I'm sorry, my laird."

Aline sobbed against his chest, and he rubbed her back, not wanting to believe the healer's words. "Leave us," he barked, watching as the woman hobbled out of the room.

"I'm going to die, aren't I? I'm too young to die." She sniffed, and tears burned behind his lids. He hated to see her like this, scared and desperate for salvation.

"The old woman is mistaken. I'll send a rider tonight to Castle Druiminn. Aedan will have Gwen come at my summons and see to ye. I know she's there visiting after the birth of Aedan and Abby's second child."

"'Twas a boy, was it not? I'm happy for them." Aline looked up at him, her beautiful face blotchy and red, either from the birthing ordeal or from crying, Ben wasn't sure. "I had hoped to give ye two strong boys, but at least we have one. I hope I've not been a disappointment to ye."

He shook his head. "You were never a disappointment to me. I know we had an odd beginning, but it's been an honor having ye as my wife. I hope I've not been a disappointment to ye, either."

Her pale hand reached out and stopped his words, her fingers cold against his lips. "You never were. 'Tis impossible for ye to be so." She slumped onto the bed. Ben studied her person and noted the ever-growing stain of red that spread upon the bedding. "I will send word straight away."

Standing, Aline reached out and grabbed his arm, shaking her head. "There is no time. Just promise me one thing, please."

Ben sat back down, taking her hand and fighting the gnawing ache opening inside his chest. "Anything, lass."

"Watch our precious lad. And as often as ye can, tell him how much I loved him. How sorry I am that I didn't get to see him grow up into the man I know he'll become. One like you: strong, capable, and kind, if not a little savage around the edges."

Her weak smile wobbled, and Ben nodded, the lump in his throat denying him the ability to speak. "Of course," he croaked out. "I'll not let a day pass without such a reminder."

"I'm so cold." The shiver that rocked her sent panic through his gut.

No!

She closed her eyes, and fear that she'd passed tore through him, followed by relief when he noted her shallow breathing. Ben lay down beside her, pulling her into the crook of his arm. Her hair smelt of roses, fresh and pretty, and he cursed the ailment that would take her life. "I have ye, lass."

"Ye always did," she said as her last breath left her body, and she stepped into the hands of the Lord.

Ben pulled her hard against him and did something he'd never done before in his life. He cried.

CHAPTER 1

Present Day, Scotland

Kenzie looked up at what was left of Castle Ross. It was hers. As of today, this massive structure, in need of a multitude of repairs, was all hers. She smiled down at the deed to the dilapidated castle.

Thanks, in part, to her own estate that she used as a bed and breakfast, and let out for weddings, and weekend cooking tutorials. Not to mention her large stable and acreage that allowed people to stable their horses for a suitable fee. After taking on Elderridge, a name her mother termed their home, Kenzie had ensured its survival by making it do what a lot of other estates were doing. She took opportunities when they came along, invested in the house, and now, thanks to her hard work, Castle Ross was hers.

In time, this too, would earn its keep. Although she was a couple of years and a lot of hard work away from such a thing.

She squealed and ran to the gate house that still stood,

after all its years of sitting on the edge of collapse. Kenzie pinched herself, unable to believe it.

Now, she just had to work with the English National Trust and have them approve all the repairs she wanted. Luckily, she wanted to keep the building exactly the same as it was when it was first built in 1435, although she was looking to add a modernized kitchen, bathrooms, and electrical work throughout.

"I cannot believe you bought this place. And I cannot believe you were allowed to."

Kenzie smiled as her oldest friend, Ann, slammed her car door shut and joined her at the gate. "I suppose you'll need help building it and bringing Castle Ross back to its past grandeur."

"Are ye offering to help me then?" Kenzie asked, smiling at Ann as she looked about the fallen walls and the tree that was well established within what was once the great hall.

"Perhaps, on weekends at least. It's not like I have a life, so I suppose I better keep my friend, who also does not have a life, company."

Kenzie laughed, wrapping her arm about Ann's shoulders and squeezing her. "Thank ye, sweetheart. I knew I could count on you."

"*Hmm,*" Ann said, walking toward the front doors of the building, which was really just remnants of the old entrance. "I gather with this new business venture that you'll not be working at Castle Druiminn for the Laird Macleod anymore. Is he happy with you branching off in this way?"

"Richard is happy for me, and I only helped out at Druiminn while I got my own business up and running. It was only a temporary thing." Kenzie walked through what was left of the front door. There wasn't much left of the place, but Kenzie had support on the way. In two months, university students studying archaeology and architectural studies were due to arrive and help her restore the castle. It was a fantastic program that allowed her free help from skilled students, which in turn, allowed them to use their abilities to restore period and historical buildings.

Not to mention, she planned on opening Castle Ross to the public for tours and hopefully, bring the castle back to its former glory so in the long run, it would pay for itself.

The castle itself wasn't overly large, certainly smaller than Druiminn castle, her ancestor's estate up near the Isle of Skye, but it was not a small dwelling either. And with the support of her cousin, the laird, she'd gained consent to purchase the castle, under strict rules that she would have to abide by in the reconstruction.

Everything she used to restore the building would have to be the exact material used during its construction. Any stone that was required to replace missing or broken stone must be hand carved, sourced from the same quarry or the closest if said quarry was no longer available. The mortar would need to be a mixture of lime, sand, and seashells, since that was what had been used, being so close to the coast as they were. Wooden beams would also need to be cut and crafted by hand; everything would be as it was, except for the modern luxuries that were approved for the inside.

It was no small task and would take months, years even, of work, but Kenzie was happy to do it, especially as she had always been fascinated with the house and the legend who had once lived within its walls.

All her life, she'd heard stories of the last laird who had lived here, the Laird of Ross, Black Ben. The painting her ancestor Gwendolyn Macleod had painted of him that hung in Druiminn Castle had made her wonder about the man all her life.

Black Ben, a devilishly handsome Scot who was famous throughout Scotland for being a brilliant swordsman and loyal to a fault, remained one of the country's biggest mysteries—his disappearance from the history books, to this day, had never been solved.

Not that anyone other than Ann was aware of Kenzie's plan, but that unknown factor of Black Ben's life would hopefully be solved.

If she were game enough to try…

"You're lucky most of the outer walls still stand. At least they can be strengthened and give you a good base to work from."

"Yes, and that most of the stones removed from the castle proper have been used in a stone fence just up the hill, which we can easily fetch and bring back, since that land was also part of my purchase. Anything else that's needed can be sourced from the local quarry, the same place the building material came from back in 1435."

"I'm so proud of you, Kenzie. I know you'll make this castle come back to life, just as you've always wanted."

Kenzie nodded, marveling at the massive step she'd taken. She walked into the old keep. The fireplace still stood, funny enough, and probably held up an outer wall, by the looks of it. She walked over to it, her hand gliding across the stone mantel, thoughts of Black Ben running through her mind.

Had he stood at this very spot, deep in thought, and touched the stone, watching the fire lick at the wood? He had been one seriously hot Scot, and she liked to imagine him here, thinking, living, drinking, and enjoying his life to the fullest, as he was rumored to have done.

"When are you heading back to Druiminn?"

"Tonight. I brought my car. Had I known you were going to turn up here and surprise me, I would've come down with you."

"Ah, well, as to that," Ann said, her voice echoing as she came out of a room that still had a partial roof, "I'm heading down to London. My mother wants me to meet her there, some appointment she's worried about going to alone."

Kenzie frowned. "Is it bad, do you think?"

Ann laughed, shaking her head. "Oh no, nothing like that. She's seeing her accountant, and no doubt she's spent too much of the allowance that father left her and he's going to tell her to rein it in."

Ann came from the States, and her father had made a fortune by investing in an internet company that was now a worldwide conglomerate. "I'm sure he's not going to tell her off at all. You tease," Kenzie said. "Come on, we better get going since we both have long drives ahead of us. I want to make it back to Druiminn before midnight."

"Are you still planning on traveling back to the time when all of this was still in its glory?" Anne asked, gesturing to the ruins.

"I am, and after being here today, it's solidified my decision. There has to be a reason all of this burned down, was destroyed. Why, after the fire of 1605, Black Ben's remains were never found, nor was he ever seen again?"

"You know, it is possible for people to be so badly burned in such fires that there isn't anything left to find. Just like the history scholars, you may never find out what happened to him."

"I'd love to solve one of Scotland's enduring mysteries, but I'm delusional, I do understand it's a long shot. But the trip will give me an opportunity to see how this castle was laid out, for the reconstruction here." Not that anyone would believe what she found out about Black Ben, but at least *she* would know the truth.

"And I can't talk you out of it? What if you never return and die in their time? Your mother will be devastated, not to mention Laird Macleod. I'm sure he doesn't wish for you to go."

Her cousin, the current Laird MacLeod, had made if perfectly clear that he didn't wish her to go back, and yet, at the end of the day, it was her choice. Her mama was aware of her plans, and she would ring her tonight and let her know she was going. Not that she planned on staying long, but at least if those she loved knew what she was doing, none of them would submit a missing persons file and have everyone asking nosy questions on her return.

"You know it's something I've wanted to do for a long time. And now that I can control my gift better, I think it's time."

Ann narrowed her eyes. "How have you controlled your gift? Have you been doing stuff that you've not told me of?"

Kenzie picked up a piece of broken pottery and cleared the dirt off the small chip. "I may have tested my ability to choose where I land when I travel. So far, it's been a success."

"Where have you been going? What times have you travelled to?"

"I've travelled to a couple of places, 1818 and the turn of the nineteenth century. During my chant I added a time and place and it worked. I landed each time exactly as I asked. So I'm assuming I can travel from anywhere to anytime should I say the words correctly."

Ann shook her head, walking toward her. "Please take care. All of your family, and me included, would hate for anything to happen to you."

"I know you would. Now come on," Kenzie said, heading toward where their cars were parked. "We better get going."

Ann sighed. "Fine," she said, giving her a hug before getting in the car, reversing on the drive, and heading south. Kenzie watched for a bit before she got in her car, the castle looming above her, the shadows of dusk making it eerie. She shivered as if someone had walked over her grave. Then she, too, started the engine.

Time to prepare to find out exactly what this old stone building was hiding.

Kenzie thought about all the things she wanted to do and see in medieval Scotland. After meeting Abby Cross and ensuring the woman traveled back to her soulmate Laird Aedan Macleod, the thought of doing the same and meeting her ancestors had almost become an obsession. Her ancestor Gwen had the gift of sight, being able to see into the future, and had picked Abby out as the best match for her brother the Laird Macleod. But when their castle had been stormed by a rival clan, Gwen had sent Abby back to her own time, and due to injuries sustained that night, Gwen had not been able to bring Abby back.

Poor Abby had been devastated, thinking that she'd be separated forever from the Laird Macleod. Abby had gone back to Druiminn Castle, heartbroken and resolved to leave the love of her life behind in history. But what Abby hadn't known was that Kenzie held the same ability as her ancestor and could send her back to seventeenth century Scotland. And that's exactly what she had done.

To be able to manipulate time was a gift she wasn't afraid to use, especially if it meant two souls, born in different times, were reunited.

Her great great great grandmother—too many greats to count—was the sole reason she had the ability to time travel. Her ancestor's gift had been passed on through the female blood line. Of course, not everything had been inherited; while Kenzie could time travel, she didn't have ability to see into the future like Gwen, nor was she very good at helping people if they were injured. But she could read people well and knew to trust her instincts when it came to reading the character of people she'd just met.

There were stories about Gwendolyn Macleod that her mother used to tell, of the woman's passion for life and family, a great healer and possibly even a witch. How she'd risked her life numerous times to save those she'd loved. Kenzie had grown up thinking the woman was Scotland's very own Joan of Arc, although that was probably a little fanciful.

Soon, the gates to her home loomed out of the darkness, and turning down a small drive, Kenzie pulled up in front of the house. Lights blazed inside, and she was thankful the house had guests so that she wasn't coming home to an empty home. Mrs. Gibbs, her cook, would no doubt be watching TV in the private living room. She'd been part of the family for as long as Kenzie could remember and looked after the guests very well while she was away.

Coming into the foyer, she shouted out hello to Mrs. Gibbs who shouted back that her dinner was in the oven. "Thank you," she said, heading toward the kitchen.

Tomorrow, as planned, Mrs. Gibbs was taking a well-earned holiday. The guests would check out before ten o'clock, and with her mama in London, Kenzie would be free to go back to the year 1605.

She spooned the leek and potato soup into her mouth and daydreamed about medieval Scotland. What she would see and do. What would Gwendolyn think of her arrival? Shock, concern, or happiness? Kenzie would soon find out.

~

The following evening, alone in the house, Kenzie went to the library, over to an old tome that had all of her ancestor's recipes for different ailments. The leather-bound book all but vibrated with history, and although Kenzie didn't need to be anywhere specific to travel back to the seventeenth century, it seemed only right that she was near what was once her ancestor's.

She collected the bags she'd packed a few days before, and she checked that everything that she needed for the trip was in them. She hadn't left a stone unturned in planning this journey. Kenzie had scoured Scotland for clothing that would suit the early seventeenth century. The shoes were the only items that she'd struggled with and, finally, had gone with ankle high boots and a few slip-on shoes that resembled slippers, but were sturdier. No one would be looking at her feet in any case.

The gown she wore today was a beautiful piece of clothing, with its elbow length sleeves and corseted waist. It truly was a dress reminiscent of a time long gone. She'd hired a seamstress to make three of the gowns, and the brilliant woman had sewn the corset into the gown, eliminating the need for others to help her dress. It was a perfect solution for someone not of the time period.

Her hair already up in a messy bun, she wrapped a woolen shawl about her shoulders and deemed herself ready enough for the seventeenth century.

"Right then." Kenzie picked up her bags, and taking a deep breath, she started to chant the Gaelic words that would take her back in time. The room spun, slow at first, before gaining speed to the point where her stomach churned. Voices and sounds shouted out around her, the layers of time that separated past and present thinned and allowed the past to intersect with the future.

Kenzie focused on the time and place that her ancestor Gwen MacLeod had lived in 1605 and ignored all the distractions until time morphed into alternate angles, before Kenzie collapsed on the ground and everything went black.

CHAPTER 2

*B*lack Ben, formally known as the Laird of Ross, woke up in a tangle of blankets and straw. The pounding in his head caused vomit to rise in his throat, and he grappled for the cup beside the bed for relief. As the burning liquid of whisky slid down his throat, his body heaved and he cast up his innards onto the floor, ignoring the loathing he had for himself being in such a state.

Ben flopped back onto the pillow, some of the straw filling prickling the back of his head. One thing he hated about being away from home was the comforts of his bed, the soft linen and feathered mattress. Nothing like the hard boards that came up to greet his back, or the bugs that fed on his person at night—enough to make a man scratch his skin off.

He rolled over and groaned as the movement churned his stomach once again. Perhaps he would partake less of the fine ale and Scottish whisky tonight and concentrate on the pleasurable flesh about the place instead. Waking up in this condition would not do.

The sun moved out from beneath some clouds, and the

room lightened considerably. Ben flung his arm over his eyes, not wanting another part of his body to hurt. Everything below his neckline was hurting enough.

The sound of the inn's door slamming ricocheted through his brain, and he made a note to speak to the publican about his rowdy guests. As the Laird of Ross, his comfort while staying here should be the owner's priority.

How long he lay there, the smell of vomit permeating the air, Ben couldn't say, but as night fell, and his stomach finally stopped protesting its abuse, he gathered his things, threw some chilling water onto his face, and made his way downstairs for a liquid dinner. Damn the food, he needed a drink.

Shouts of welcome abounded as he made the dining room. The smoky peat fire burning bright in the corner of the room gave the ambiance of comfort and warmth, when in reality, the lodge, situated at the foot of the Waternish peninsula, was anything but homey. A whorehouse in the middle of nowhere would be a better term.

"The usual, Laird?" the barmaid said, her teasing grin ruined only when she smiled, and the full extent of her rotten teeth appeared. But then, he didn't have to kiss her.

"Aye, lass. Ye know me well."

She winked and poured him a good cup of the golden liquid. "I'm more than willin' to know ye better. Just say the word, Laird, and I'm all yours."

Ben smiled, liking the lass even more. "I'll hold ye to ye words, lass, so ye better mean them."

"I do," she said, moving away to serve another patron.

Ben looked about the room and caught sight of himself in a mirror just beside the dining room door. His shoulder-length hair was matted, dirty, and in need of a good wash. Well, perhaps tomorrow he'd go down to the shore and bathe. He could, of course, send for warm water here, but the cooling ocean was more appealing. The inn's water was dirtier than himself.

Ben downed a few more whiskys and ate a bowl of stew for good measure. He nearly choked on his mouthful when a hand came down hard on his back, sending him forward in his chair. "Aye, I thought it was ye, Laird of Ross. What brings ye into Macleod land?"

Ben stood. "Braxton, lad. 'Tis been a long time."

The man laughed and then frowned. "Aye, too long. 'Tis good to see ye. And Gwen will be happy to see ye as well. She's outside, probably demanding all sorts of things from the publican's wife. We don't normally stay here, but Gwen couldn't stand a minute more in the carriage and asked to stop for the night."

Damn. Ben clenched his jaw, not wanting to see a happily married couple, and certainly not his best friends' sister whom he'd liked more than he ought as a young lad. "Aye, I can see Gwen, lass doing such a thing."

Braxton sat beside him, smiling politely to the barmaid when she asked what he'd like.

Ben frowned at the lass when she used the same beguiling tone on Braxton that she'd used on him. When Braxton ordered a lager and didn't react to the wench's flirtation, she slammed the drink down and walked off in a decided huff. Ben grinned.

"How are ye, Laird? You seem well, other than the bloodshot eyes or the fact that ye stink of vomit." Braxton flicked at Ben's tunic. "Ye have a great dollop of it still on ye clothes." Braxton took a sip of his beer, his eyes contemplative.

"Och, I may have drunk more than I ought the previous evening, but that's not up for discussion and neither are my clothes. What is, though," he said, sitting back down, "is what are ye all doing traveling about? I would've thought Gwen would be at Castle Druiminn looking after Abby and the new bairn."

"Aedan has gifted me and Gwen land and a larger estate not far from their own. We inspected the property a few months past and will occupy the place from tomorrow. It'll do us nicely, I believe. Be a safe and happy place for our bairns."

Ben finished off his drink as the thought of Aline flittered through his mind. Of how excited she'd been upon first seeing his estate. It was nice that she'd been pleased with what she'd settled for. If anything, at least he'd given her a good home with an abundance of servants.

"I'm happy for ye, Braxton, as I'm sure Gwen is, too, being so close to Aedan and Abby once again. Are the bairns with ye, then?"

"Aye, she is and yes, they are, although they've probably gone running down to the beach with Nurse," he said, turning as the door opened. "And here's Gwen now."

Ben met Gwen's gaze and smiled, standing to pull the lass into his arms. Holding her was like he'd stepped back through the doors of his keep. Home. "How are ye, Gwen, lass? You're looking as pretty as Bell Heather in full bloom."

She laughed, patting his cheek as she took in his attire, not liking what she saw if the frown between her perfectly arched brows were any indication. "Very well, looking forward to settling at our new estate and making it a home. I'm getting too old to be going here and there about the country. My poor, old bones cannot stand the jarring."

Ben laughed, an odd sound since he'd not heard it for an age. "Old bones? I think ye're a little too young to be talking of such things, but I have to agree, the roads about here are rough enough to break one's back on a horse."

Gwen gestured to the publican. "Please have someone tend the horses, and I've ordered some clean hot water, so if ye could have it carried up to our rooms, I'll be thankful." Gwen turned to him. "Are ye on your way to see Aedan and Abby? I know they'd only be too happy to see ye again. It's been more than two years since ye visited us last."

"A lot has happened since then, and I'm content to stay where I am at present. Mayhap I'll travel over and see ye all, but I can't promise ye anything."

"Well, when you're able, the door is always open." Gwen's gaze turned serious, and Ben armed himself for what was coming next. It was the same forlorn look everyone got when they wished to bring up old wounds. "I was sorry to hear about Aline. I know I didn't get along with her very well, but I never wished her ill. How is your son? Aedan told me he survived the birth."

Warmth threaded through Ben's veins at the thought of his child, even if guilt soon followed due to his abandonment. He told himself it had been necessary—to get away from his holdings, the people who looked at him with pity and concern. He couldn't stand a second more of it. Life was for the living, and there had been a time when he'd travel about for months, enjoying his homeland and the merry lasses who occupied it.

He was a selfish bastard, mayhap, unforgivable even, but he wasn't ready to return to Castle Ross, to be a father or a laird. He needed to mourn. To eradicate the guilt that had plagued him every day since he'd handfasted with Aline.

Aye, he'd married the lass to ensure his friend Laird

Macleod could marry his soulmate, but in the two years that they were married, Aline had grown more and more unhappy by the day. As much as he'd cared for her, given her his body, and lathered her in affection, he'd not loved her. Ben had hoped, in time, that the elusive emotion would blast upon him and he'd feel some such toward the lass, but it had never happened. Now, he doubted he was capable of such feelings. And it was only right, for Aline had never loved him either.

"The babe is doing well and in the safe hands of his wet nurse. He's not wanting for anything while I'm away."

"And how long might that be?"

Ben chose to ignore the slight censure he could hear in Gwen's voice. Only certain battles would he choose to fight with her, and it was not often he won against Gwendolyn Macleod. "Dinna fret lass. As the Laird of Ross, I will return." His tone brooked no argument, and Gwen seemed to understand his meaning.

She scoffed and dusted down her gown, wrapping her arm about her husband's. "Come, we need to get the children inside so they rest before dinner." Gwen turned before they left the bar. "Will ye join us for a meal? It looks like you could use a good feeding."

"Another time mayhap, lass," he said, waving his cup at the barmaid for a refill.

Gwen shook her head. "Please yourself, but the invitation is there should ye change your mind."

"Aye." Ben watched them go, glad the lass he had once favored was happy and settled. He took a sip of whisky, finishing off his drink and admitted that as much as he'd fancied Gwen, a woman he liked and respected above any other, he'd not felt the elusive emotion of love for her either. He'd desired her yes, but love? No.

CHAPTER 3

Kenzie marveled at the stone home that looked so different from the one she'd inherited only a few years ago. Her ancestor's home had changed quite a bit in the past four hundred years. Before her stood a square keep with a little circular turret that went from ground height past the roof. The house, in its original state, was quite nicer looking without the many alterations and additions that had happened to it over the centuries. It looked welcoming and homey, whereas in the twenty-first century, it looked like a monolith that had something of each era imprinted upon it.

Knocking on the door, Kenzie checked her gown and pulled her woolen shawl tighter as a chilling wind blew up from the coast. She'd woken on the shore in front of the house and had dusted herself off, happy to see her bags had joined her on the beach.

No sound came from inside, and she stepped down the couple of stairs at the entrance to look about the yard. It, too, seemed deserted. She pursed her lips, puzzled. Had she landed in the wrong time? Made a mistake as to where her ancestor was supposed to be in 1605? Her stomach churned before the sound of a carriage caught her attention, and she stood to the side of the door, waiting and hoping beyond hope that it wasn't a sword-wielding barbarian looking for someone to kill. Namely her.

A cart carrying an array of furniture and trunks passed her by and went around the back of the house before a carriage came into view, along with a group of riders. Kenzie swallowed her nerves, having had no way of informing her ancestor of her arrival. She wasn't sure how Gwen would take her visit. She hoped it would be welcoming, but then, they were strangers when all was told, and she'd yet to see the woman's face that she knew as well as her own—from the portraits that hung of her in Castle Druiminn and this very house behind her.

The carriage rocked to a halt, and a woman, much shorter than herself, stepped out, stretched her back, and mumbled her relief at being out of the vehicle. A horde of children followed, all squealing and running off toward the gardens, not paying the least mind to their visitor.

Not sure if she should curtsy or speak, Kenzie waited to see what Gwen's reaction would be. To be so patient and quiet wasn't easy for her. As a woman who ran her own estate as a profitable business, she wasn't used to not speaking out.

"Gwendolyn Macleod?" she said at last, finally catching the woman's attention.

"Aye." Her ancestor walked toward her, and Kenzie realized she was quite possibly the most beautiful woman she'd ever met. Fiery red hair and intelligent, deep green eyes took her measure, before Gwen grinned. "I have a feeling I should know ye, lass. Is that right?"

Kenzie nodded. "Yes, that's right. I'm Kenzie Jacobs of

Clan Macleod, and I'm your granddaughter, many times removed."

Gwen closed the space between them, clasping Kenzie's cheeks, taking in her every feature. "Aye, I know in my blood ye are who you say. Oh, my dear, dear child," she said, taking Kenzie into her arms. "Is everything well? Why are ye gifting me with such a visit?"

"Do not fear, all is well, but I wanted to see you, meet ye." She went willingly into Gwen's arms once more and only looked up when a man of similar age walked up to them, a curious look on his face.

"And who's our guest that ye're so fond of, Gwen, lass? I don't think I've ever met this young lady before."

Gwen laughed, going to the man and wrapping her arm about his own. "Come inside, Braxton, for it is the best of news, but we should not discuss it here."

Kenzie followed them inside and noted the large wooden staircase that threaded up to the second floor. Large animal heads graced the wall, most of which were no longer hanging in the home due to the fact her mother hated taxidermy and the killing of innocent animals for the pleasure of men.

But in this time, it suited the home, along with the iron chandelier and large rectangular table that sat in the foyer with nothing other than a vase of native flowers to cheer up the room.

Gwen clasped Kenzie's hand and pulled her into an adjoining room, ordering mead and bread from a waiting servant before shutting the door. Gwen seemed to prepare herself for her speech before taking Kenzie's hand and squeezing it kindly.

"Braxton, my love, this is Kenzie Jacobs Macleod, and I do believe she's our descendant."

Braxton's smiled dissipated, and Kenzie hoped she'd not disappointed him with her visit. She only wanted to bring joy to them all, not to be a burden or a cause of trouble.

"Our descendant," he repeated, frowning. "How so?"

Gwen gestured for her to explain. Kenzie clasped her hands to stop them from shaking. "I'm your great great, many times over, granddaughter. My family line comes from your daughter Madeline." She shrugged. "And so, here I am."

"Yes, here ye are." Gwen pulled her into another hug. "How wonderful to hear that wee Madeline's line thrives to the your time."

Kenzie nodded, knowing that such knowledge would be welcome for a parent. To know their children survived long enough to have a marriage and bairns of their own. "From what I know of the family tree and from reading letters and journals—all the marriages in my line were happy ones, barring my own mother's, but I'll tell you about that another time."

A light knock sounded on the door, and Gwen bade the servant enter. The young lass in a grey, heavy skirt came into the room, her shirt tied up right to her neck and her hair tied back in a simple knot. She looked at Kenzie with large brown eyes, taking in everything, before walking out and closing the door behind her.

"I fear you'll be a curiosity for the next few weeks until the staff get to know ye. Ye are staying for a few weeks, are ye not?"

"I hope to if you'll have me."

Braxton laughed. "If we'll have ye? Of course, we'll have ye," he said, finally closing the distance between them and hugging her soundly. "I can see my mama in yer eyes. 'Tis extraordinary."

"I look like your mother?" Kenzie's eyes smarted. "That's so lovely to hear."

"But ye sound slightly English for a Scottish lass. Why is that?"

Gwen ushered her to a chair, and they all sat while Gwen poured her a cup of mead.

"Mama divorced Papa; the marriage was anything but a love match. They hated each other in the end, and because Father refused to leave the estate, Mama took me to England and raised me in London. Mama is still in London, but Father passed away last year."

Braxton made what sounded like a growl.

"Life happens, people make mistakes, but I didn't come here to make you upset. I came to meet ye. And, I gather, from seeing a little girl race off toward the beach and a woman madly chasing after her, that was Madeline? Can I ask who the other children are?"

Gwen laughed, her eyes lighting up with the mention of her babe. "Aye, Madeline is the most precious doll. She's almost two now, and no doubt, she's busy with Nurse collecting shells. The other children you saw are the Nurse's babes. She's a widower ye see, and while caring for Madeline, she's also able to care for and educate her own."

"She sounds adorable, and in my time, there's a painting that hangs in this very room, of her as a young lady. I do believe I should warn you she's a beauty, and very much sought after, if history has any truth in it."

Braxton growled again, and Gwen beamed. "It's so lovely to hear that. Although, by the reaction of Braxton here, he wishes her to grow into a haggard, old woman. "You do realize, my love, that children grow up and marry their own loves. As will Madeline, and eventually, as will our Kenzie."

Kenzie shook her head. "I'm never marrying. Ever."

Gwen frowned. "But ye must. How will ye have children and ensure the estate stays in the family for generations to come?"

Kenzie could think of a few ways that would be possible. "That is a conversation for another day. For now, let us just enjoy each other, but there is probably one thing we must discuss before my stay here goes any further."

"Of course, what is it, my dear?"

"What do you wish for me to call you? Somehow, I don't believe grandmamma or grandpapa would be suitable."

Braxton came and sat on the table, laughter in his gaze. "I think Braxton and Gwen would suit just fine, and we shall call you Kenzie. A distant relative of Gwen's will suffice and allow the staff not to be suspicious of ye. What say you?"

"I say, yes." Kenzie took in their features and could see a resemblance to herself in Gwen's high cheekbones and full lips.

Gwen ran a hand over her cheek almost as if Kenzie's own thoughts brought forth the action. "How old are ye, Kenzie? If ye don't mind me asking."

"I just turned twenty-five last month." Braxton's burst of laughter startled her. "What is it?" she asked, not sure why her age was so amusing.

"You're older than we are now," Braxton said, his smile warm and full of mirth.

"Ye are, lass. We're not far off ye in age, but certainly not yet twenty-five." Gwen smiled, before pulling her to stand. "Now come, my dear. I want to show ye to your room and get ye settled. Would you like a bath brought up before we sup tonight? Even though we're only moving in today, some staff have been here for a week or more, and we're perfectly able to attend to any wish ye may have."

The thought of a bath seemed heavenly, and Kenzie was tired after her travel. "I would love one, if it's not too much trouble."

"'Tis no trouble at all, lass."

They walked from the room and headed up the familiar staircase. To know that her ancestor really had lived in and enjoyed a house that she now called her own was truly an amazing, wonderful thing. So many great memories, of family, children, births, and unfortunately, even deaths had happened under this roof. *Life can't get much better than it is now.*

Her room was inlaid with the same dark wood that the staircase was made of, and funny enough, it was the room Kenzie had used as a child, before her mother had packed them up and left for London.

Kenzie pulled out the few gowns she'd brought with her and hung them in the armoire before looking out the window, watching as day gave way to late afternoon. Gwen fussed about her room, making sure the maids understood their duties to her new guest and ensuring the bath and linens were brought up promptly. Kenzie smiled at Gwen's fretting like an old mother hen about her chick.

"There we are, dear. I think the water is at the right temperature now."

"Thank you, Gwen," Kenzie said, sitting down and pulling off her shoes. "And thank you so much for making me welcome. I wasn't sure how you'd take my arrival here. I'm so happy that you approve."

"Well..." Gwen went to the dressing table and picked

up a ribbon, coming over and tying Kenzie's hair back to keep it from getting wet. "I canna lie, it does make me a little nervous that you're here. This time is hard, and I certainly don't want anything happening to ye, but it also fills my heart with joy, knowing my children, my lineage, survives through the next few centuries, right up to yer own time."

Kenzie could see how such knowledge would be pleasing for someone who'd otherwise never know. "Do you think it's possible for me to visit with Abby Cross, your brother's wife? I should so like to see her again."

"Oh aye, we're due to travel there in a few weeks for the christening of their new bairn. I know Abby was so thankful to ye, and so I have no qualms with them seeing ye. And I would also think Aedan would love to thank the lass who secured his future happiness."

"I'm glad to hear it."

Gwen sighed. "Well, I'll leave ye for now to have ye bath. Come downstairs when you're ready, and we'll have supper."

Kenzie watched her go, grateful that Gwen was so loving. She looked around the room, the animal furs on her bed, the roaring fire next to the small wooden tub. She undressed quickly, wondering if, when they traveled to Druiminn Castle, the Laird of Ross would also be there to congratulate the couple on their new baby. Needing the ladies room, Kenzie looked behind the screen in the corner of her room. She had hoped against hope for a lovely flushable toilet, but no, there was none. Instead, a pretty pink bowl sat on the floor. How was she going to squat over that? There was also no sign of toilet paper either, merely some torn up pieces of cloth. Lovely...

Thankfully, she could bathe after relieving herself.

Kenzie lowered herself into the tub, hoping the Laird of Ross would show his face at some point. She was in the seventeenth century after all, to see the man and possibly find out how and why he had disappeared without a trace.

Kenzie soaped her arms, liking the smell of lemon and trying to ignore the small amount of guilt that pressed on her conscience about not being totally honest with Gwen as to why she was here. It was probably best they didn't know, for they'd probably try and keep her from meeting Black Ben, and then she'd never learn the truth behind the old Scottish mystery.

This was going to be a great trip. One she'd never forget.

~

*K*enzie sat up in bed with a start at the sound of loud banging coming from below stairs. She fumbled about on her bed, trying to find the shawl that Gwen had given her to use and toppled off the bed when she reached into nothing but thin air.

Feeling her way toward the windows, she pulled the thick, heavy drapes aside, allowing the glow of the moon to light the room. The fire had long burned down to nothing but embers, and she tiptoed toward the door, hoping the house wasn't under attack by some thieving, barbaric Scots.

She opened up the door a slither, the sound of swords being drawn and whispers from the men below stairs making her pause. What was going on? Were they under attack? The pit of her stomach clenched, and Kenzie thought she might be sick. Gwen rushed past her, most decidedly rumpled, and looked over the balustrade, her long, red hair hanging down her back. She stayed frozen on the spot as the men downstairs opened the door and shouts rang out.

Gwen gasped and raced downstairs, and when she heard Gwen tell her men to lay down their weapons, Kenzie tiptoed to the banister and looked to see who was at the door.

Kenzie stifled a gasp of her own at viewing the man below. He was filthy and looked like he'd not bathed in weeks, not to mention…was that vomit on his shirt? Dark locks limply hung over his eyes, as dark as a Spaniard's but clumping together due to its lack of wash. His cheekbones were sharp, his jaw strong and covered in dark facial hair.

Eww.

Braxton hoisted the man's limp body from the front step of the door after he collapsed and carried him into the room where they'd earlier had bread and mead. Kenzie noted the guards dispersed after checking outside, some staying outdoors while others headed to their quarters near the rear of the house.

Wanting to help in any way she could, even if she could catch lice from the dirty fellow, Kenzie headed downstairs to join her ancestors.

She found them both huddled over the stranger, Gwen's brow furrowed in worry. Kenzie studied the man as she came closer. He didn't look like any of her ancestors she'd seen in portraits and yet, she had the oddest feeling she'd seen him before.

Gwen called for cooling water and cloths, along with the request that a servant head below stairs to light the candles in her healer's room. The man lay, without speaking, on the settee, every now and then moaning, coughing, and looking as if he had some sort of flu or pneumonia. Either way, he seemed very ill.

"What do you think is wrong with him?" Kenzie asked, coming a little closer.

"I'm not sure as yet, lass," Gwen said, before thanking the maid as they brought in what she'd asked for. Gwen started to pat down his brow, cleaning away what looked like days of grime, sweat, and dried vomit. Yes, it was definitely vomit that soaked his shirt and parts of his chin. "He's got the ague and is no very well at all." She pushed the man's hair back, long locks that were as dark as night itself. Kenzie's mouth turned up at the sight of him up close.

The word *eww* again reverberated around in her brain.

"I must make up a tisane. I'll be back forthwith." Gwen met Kenzie's gaze. "Come sit by Ben, and keep the cooling cloth on his brow. 'Twill help until I can give him some wormwood and mint elixir. If that doesn't work, I'll try some horehound syrup to bring down his fever."

Ben… Could it be? "Gwen, this isn't the Laird of Ross, is it? Also known as Black Ben?"

Gwen nodded as she strode toward the door. "Aye, the very same. His correct name is Abhainn, Laird of Ross, but Ben to his friends. I'll be back right quick."

"Of course." Kenzie did as she was told. The laird was even more intimidating than he was at a distance or in any painting she'd ever beheld. Braxton looked in on her, and seeing all was well, left as soon as he arrived. Through the open doors, Kenzie could hear the men talking outside, a whisper of words all about the man lying unresponsive before her.

"Do not worry, sir, I'm sure you'll be feeling a lot better soon enough." Kenzie wiped his brow, bringing the cloth down his cheek and wiping away what was left of his vomit. "And with Gwen looking after you, a wonderful healer, I might add, you'll be up and walking before you know it."

He rasped something, and Kenzie leaned close to hear what he was saying. A putrid odor, more awful than she'd ever smelled before, wafted from his skin, and she pulled back, gasping for air. It was rude of her, but thankfully, the man was so out of his mind that he did not notice her reaction to his stench.

For that was exactly what it was, a smell that reminded her of sweat that was weeks old, along with teeth that were not much better. It was no wonder the man had caught some disease. If not from someone else, the air that hung about his head was enough to make anyone ill.

Kenzie wiped his chiseled cheek. Under all his filth, the laird was attractive, and should he eat a few meals, would probably look even more so, but now he looked like nothing but a drunk who'd made himself sick by lack of respect for himself. What had made him do this? He certainly didn't resemble the man she'd seen in paintings—a tall, athletic, virile laird of his time.

"Did you wish for a drink, sir?" she asked, noting for the first time his eyes were open a little, showing off orbs that were nearly as dark as his hair.

"Aye. Whisky."

She snorted, and he frowned a little. No way in hell was she going to give in to his request and supply him with more alcohol.

"Drink," he repeated, and she poured a cup of ale from the pitcher on the table. Holding the cup to his lips, she helped him sit up a little as he had a small sip.

He swore, sputtered out the ale, and knocked the cup

out of her hand. Kenzie stood as the man sat up, no longer so faint, but fully awake.

"What are ye trying to do, woman? Kill me? What was that vile concoction ye thought to give me?"

Kenzie picked up the cup, meeting his glare with one of her own. "Well, it's the funniest thing, but I do believe it's called beer. And even more fascinating, you should drink it, instead of the muck you've obviously been imbibing the past few days. Water would be better, but there doesn't seem to be any on hand here."

One brow rose before his eyes narrowed, pinning her to her spot. Kenzie swallowed, reminded herself that Gwen cared for this man in some small way, and surely, since she was a friend of the family, he'd not hurt her. She had nothing to fear. Nothing at all, and yet, her nerves kept jumping each time he moved or spoke. She had no idea why.

He sank back down on the settee, his burst of energy seemingly short-lived. "Who are ye? I've never see ye afore."

Kenzie sat down on the chair once again, and rinsing the cloth, placed it on the Scotsman's forehead. "I'm a distant relative of Gwen and Braxton's."

His contemplative gaze raked over her form, and she shivered. What was it about this man that made her react in such a way? For a start, he stank, seemed to be an alcoholic, and was nosy, to boot.

Dismissing her stupid reaction, Kenzie concentrated on rubbing the cloth over his temples and working her way down his neck. The scattering of hair peeking through the top of his shirt gave her pause, and she wondered if he was overly hairy or just a little as she preferred. No one wanted to sleep with a bear, after all.

"A relative of both of theirs, eh?" He groaned and rolled to his side, forcing her off the chair. "A bucket. Quickly, lass."

"Oh my God, seriously?" Kenzie looked about the room, and spying a peat bucket beside the fire, she tipped the little bricks of peat onto the ground and raced back to his side.

Great heaving and the sound of a lot of whisky coming up filled the room for the next few minutes, along with a smell that Kenzie never wanted to experience again. Rinsing the cloth, she passed it to him when he seemed to be finished and watched as he wiped his mouth and chin.

"You're very pretty lass, and very similar to my Gwen."

The word 'my' wasn't lost on her, nor did she like hearing it. "Gwen isn't yours, sir. And I don't care if you find me pretty or I remind you of Gwen. You, sir, are a sickly drunk who doesn't have any respect for his own wellbeing."

It was his turn to look stunned. "Sickly drunk? I've been called a lot of things in my life, but those two terms have never been two of them. Perhaps you ought——"

Kenzie held up her hand. "I don't want to 'ought' anything. All I wish is to get you better so you may leave and get on with ruining your own life, which, if your appearance here this evening is any indication, you're quite on the road to doing. Laird indeed…"

The door opened, and Gwen walked into the room, a small bowl and spoon in her hand. "Ay, Ben, you're awake." She sat beside him, and Kenzie noted the subtle change in the man, a slight relaxing of muscles, his brow eased of tension, the glitter of triumph in his eyes when he caught Kenzie staring at him.

What a dick.

"The Laird of Ross, hey, Gwen?" Kenzie said, not bothering to hide her distaste.

"Aye, the very one. Although most folks like to call him Black Ben."

What a waste... Disappointment stabbed at her. *This* was one of the most ferocious warriors Scotland had ever seen? *This* stinky drunk ass who seemed to think her married ancestor was his? *He* was who she had wanted to try and change history for? Or, at least, find out how and why he'd disappeared without a trace?

"I wish I could say it was a pleasure to meet you, Laird Ross, but well, it's not." Kenzie caught Gwen's gaze and said, "He vomited in your peat bucket, just so you know."

Ben took a cup of ale that Gwen held out to him and without a word of complaint, sipped. "'Tis no trouble, I would like to stay for a time." He turned a beguiling gaze onto Gwen, and she was pleased to see that, although Gwen looked at him with kindness, there was no affection other than a platonic one. "I'm sorry I've arrived so unwell, lass, but after ye invited me to visit, I could not return to Castle Ross without seeing ye all one last time. I'm not sure when I'll be back in this part of Scotland again."

"Of course, ye're more than welcome to stay, and Braxton has ordered the staff to ready a room for ye, and a bath, which should help with bringing down ye fever. But my rule is that you're to stay in bed until I say otherwise."

The man took Gwen's hand and kissed it. "Och, lass, ye've always been so kind to me. What a shame it is that ye didn't marry me instead of Braxton. I could've had such caring from ye for all of my days."

"Were you engaged to him?" Kenzie amended her accusing tone. "I apologize, it's just, he's so, so…"

"Sickly and drunk, I believe ye said." The rascal threw her a smile that bordered on sexy, and it was certainly triumphant. Kenzie ground her teeth, hating that her body reacted the opposite of how it should in front of such a womanizing jerk.

"Kenzie, tell me you didn't call Ben such names. That's not how we speak to any of our guests."

Chastised, Kenzie bit her tongue, wanting to retort that she'd speak to the drunk in any way she wished. After reacting to ale as if she was feeding the man the devil's drink, what kind of person was he? A simpleton? An ass? The latter seemed to suit him more.

"Kenzie, is it? Weel, what a sweet name for such a pretty lass."

"That's enough talking from ye." Gwen threw a warning glance at the laird and pulled Kenzie to the side of the room. "What's the matter, lass. Do ye not like the laird?"

"I don't believe there's anything wrong with him other than he's drunk, has had no food, and is in need of a good wash and sleep. And as soon as he opened his eyes when you were making his medicine, he was stating how pretty I was and how you were 'his Gwen.'"

Understanding dawned in Gwen's gaze, and she chuckled. "Kenzie, I will admit there was a time that Black Ben courted me, but I never loved him, and I never would have married him, even if he wished it. And he is married to another."

"Is? He's married still? I thought..." Why this revelation made the air in her lungs expel, Kenzie didn't know, nor did she wish to analyze it, certainly not now with him looking at her again, taking in her every detail and probably making an inventory of her failings.

Gwen shook her head. "No, let me rephrase that. He was married. Aline, his wife, died after the birth of their first child, only a few months ago. The babe is fine, but I think Ben is suffering from the loss of her. We need to be kind and understanding. Please try, my dear. Once ye get to know the laird, you'll find he really is a lot of fun and quite charming in his own way."

Kenzie studied him again. Maybe she had been too harsh in judging the guy. It wouldn't be easy losing the one you loved and having a child to raise on your own. She sighed, her annoyance lessening a little.

"Fine. I'll be civil, but if he annoys me in any way, doesn't show respect to you or your marriage to Braxton, you must give me leave to remind him of his honor as a gentleman. If he has any, that is." Which Kenzie highly doubted.

"He's not a threat to me or Braxton if that is ye concern."

The man himself cleared his throat. "Excuse me, I can hear ye, and by the way, now that the both of ye are side by side, I can't help but notice—the similarities are striking." He paused, tipping his head to the side. "Gwen, lass, you've not been playing about with ye spells again, have ye?"

Kenzie gasped, meeting Ben's gaze. Did he know of their "gifts"? And what would he do with such knowledge?

"Nay, you know I cannot since I lost my abilities after the fire, but I cannot say the same for my relatives in the future." Gwen walked to the door and summoned a servant. "Kenzie, please explain as best ye can to Ben, while I organize what's required to attend him."

Kenzie watched her ancestor leave her alone with the smelly male and turned to catch him studying her intently. She narrowed her eyes. "If you must know, and since it seems Gwen trusts you, I'll tell you exactly who I am."

He crossed his arms over his chest. "Aye, very good, lass, but first, do ye think ye could put a woolen throw over my legs. I'm a wee bit cold."

She sighed, but did as he asked, all the while thinking that the blanket would be ruined after being placed on such dirty trousers. Not that she wanted to be so anal about things. Normally, she didn't have a problem helping someone in need, but there was something about this man, something that instantly put her on guard, that she didn't trust. "Anything else, your highness?"

He chuckled and commenced coughing, as if his lungs would soon spill out into the sick bucket. Instinctively, she touched his brow and found it overly warm, and she wondered if he was sicker than she thought.

"Ale," he rasped. Kenzie did as he asked and sat on a chair nearby, waiting for him to catch his breath. "Are you okay? Do you want me to get Gwen again?"

"Nay, lass. I'll be well in a few days." He paused, taking some steadying breaths. "Now, tell me from where ye come."

Kenzie thought about how to go about telling someone such a thing and then decided to jump straight in. "I'm Gwen and Braxton's descendant from the future. I've come back to see them."

"Aye, makes sense, since ye look so familiar, but tell me, lass, what brings ye to our time. 'Tis not an easy era to be visiting."

Kenzie didn't disagree, but then, if she wanted to visit the matriarch of the family, this was the only time she could. Not to mention, she'd had a fascination with history, and the man before her, since forever. Not that she'd be telling *him* any of that.

"Your time is quite different to mine, of course, but I've become fascinated in particularly with this time, especially after I sent Abby back." She paused as Gwen came in carrying a tray with an array of bowls, medicinal bottles, and flasks of liquid, presumably some herbal concoctions. "How do ye know my time is less savage than this one? I never stated what year I hailed from."

"From Abby, of course. I've had the pleasure of many interesting conversations with her. You seem very similar to her and it isn't hard to guess you were from a similar time."

"Of course." Kenzie moved out of the way as Gwen started to fuss with Ben. She watched as she removed his dirty shirt and using another bowl brought in by a servant, started to bathe him. Braxton came in and offered his assistance, which Gwen was only too happy to accept.

"What century, Kenzie?" Ben rasped, seemingly half-conscious.

"The twenty-first, my Laird."

Gwen and Braxton cleaned him up as best they could and with the help of some male servants, carried the laird upstairs.

Over the next hour, the laird's health deteriorated, and no longer did he speak or acknowledge them in any way.

"He's very ill, and there's a distinct rattle in his lungs that makes my blood uneasy. I do hope he'll pull through. He's been through so much already." Gwen paused, turning to a servant. "Forget the laird's bath. He's too ill to be moved."

Kenzie didn't know what Gwen meant by such words, but with the worry etched on her face, now wasn't the time to pry. Helping her clean up, they soon had the little room they'd carried Ben into back to its former self, before they both headed upstairs. "You're fond of this man, Gwen?"

"Aye, very much so. And before ye go back to ye time, I may tell ye our history. But not tonight, 'Tis very late, and ye should be off to bed. What a day you've had already, what with coming here and then all this with the Laird of Ross. You must be exhausted."

They climbed the stairs together, Kenzie noting for the first time there was no carpet run on the steps beneath her feet. "A little, but I'm energized by just being here." She paused. "Are ye sure you do not mind me staying for a while? I so wish to get to know you and this time better."

Gwen met her gaze as they reached Kenzie's room. "We love to have ye here, never doubt that, but the time is fraught with danger, so ye must promise to listen to me if I say ye should or should not do something. Can I trust ye to obey me at all times?"

"Of course, I'd never do anything to put myself, you, or your family in danger. I promise."

Gwen smiled, and Kenzie recognized her mama in her great great great grandmother many-times-over. How amazing that the family line, even now, resembled those from the past.

"Now, 'tis best ye get back to bed," Gwen said. "Morn will be here before we know it."

Kenzie walked into her room and noted the servants must've been in and lit some candles for her. "If you need any help with the Laird of Ross, please don't hesitate to wake me. I want to be helpful while I'm here."

"I know ye do, lass, and ye will be." Gwen kissed her cheek, giving her a small hug. "I will see ye on the morn."

"Good night," Kenzie said, getting into bed and studying the ornate plasterwork on the ceiling. How wonderful to be here. And to think they would travel to Druiminn castle and she would see Abby, a woman from the twenty-first century who'd made this time her own. Excitement thrummed through her veins, and sleep proved elusive.

CHAPTER 4

*T*he following week was full with running around nursing the sick laird. There were rounds of bathing, dressing, cooling down and heating up the man, as he lay abed, sweating, swearing, mumbling incoherent words that were brought on by his fever.

And even with all this care, the man still seemed as ill as the day he arrived. Kenzie sat, watching his labored breathing, the line of sweat that beaded his top lip. She had to do something. Anything was better than this continual state of hell.

"Gwen, may I have a word?" Kenzie asked, catching the woman as she walked swiftly toward the kitchens. Gwen's healing abilities, her knowledge of herbs that could heal the sick or injured were wonderful and well documented in the family history, but in this case, something stronger, possibly twenty-first-century prepared, was required.

"Of course, my dear." Gwen wrapped her arm in hers and walked them toward the front parlor. "What is it you wished to discuss?"

Kenzie shut the door behind them, wanting to make sure no servants heard what she was about to suggest. "I brought some medicine back in time with me. Just in case I needed it, you see. I didn't wish to fall ill in this century. I took precautions and such before leaving but this is different." Gwen stared, clearly confused by what she was saying. "The medications I have could possibly help the laird if you'll let him take it."

"Truly?" Gwen sat and waved her over to join her on the lounge. "Like what, lass?"

"Just small things, like cough medicine, and paracetamol, which helps bring fevers down. It may help him, or at least relieve his symptoms a little."

"Why did ye not mention them before? Ben's been here a week already."

"I know, and I'm sorry." Kenzie didn't like the slight timbre of Gwen's chastisement, but she was right. The man had been here for seven days, and she should've spoken up about her idea sooner, but... "Truly, I didn't mean not to help, but I wasn't sure if it was something I should do. No one in this time has ever been exposed to the kinds of medicine I have, and it worried me that by giving it to the laird I may make him sicker, or even worse, kill him."

Gwen patted her hand, understanding dawning in her eyes. "Nay, lass, I understand. Of course, ye were worried and rightfully so. But I think in this case, it's a risk we need to take. Nothing I've tried has helped him, and his fever is something I canna get down."

"The paracetamol will help best with that. I'll retrieve it and meet you in the laird's room, if you like."

"I'll fetch another pitcher of cool water and meet ye there."

Kenzie did as Gwen bade and collected the medicine. The day she'd arrived she'd hidden it behind a loose board next to the fireplace, not wanting any of the staff to find it. A box with smart packaging and pretty little tablets and a bottle of liquid with a child-proof cap wouldn't be the easiest items to explain.

Gwen was already beside the laird when Kenzie arrived, and she quickly passed the two tablets over.

"Leave us," Gwen commanded to the two maids who bustled about the room, stoking fires and taking away dirty linen. The two girls did as they were told, closing the wooden door silently behind them.

"Does he swallow them whole, or can I crush them into a drinkable solution?"

"You can do either, but I'd suggest you crush them. In his current condition, I don't think the laird is capable of swallowing them whole." Her ancestor looked at the little tablets, running her finger over them, before placing them in a mortar and pestle and crushing them to powder.

"They're the oddest little things. You'll have to tell me what's in them, so I may be able to reproduce them in some way here. If they work, of course."

Kenzie smiled. "They'll bring his temperature down, of that I have no doubt, but as for the infection in his lungs... Well, we could try the cough medicine and see if that alleviates his symptoms a little." Or not. She was unsure if any of it would work. She watched as Gwen placed the crushed tablets into a cup and mixed them with ale.

The laird tossed and turned on the bed, sweat beading his brow and his cheeks as red as a beetroot. Kenzie wasn't sure if the pills would help the infection that was raging through his body, but she hoped so. Gwen did seem very fond of the man, and although he'd been quite annoying the first time she'd met him, the past seven days had been different.

Probably due to the fact he was mostly in a comatose state, but even so, he was easy to look at, even as ill as he was. His ebony locks hung loose about his shoulders. Kenzie was shocked to feel a pull of some sort of emotion she'd never experienced before. Of course, it wasn't because he was very handsome with high cheekbones, a perfect straight nose, and lovely brows that were a lot more obvious now that he was cleaned up a little. She wasn't that shallow to crush on a guy near his death bed.

Kenzie helped sit the laird up, and with a little coaxing, Gwen was able to get the paracetamol down without too much spillage. He flopped back onto the bedding, his face a mixture of pain and annoyance.

Over the next few hours, the fever, which had wrecked his body, abated a little, but in the following days, the Laird of Ross's health fluctuated wildly. Kenzie gave an abundance of paracetamol to him, along with the cough medicine, but still, the cough rattled the man's chest and sounded painful whenever he breathed.

"A drink." He coughed again. "Please, lass."

Kenzie poured a cup and rushed over to his bedside, pleased to see him trying to sit up for the first time in what seemed like weeks.

"You're awake. I'd not thought I'd ever see the day." She helped him to drink. His skin still felt damp, but the fever had broken if the coolness that touched her palm was any indication.

He drank soundly, finishing the cup. "Thank ye."

"You're welcome." She sat down beside the bed, wiping his brow with a damp cloth. "Can you remember anything over the past few weeks? Do you know where you are?"

His eyes took in the room before narrowing in contemplation. "I've no blasted idea where the hell I am. Although ye're familiar to me."

"That's probably because I've been looking after you. You're in Gwen Macleod's home. It was gifted to her and Braxton from her brother, Laird Macleod."

"I dinna need a history lesson, lass. I know who Gwendolyn is."

He pushed himself up, leaning against the headboard, and the blankets that were previously covering his chest slipped, exposing a very fine body. Kenzie bit her lip as she watched it flex with the movement of him pushing his hair out of his face. Standing, she walked over to the basin of water and rinsed the cloth in her hands, fiddling with anything so she didn't have to look at him. When he'd been ill, laying limp and stinking to high heaven, she'd tried to keep her mind on the task of keeping him alive.

But now. *Wow*. With a body like Black Ben's, and a voice of Scottish sin, he was every twenty-first-century woman's fantasy.

"Did we not argue the last time we met? I believe ye didn't like me verra much." He nodded, sitting up further. "Aye yes, ye were a right banshee and one from the future even. Just like the delightful Abby Macleod."

"That's right, but you were extremely obnoxious, and if you should be again, we'll argue some more."

"Seems to me we're arguing already—about arguing." He smiled, meeting her gaze.

Kenzie's tummy fluttered at the amused look he threw her that made him look five years younger, carefree, and happy. And yet, there was something in his eyes that was far from jovial. If anything, it was dark, dangerous, and tinged with anger. She placed the cloth back on his brow.

Do you think you're capable of bathing? I can have the servants bring up a bath for you. But only if you're feeling up to it. You have been very sick."

"That would be most welcome, and, lass," he said, groaning as he slid to the side of the bed, putting pressure on his feet for the first time in days. "Thank ye for ye kindness. I'll not forget it."

Kenzie did as he asked, finding a maid in the corridor and sending her down to prepare water and have the menservants carry up the bath. She didn't immediately go back into the laird's room and instead, went to her own, wanting to change as she'd taken the night shift the previous evening and needed to feel a little more human. She would sleep a thousand years after last night. And as soon as the laird was bathed and dressed, Gwen should be in to take over his care.

A loud crash sounded in Black Ben's room, and she hurried back to it, only to open the door and see the laird as naked as the day he was born, fighting to pull off his pants.

"Ye either going to keep staring at me ass, lass, or are ye goin' to help pull off my trews? I'm not as strong as I was, and they seem to be stuck about my feet."

For the life of her, Kenzie couldn't drag her gaze upward from his groin. Seriously, what other assets did this man have? She swallowed hard, finally managing to turn around and give him privacy. "*Umm.* Maybe if you sit on the bed and cover yourself that would be better, before I help you, that is."

"Ye've been bathing me these last few weeks, why the modesty now?"

47

Her cheeks burned. "*I* have not been doing anything of the kind. So, turn around and sit down, or you can ask someone else to help you." Kenzie heard mumbling, with words like, minx, annoying wench, and damn it. The list went on until he called out that he was ready.

Kenzie was relieved to see he'd pulled a woolen shawl across his lap as she came to his side. Lifting his foot, she pulled off the stiff pants, which took her some, since his body was so filthy. She threw them toward the door, coughing as the stench wafted up to her nose.

"I dinna stink that much, lass," he said, looking offended.

"May we enter, m'lady?" a maid asked from the door.

"Of course." Kenzie waved them in. "If you would set the bath up beside the fire, that would be great. Thank you." She watched as a steady stream of servants came in and out of the room, carrying buckets and linen cloths similar to what she'd call a towel. Two of the maids stripped the linen off the bed, right down to the hay, replacing that, as well, before throwing down two large animals furs and making the bed up as it was before. Ben sat on a chair near the fire, neither watching nor taking any interest in the goings-on in his room, quietly contemplating the flames.

At last, the door closed, and they were alone. "Your bath is ready. Are you going to be okay getting into it?" She checked the temperature of the water, and it was hotter than she thought it would be.

"Of course, but if ye want to stay, lass, you're more than welcome to clean me. I could do with a good lather." He came and stood behind her and every nerve in her body sparked to life. What a flirt he was, and a good one, since she contemplated it for all of one second.

"I think not, my lord. Now," she said, stepping away while fighting her impulse to remain. To be this close to the laird was too dangerous to ignore. Her body didn't want to refuse his offer, no matter that her mind did. "And let me remind you of a few things, Laird Ross, just in case you've forgotten," she said, angry that her body seemed to have a mind of its own.

Kenzie pushed him toward the bath, ripping the towel away from his hips and fighting not to look. "You smell. In fact, the stench that is wafting from you is beyond anything I've ever smelled in my life. Not to mention, your teeth need a thorough brushing as your breath isn't much better than your body odor. So, no, I neither want to wash you or join you in the bath. But I will show you where the soap is, so you may get started."

"No need. I can find it myself." He gestured toward the door. "If ye don't mind, I'd like to be alone."

"Great. I hope not to smell you soon." Kenzie left the room and shut the door with a bang, a full stop on his suggestion and her ridiculous mind that had actually considered it. Smelly or not, it wouldn't take her long to right that wrong, and it had been so very long since she'd had a boyfriend. She wasn't so innocent not to know what a man could do with his hands...or his mouth.

She stormed into her room and paced before the windows, opening one and standing before it. The cool air kissed her skin and went some way in reminding her she didn't want to just throw herself at anyone who was willing. And she definitely did not even like Black Ben enough to do the dirty with him. An atrocious flirt, if ever there was one, and definitely a man no woman could trust. His life-style after the death of his wife was proof of that.

⁓

*B*en glared at the door as it closed behind Kenzie and then, holding the edges of the wooden bath, lowered himself into the water. Och, he needed this. The warm water smelled of herbs and knowing Gwen, had some sort of healing properties as well. Soon the heat helped his aching bones, and he lay back, enjoying being anywhere but his bed. He'd been stuck in this room for far too long, and he longed to get outside, have some sunlight on his face and perhaps a good spar or two.

An image of Kenzie outdoors alongside him flittered through his mind, and instantly the thought soured his mood. "Menacing wench," he mumbled, finding the lavender soap and washing his arms. If she wasn't so damn sweet looking, he'd demand Gwen send her home.

What was it with these women from the future who were self-assured and tough? Not like the women of his time. Women who took no bullocks from their husbands and ran a home with an iron fist.

He looked over at the bed and wondered how long he'd been here. He really ought to return home, check on Alasdair, and ensure all was well with the estate. Guilt pricked his conscience that he'd not been the father he'd promised to be. Was his boy crawling now? Had his hair grown, did he still have his mother's striking, blue eyes?

Not to mention, should Aedan hear of his dissolution, his closest ally would hunt him down and give him a good wallop. And in truth, he deserved one. He'd been less than what he was brought up to be. Aline, may her sweet soul rest in peace, would be disappointed in him. Just as he was, now that he was sober enough to know it.

With a large amount of effort, he managed to get out

of the bath, dress, and clean his teeth, just in case the wench from the future was right, and his breath did stink. His exertions left him drained and leaving only his tunic on, he crawled back into bed.

The door swung open, and he looked up, hoping to see the brown-haired lass, but only to see his fiery-red-haired Gwen.

"Ah, you're about, just as Kenzie said ye were. 'Tis a happy day, and I'm glad ye're getting better." Gwen came to sit on his bed, and Ben gave her a weak smile.

"I'm so tired. I feel like I've been in battle."

"Well, ye have, in a way. You've been very ill, Ben. I thought for a few days there, we were going to lose ye, but luckily for you, my clever Kenzie saved ye life."

Ben frowned, not sure if he should feel alarmed or comforted by that fact. Kenzie had saved his life? "How so?"

"Ye were drunk, but ye also caught a terrible ailment of the lungs. Ye breathing was labored, and ye breath cracked on exhale. Kenzie had some medicines she brought from the future, and they seemed to help bring ye temperature down and to soothe your cough. Ye are very lucky she was here."

"Damn it," he mumbled, not wanting to be in debt to the lass. "Now I'll have to thank her." He looked over at Gwen, thankful to have her as a friend. "She doesn't like me."

"Who? Kenzie?" Gwen grinned and opened the heavy curtains that covered the windows, spilling light into the room. "Of course, she does. Ye just have to be your charming self. Not the sword-wielding, overbearing High-land ass ye sometimes can be."

Ben ignored her insult. "She hates me innards with a

passion. Hell, had I died, she would've probably danced a jig on my grave."

Gwen raised her brow, and he grasped what she was thinking. That he was acting all piqued over a lass he had no right to feel piqued over. "Over-exaggerating much? I'm sure ye're wrong."

"'Tis not my concern, in any case. She's your problem." He sighed, hating the fact that his words rang false, even to his own ears. "I need to return to Castle Ross and soon. I've not been the best laird I could have been." He paused. "I feel I've let Aline down."

"Aye, when you're able to ride, I'll allow ye to leave. Until then, ye're to stay here and gather your strength. I'll not hear another word about it. And secondly," Gwen said, coming to sit on the bed and taking his hand. "Should I hear about ye whoring in any more inns across Scotland, I'll be letting my brother know about it, and then you'll really get what's coming to ye. Do ye understand, my friend?"

Ben narrowed his eyes, not liking the chastisement by two women in one day. One was enough. "I'm not going to live my life as a monk, Gwen. Will ye let me visit my lady companions so long as I stay sober and discreet?" He grinned.

Gwen threw him a scathing look, and he laughed. How he adored her, always had. She was the one person in the world who'd never shied away from telling him the truth. Most people, after meeting him, agreed with every word he said and wouldn't dare naysay the towering, sword-wielding Black Ben.

He supposed it was one of the reasons he liked this Kenzie lass, too. Just like Gwen, she wasn't afraid of him.

Quite the opposite if her banshee mouth was any indication.

"If ye behave and act like the laird that ye are, I'm sure it'll be fine. But heed me, Ben. Should I hear of anymore of this shocking, dissolute lifestyle you've adopted, I'll be putting a stop to it."

Gwen left, and not long after, a bowl of vegetable broth arrived, along with a cup of ale. Ben looked out the windows, seeing the ocean and its vastness beyond the shore. Gwen was right and had voiced what he himself had already known. It was time he returned home, stopped acting like an ass, and became the father he longed to be. The sound of a door closing in the room adjoining his sounded, along with muffled voices—one he recognized as Kenzie's.

She had a soft voice, but it was laced with strength. Mayhap in the days ahead, he could come to be friends with the lass from the future. Learn a little more about her time that had endlessly fascinated him after talking to Abby Cross.

Kenzie was his last thought before sleep captured him again.

CHAPTER 5

a week later, the Laird of Ross was well enough to dine with the family downstairs. Kenzie was not pleased about it. Just his presence was enough to set her on edge. Too manly by far, and only too willing to give her looks that set a woman's skirts on fire. He could probably lift her up as if she weighed nothing at all. Hold her against a wall and—

"Are ye enjoying ye meal, my dear?" Gwen asked, smiling. "Is there something wrong with the broth?"

Kenzie took a sip of her mead, needing to cool down her core temperature. Tomorrow night she'd be sure not to sit so close to the fire. "Not at all. It's very tasty. Why do you ask?"

"Only that ye've stopped eating, but as long as all's well…"

"All is very well. I promise." Kenzie smiled.

Gwen's gaze moved to Ben who sat beside her, and Kenzie didn't need to be a nuclear scientist to know Gwen was aware of what Kenzie was thinking. Or more truthfully, who she was thinking of. Like the maid who stood near the window. The young woman had practically been salivating over Ben the entire night, and he'd been lapping it up like the bachelor he was.

"Ye're not pleased with me, lass. Am I not what ye thought a Highland lord ought to be?"

It was an odd question, and Kenzie studied him while gathering her thoughts. "What makes you think I'd expect anything more than what I've found?"

"Ye remember Abby Cross…the lass ye helped to return to our time."

"Of course," she said.

"She told me of a certain type of book that you women like to read. Books that are filled with muscular sword-wielding men, with long, flowing locks, and big—"

"I get the point," she said, cutting him off before he said something she neither wanted to hear or imagine. Or imagine more than she'd already been imagining. It was bad enough to be beside a man who encompassed all that romance novels stated and more. He certainly had the hair thing going. Lovely, long locks she could clasp in her fist, to hold him against her mouth or other delectable places.

Kenzie poured more mead, she didn't mind this drink as it had a distinct honey taste to it. Much more preferable to water that could make you ill, or the ale that was too bitter for her palate. She should've really stopped reading those romance novels before coming back to this time. It was giving her ideas she had no right to be thinking. "What Abby may have mentioned, but you've chosen to ignore, is that all the heroes in those books were kind, gentle, and had spades of honor." Kenzie fought to eat her food with the wooden spoon and used the small knife instead. She narrowed her eyes when she caught Ben watching her. "Do you have any of those traits, my lord?"

His gaze met hers. "Och, lass, ye wound me." Ben clasped his chest, mocking laughter in his eyes. "I have all of those qualities, and furthermore, I've been told my hands are very gentle, if not a little maddening." He winked, and her stomach flipped. Damn his sex appeal. He was like a walking Viagra pill for women. "I'm more than willing to prove my words are true if ye were interested."

"I'll pass, but thanks for the offer." Kenzie ignored his chuckle and settled down to eat her dinner, but her mind refused to cooperate. With each spoon of broth and sip of her drink she could feel his attention on her, burning her like a brand. It left her hot and discombobulated.

"Do ye really find me so repulsive?" he asked, waiting for her to look at him. "I know we didn't have the best introduction, but as a descendant of Gwen's, I would like us to be friends. May we start afresh?"

Kenzie wasn't sure if that was a good idea. If she actually grew to like the man, what would her hormones do then? She bit her lip, knowing exactly how her body would react and that was one road she refused to go down. But then, if she befriended the man, she could find out who he socialized with outside of her family. Someone obviously had killed him at some point, and from what history had assumed, it was someone he knew. Being around Black Ben could help her solve the mystery of what had happened to the Laird of Ross.

He continued to eat, and she studied him covertly. He laughed at a tale that Braxton told, and Kenzie watched as his Adams apple bobbed with his reply. Three months and this man would be no more, would be as dead as his wife. She shook her head. No matter his sexual innuendoes, and her reactions to them, no one deserved to die for nothing. And it was sad that he would pass away so young.

Ben caught her gaze, his eyes dark and intense, and heat sizzled between them. "Well, lass. Can we be friends?"

She nodded, her body on edge and not at all calm and assured as she prided herself on being. "I'd like to try." And in truth she did. Black Ben was a Scottish historical icon. Who *wouldn't* want to learn about the man? But that wasn't her only reason. He fascinated her in a way no man ever had. Whether this was because the date he'd died was etched into her brain, or because the way he lived his life, or his friendship with her ancestral family, Kenzie wasn't sure, but she wanted to know what made him tick.

"I have a suggestion as to how we may start our new friendship."

"You do?" Kenzie pushed her plate away and took a cob of bread from the bowl. "And?"

"Do ye ride?"

"Horses?"

He grinned, biting his lip a little. Kenzie couldn't look away at his perfectly straight, white teeth, that were absolutely clean. "What did ye think I meant when I said ride?" He chuckled.

Heat bloomed on her face. "Very funny. Do be serious."

"My apologies," he said, placing a hand over his heart and bowing a little. "But yes, I meant horses, although the direction yer mind went certainly has sparked another image of how we could spend the day."

"Do you never stop?"

He shrugged, leaning back in his chair. "Sometimes." He paused. "I was going to suggest we spend the day riding ye family's land. With me, you'll be safe enough, and I could use some exercise, having been kept indoors these last few weeks. And it would give me some time to quiz ye on where ye came from."

Kenzie thought about it. A day out riding with Black Ben. To some, this would be a dream come true. A historian's lotto win. And it would be enjoyable. Yes, he flirted, but it was nothing she couldn't handle, and no matter what he said, or had said in the past, there was something about the man that resonated trust. He had a violent past with battles and clan disputes, but Gwen trusted him, and Kenzie was certain that he would never hurt her or force anything on her she didn't wish.

"That sounds wonderful. I'd love to see the lands. Thank you."

"Ye're very welcome. We'll break our fast and meet outdoors first light tomorrow."

~

Kenzie woke, her blood singing. She jumped from the bed and dressed quickly, not bothering to ring for her appointed maid. It seemed silly of her to use another person to help her dress or clean, and she'd much prefer to do everything in private, especially since her clothing wasn't handmade or historically accurate. A maid would notice such things immediately. Having servants wasn't something she'd ever get used to as she pulled her hair back into a ribbon and tied it up.

The sound of voices floated up to her room, and she headed downstairs, following the smell of a hot meal to the breakfast room. Candles were lit along the length of the table, as full light had yet to make its mark across the land, and Kenzie spooned some eggs onto the seventeenth-century version of toast, which actually looked like burned bread.

"Ye beat me this morning, lass. And here I thought I was up before the house itself."

"I was excited about getting out and looking around and came down as soon as I could. I assume we're still going?"

"Aye. Of course." Ben served up his own breakfast and sat beside her. It surprised Kenzie that he wished to be this close to her and not seated anywhere else at the table. But then, they were starting their friendship fresh, and it was much easier to converse when beside one another than at opposite ends of a table.

"Do you think our outing will take all day?"

"Mayhap it will. Ye will have to wait and see."

They finished their meal in companionable silence before Ben walked them out to the stable. A young lad held two saddled horses. Kenzie's mount was higher than she'd ever ridden before, and nerves skittered in her belly.

"Is the horse safe?" She patted the bay mare's nose, smiling when it nuzzled into her palm. "You know what I mean. Is she placid?"

"Aye, she's placid enough. You'll be fine, lass. I'll not let ye fall."

The sureness in his tone settled Kenzie's concerns, and with the help of a mounting block, she climbed onto the saddle and settled herself.

"We'll head east along the coast and come back through the small forest the estate is flanked by to the west. You'll see the best of both locations that way."

"Lead on." Kenzie trotted out after Ben, and slowly, thankfully, he guided them toward the beach. Kenzie had been this way many times. It was the same well-worn walking track that she used in her own time when going down to the shore.

"Does it look familiar to ye?" He cast a look her way before gazing back toward the shore.

"It does. In fact, it's still the same route to get to the beach." She chuckled. "I was just thinking how weird that was and yet how wonderful that no matter how much time has passed, some things never change."

"Nay, they don't, do they?" He looked contemplative before guiding his horse onto the shore, where Kenzie came up abreast of him.

"Is it reasonably safe around these parts?"

"Are ye scared, lass?" Ben asked, not looking at her but watching the ocean instead.

"A little," she conceded. "I've read so much about clan battles and how violent they can be. Most often, the attack happens when one least expects it. I don't know how to fight. I wouldn't know what to do should such a thing happen to us out here."

"Well, 'tis lucky I do." He reached over, slipping a stray hair that had come loose of her pony tail behind her ear. The contact sent shivers down her spine and her stomach clenched. "I'll protect ye lass, with my life."

"Even though only a few days ago we were not the best of friends?"

"Of course. Ye're a woman. So, unless ye come at me with a sword, I'll protect ye at my own cost."

Kenzie wondered how it was that anyone could be so selfless with their life. To protect others, even if it cost you your life, was a sacrifice she wasn't sure she could make. How was it that the men of this era never second-guessed themselves? Never doubted what they should do, who they should protect?

"I find it infinitely fascinating that you could sacrifice yourself for me. Not," she said, gesturing to the woods that grew denser beside the beach, "that I would like us to be stormed by an enemy to test your honor, but how do you do it? How do you know that you would gladly give up your life so that someone you hardly know can live?"

He threw her an odd look before he shrugged. "Because no matter what ye may have read about me in your history books, or know of this time, I'm an honorable man. But do not be fooled that everyone is, lass. Should we be ambushed, if I tell ye to run, get away, or hide, ye must do as ye're told."

Kenzie nodded. "I understand, and Gwen said something similar to me not long after I arrived. And, of course, I will, I promise. I don't want to die."

"Very good. Now, there is a track up ahead we could take into the forest, which will bring us to the point on the cliffs. Did ye wish to see the view?"

She pulled her horse to a stop and looked up at the hill that came to a head overlooking the sea. From this point, the hill reminded Kenzie of the white cliffs of Dover, except not as high or steep. And instead of the crystal-white chalk, this hill was covered in moss and rocks, right down to the surf, which was a little wilder than the flowing waves now beside them. "I would love to see it." She'd often hiked up to the spot, spent hours reading on the clifftop with nothing but the sound of the sea crashing against the land. To see if it had changed between this time and hers was exactly what she wanted to do.

They rode into the forest and Kenzie was thankful she'd brought a warm woolen shawl with her. Under the cover of the large trees and dense foliage, the air was moist and cooler. Ben worked their way in the direction of the lookout but stopped suddenly, lifting a hand for her to be silent.

Kenzie did as he told her and the hair at the back of her neck rose.

"Get off the horse, lass."

She quickly did as he bade, and with a gesture, Ben walked the horses off the little track and into the forest. Within only a few yards, the track was no longer visible, but Ben didn't stop, just kept walking the horses farther in, as if to hide them.

"What did you hear?" she whispered, bumping into the back of Ben when he stopped.

"Men."

Kenzie looked back toward where they'd come and listened, and finally she heard it, too. The muffled chatter of men. Why were they in the forest not far from Gwen's home? And did Gwen know? What if they were on their way to kill her family?

"Shush, lass." The whispered words against her ear made Kenzie aware of another danger—the one that stood beside her. Clad in a tunic, with his tartan kilt, Black Ben looked the part of a warrior Scot. A mixture of danger and delicious temptation.

"Do you know who they are?"

"Nay, I don't recognize the voices." Ben took a step toward where they'd come and moved some ferns to get a better look. "Ah, McDonnel men. Deserters, by the look of their filthy tartans."

Kenzie came up behind Ben and peeked about his shoulder. Unconsciously, she clasped his hips to steady herself and regretted the action as soon as she did it. He was solid muscle. She wanted to run her hands downward to see if his ass was just as solid, just as firm.

Of course, she'd seen him naked, so she was very aware that he was well endowed. His body was practically perfect.

Shouts sounded from the trail, and Ben pulled her onto the ground, muffling her mouth with his hand. Kenzie couldn't breathe, but she wasn't sure if it was from the fright or that Ben was laying over her, his mouth awfully close to her cheek and his form running the length of her body.

Oh, dear Lord, I really should have stopped reading those romance novels…

"Horses have been here and not long ago. Let's go, lads, before we're caught."

Everyone seemed to be in agreement, and not long after, Kenzie heard the sound of horses cantering away from their location. "Do you think it's safe now?" she muttered under his palm.

Ben removed his hand, and she gazed up at him just as he looked down at her. Another mistake. He was so close.

"Ye have dirt on ye cheeks." Ben wiped her skin with his thumb, his attention snapping to her lips.

Was he going to kiss her? *Oh please, God, let it be so.* Kenzie wanted to know what it would feel like to act on this overwhelming desire for the man. A man who was not meant for her, no matter how much she found him physically attractive.

"We should go. Come, lass," he said, standing and pulling her up. "Those men are long gone, and we can still make the point, if we go now."

"Okay." Kenzie walked to her horse and with Ben's help, mounted. His hands stayed on her hips longer than they needed to, and she adjusted her seat, trying to calm the heart that beat a million times too fast in her chest.

She watched as he swung up on his horse, his kilt lifting a little and giving her a view of a muscled thigh. "Oh, for crying out loud."

"Did ye say something, lass?"

Kenzie kicked her mount on. "No, nothing. Lead on."

They rode for a time in silence, and Kenzie assumed it was because Ben wanted to listen for the men, no matter that he'd said they were gone. And Kenzie was happy for the silence. She needed to compose herself. This attraction she had to the man was beyond annoying and truly illogical. She would be going back to her own time shortly, and she couldn't forget there was the pesky problem of Ben disappearing or being killed by a never-known source.

As they climbed upward, the forest thinned, until the trees were sporadic and the ferns were replaced with small shrubs and heather.

At the top, Kenzie looked out over the ocean, its blue depths never changing, no matter the era. Rocks that she'd sat on in her time were in their rightful places. How wonderful that the earth could be so similar even after all the years.

"Have ye ever been up here before, lass? I know this is ye home in the future, but ye're looking at the sea as if you've never seen such beauty."

"I grew up in England, and only moved back to Scotland a couple of years ago, after my father died. I come up here often to read and relax. The view is as spectacular as it always has been."

At a thumping sound, Kenzie turned in her seat and looked behind them, only to see the men from earlier riding hard toward them, swords drawn and raised.

"Ben, we have company."

Before the words had left her lips, the ting of metal

being drawn sounded beside her as Ben pulled a second long and deadly blade from his hip. "Stay on ye horse, and stay behind me for as long as ye can. And when I say so, ride hard for the trees. Head home and sound the alarm to Braxton."

"I will." Fear curled about her, and her horse shifted, stomping its feet the closer the four riders came. Kenzie pulled out a knife she'd hidden in her boot; it was pathetically small, but she only needed to stab a hand or something. Not that she wanted to get close enough to these men who, the closer they came, the angrier they looked.

On the cliff edge, Kenzie and Ben had nowhere to go, and the men slowed just before reaching them, menacing glee written across their faces.

"Ah, Black Ben, 'tis good to finally find ye. We've been looking for quite some weeks."

Ben didn't reply, but Kenzie noted his hand flexed on his sword handle.

"So ye've been hiding out on Macleod lands, hey? Didn't think a Ross would be so cowardly."

"What do ye want?" Ben asked, his back rigid, ready to defend her.

"Nothing that ye need to concern yourself about as ye will be dead within a few minutes."

"Who sent ye?" Ben asked, his voice a lot calmer than Kenzie's would've been had she been speaking.

"That also dinna concern ye, but know that once you're dead, we'll be claiming a good deal of blunt for our trouble."

With Ben's death guaranteed only a few months away, Kenzie couldn't help but think this was a lead up to the eventual raid at Castle Ross. Kenzie clasped her reins, ready to go as soon as Ben told her. These men meant trouble, and she and Ben were not getting away without a fight.

The only solace was that Ben's date of death was not today, so at least one of them was getting out of here alive. With that thought came another. Since she had traveled back in time, perhaps she'd already altered history and today *was* the day Ben would meet his fate?

A cold shiver ran through her blood, and she sent a silent prayer up to God that it wasn't so. It was too soon for him. It would always be too soon.

❦

*B*en kept his gaze locked on the man in the middle of the little pack, the one who seemed to be in control of the rabble. They all looked small enough for him to deal with, but with men who no longer followed clan rules, it was anyone's guess as to how they would react, or what they were willing to do. And he had Kenzie to keep safe.

"What are ye doing on Macleod land? The laird will not be pleased to find ye're here without his consent."

Each one laughed and snickered. "We heard the land was gifted to the laird's sister. She's a pretty lass, that Gwendolyn. Lovely and ripe, perfect for picking."

The second largest rubbed his jaw. "Just like your sweet lass. Pretty, too, nice clean skin that we'd hate to mark, but…well, it happens doesn't it, aye."

Ben clenched his jaw. The thought of Gwen and sweet Kenzie getting into such abusive hands sent rage roaring through his blood. "You'll have to get through me first, before ye touch either lass. And if ye do, dinna think to be touching her for long."

The leader pointed his sword at Ben. "Shall we see how long it'll take for us to get to your sweet lass? Shall we commence?"

"Aye, if ye're ready to die."

The man lunged, and Ben swiped his sword up, bringing it back down to slice against the man's stomach. Instead of spilling his innards across the grass below their boots, he nipped the skin, leaving a perfect line of red that seeped onto his cut tunic.

"Are ye sure you wish to continue?" Ben asked, rolling his sword in his hand.

This time, the men came at him from all angles, and it took some effort to fight off the onslaught. Ben managed to land a solid blow against one of the men's temples, and he went down, out cold, possibly dead if he was lucky.

The other two remained persistent. The fight carried on for some time, and Ben cursed his sickness that had made him weak; his stamina was not as it once had been. One of the men threw his sword in the direction of Kenzie, and before Ben could shout out to her to run, the weapon lodged firmly in her horse's chest, killing the animal instantly. The horse and Kenzie went down together, and out of the corner of his eye, Ben could see Kenzie fighting to get her leg out from under the horse's body.

"You'll pay for that," Ben said, his voice laced with deadly promise.

The third man he'd knocked out came to and joined his clansmen. The men lunged, and Ben fought hard, but three against one wasn't good odds, especially after his illness. "Run Kenzie. Now. Get out of here."

He was glad to see she was able to extricate her leg, and she bolted in the direction of home. Ben had maneuvered the men around so their backs were facing the cliff and sea, but one broke off and chased after Kenzie.

The other two laughed, and Ben lunged, striking one bastard with a killer blow to his stomach, which was already bleeding. This time, Ben was pleased to see his guts did spill out over his shoes, the man's shocked gaze watching it land at his feet before he stumbled backward over the cliff.

The last one, an idiot who stopped fighting to watch his comrade die, never saw the blow that sliced into his shoulder and neck, cutting his head partly off.

Ben grabbed his horse, mounted, and took off in the direction Kenzie had fled. Ice water rushed through his blood at the sound of her scream. He urged his mount on, coming across a scene that he never wished to see again.

Kenzie lay beside a slow-flowing river, the filthy bastard over her, ripping at her dress and pushing her legs apart. He could see she was fighting him with everything she had, but the man was large, too strong for her.

Ben jumped off his horse as it was still moving, coming up behind the man and slitting his throat, his knife sinking into the man's skin so deep Ben could feel the neck bone grind against his blade.

Ben should've pulled the man off Kenzie before killing him, and it wasn't until absolute shock registered on Kenzie's face did Ben realize what he'd done.

He threw the man to the side and pulled Kenzie into his arms, rubbing her back, hating that she shook, was cold and rigid. "All's well, lass. Ye're safe now. I have ye." She sobbed into his arms, her hands coming around to clasp his midriff.

"You killed him. I saw. I saw." She paused, taking a

deep breath. "His head nearly came off." Heaving sobs wracked her body, and Ben cringed.

"I'm sorry, lass. I should not have killed him before ye. I forgot ye're not from my time, and you've probably never seen such before."

She shivered in his arms, and he picked her up, sitting down on a nearby fallen log to hold her as she came to terms with what she'd witnessed. Not that Ben thought she'd ever get over such a sight, but he would comfort her for as long as it took. He'd seen the softer side of Abby MacLeod often enough to know that Kenzie's time wasn't as coarse, that the people of their time were not prone to such wars and violence. They no longer had to fight for survival in Scotland. They simply worked and lived with little trouble.

"I have his blood on me."

"Aye, ye do." He looked over to the slow flowing river. "Did ye want to wash it off?"

She looked toward the waterway but shook her head. "No, I just want to go home." Kenzie looked up at him, and Ben had an overwhelming urge to protect her, to care for the woman in his arms, more so than any other woman ever.

He whistled for his horse and stood, carrying Kenzie to the beast's side. He mounted and pulled her up before him, riding back to the house as fast as he could. A day that was supposed to be carefree and peaceful had turned into a nightmare.

As for the men who'd attacked them, he would be sending out Braxton's men to see if any of them recognized who they were, before they buried the bodies.

◠

*L*ater that evening, he sat in the great hall, Braxton across from him, both quiet in contemplation.

"My men had never seen the men who attacked ye today. Granted they were wearing McDonnel tartan, but they could've stolen those, been deserters of another clan. I'll send word to McDonnel to see if they're missing any clansmen, and then we'll know. But what concerns me more is why they attacked ye in the first place? Do ye know of anyone who would wish ye harm?"

"Nay, no one, although it seems someone has put a price on my head." Ben thought on the attack and what it could bode for him in the future months. "They could've just been sayin' that as well, to rattle me. Dinna forget I had Kenzie with me, and she's a pretty morsel of flesh, if ever I saw one. They could've been after her."

"Pretty morsel of flesh? Do we need to have a discussion as to why ye're not allowed to court my great-too-many-times-to-count granddaughter?"

Ben met Braxton's gaze and noted it was deadly serious. "What? I'm not good enough for ye bloodline? I think ye're forgetting I'm a laird in my own right. I've not had my position bestowed on me because of who I married."

"Watch yourself, Ben, or you'll be finding yer ass out on my front stone step faster than ye can blink."

"Will you two cease such stupidity? No one is kicking anyone out, and Ben, as much as we care for ye, consider ye a friend, Kenzie is not for you. Remember, she's not staying for long, and it would be unwise of ye to form any sort of attachment to her."

Ben downed his mead and poured another. It was too late not to form an attachment to the lass. He liked her, appreciated her company. Aye, the lass had a lovely face that just added to his pleasure when around her. "If ye think I'm going to fall in love with her, drop to my knees, and declare my life over the day she departs, ye daft in the head. I enjoy her company. That is all. There will be no further discussion on the matter."

"I'm glad we're in agreement," Braxton said, still glaring.

"Braxton." Gwen sighed, throwing her husband a quelling stare. "No matter what we say, or our reasoning behind it, Kenzie is a grown woman and will, I'm sure, make up her own mind as to who she allows courtship with. We cannot interfere in her life. It is not our place."

"Ye would allow her to form feelings for someone not of her time?" Braxton whispered, looking about for servants.

Gwen sighed again. "Ye're getting ahead of yourself and everything you are saying will probably never become an issue. Ben has stated he's not interested in her in any romantic way, and from what I know of Kenzie's feelings, she feels the same."

"She said that?" A prickle of disappointment stabbed at him that Kenzie didn't consider him in that light. He took another sip of mead, dismissing the madness in his head. "Getting back to what happened today, I think it would be best if ye placed some men on lookout and do a search throughout your land, check that no others are hiding, lying in wait to strike at us when we're unprepared. Just as I was today."

"In your condition, I'm surprised ye survived." Gwen sat beside Braxton and summoned a servant to bring some bread. "When you came back and Kenzie was covered in blood, at first, I thought it was hers. My heart has never threatened to come up through my mouth, but today I venture to say it did."

"Aye, mine, too. How is she, my love?"

"She had a bath upon returning and is now asleep, but in a little while, I'll take up her dinner and make sure she eats. Today was a great shock to her. Not one she'll ever forget, unfortunately."

Ben shut his eyes to block out the image of Kenzie on the ground, fighting off a man who would've raped her had Ben been killed or if he'd failed to get there in time. "Is there any possibility that Kenzie has come back to hide from a problem in her life? Mayhap someone has found out about her abilities to travel in time and wants it for themselves. Wants to use her to alter history or some such madness?"

Braxton leaned back in his chair. "'Tis an idea I'd not thought possible. What do ye say, Gwen? Do ye think the lass is in some sort of trouble and needs our help?" He paused. "Her arrival here was odd and not expected. Not that we don't love having the lass stay with us, but if she is in trouble, perhaps we could help her in some way."

A servant came in and placed another flask of mead on the table, along with some freshly cooked bread rolls.

"I'd not thought of such a possibility, and I suppose it could not hurt to ask her." Gwen offered Ben some food, and he waved it away. "I think it's more realistic that the men were after ye, and their words to ye were truthful. Ye have an enemy, someone who's willing to pay enough that those rabble rousers tried to take ye today. We shall increase security here, but ye need to think of ye own safety, Ben. Someone wants ye dead and ye need to find out who that someone is."

Ben nodded. "Aye, you're right, and I'll have to think

on the matter some more. I suppose I could've slept with someone's wife without knowing it and the husband is now set on seeing my head on a stake. I've been in melees and clan disputes before, but to put an actual price on my head is somewhat determined."

"You must watch yer back and keep yer guard up until we can get to the bottom of this," Braxton said, biting into a bread roll.

"Ye said Kenzie hasn't had her dinner yet. Do ye mind if I take it up to her? I want to ask her if she had a specific reason for being here and also check to see if she's well. I must admit, I probably could've handled killing the man who attacked her better, or at the very least, not right in front of her." Ben rubbed his jaw. He hated to imagine what the poor lass thought of his barbaric ways, and yet, he would kill the man again, would change nothing about his reaction, but mayhap, he would do it where Kenzie wouldn't have seen.

"Cook is fixing up a tray for her now if you want to go down and collect it. 'Tis been some hours, and I'm sure Kenzie is due to wake soon. She's probably quite hungry."

Ben stood. "I'll go and check." He left them in the great hall and went to the kitchens where he found the food being placed on a tray, ready to go. Ben took it from the servant and left. As he walked up the stairs, he wondered what to say to Kenzie. How to comfort her, make sure she was well and not fretting over what she saw. He hoped she didn't think him nothing but a Scottish savage.

He found her sitting up in bed. Candles bathed the room in light, and she looked as calm and as happy as she had been this morning before their ride.

"I brought ye dinner. I hope ye like stew."

She smiled, nodding. "I do. Thank you." She wiggled a little further up in the bed and settled the blankets over her stomach. "How are you? Were you hurt at all today?"

Ben placed the tray on her lap and sat on the bed beside her feet. She looked so small, so delicate in the large wooden bed. It was too big a bed to sleep alone in. He pushed the wayward thought aside, stupid thoughts such as those had no value in his life.

"Nay, lass. A few bruises and one cut across my shoulder, but nothing to worry about. I've had far worse. I'm more concerned for you. I know what I did in front of ye was probably not the best thing to see...and well..."

"It's okay, Ben. Even though it was nothing I'd ever seen before, I'm glad you did it. He would have raped me had you not come. I'm glad he's dead. At least the vile, human scum cannot do it to anyone else."

"Eat," he said, gesturing to her untouched meal. "I hope today has not frightened ye so much that you wish to return home."

"Not at all." Kenzie started to eat, and Ben was pleased to see some color come back into her cheeks.

"There is something else, something that Braxton thought may be the reason why the men attacked us in the first place. Now, hear me out before ye reply, and just know that we're here to support and protect ye. We'll not let anything happen to ye while you're here."

"I know you will." She threw him a smile and took another spoonful of stew. "What did you want to ask?"

"We wondered if mayhap you had come back to our time to get away from someone who may be threatening harm against ye person. Is that so, lass? Did ye come back because someone was aware of your time-traveling abilities and wished the gift themselves or to use it to their advantage?"

Kenzie sat back against the headboard, and the action made Ben aware of her bedclothes. The sheerness of the tunic she wore. He shifted on the bed, conscious of how intimate the setting was.

"There is no one after me, and other than my mother, my friend Ann, and my cousin, the current Laird Macleod, no one knows of the gift I have and what I can do. I think you should look to yourself and who has a score to settle. They did state there was a price on your head. You need to find out why."

All true, but still, Ben needed to be sure before finding out who his enemy was. "On ye travels to Gwen and Braxton's home, ye encountered no one who would now wish ye harm?" A frown line blemished her brow before she shook her head.

"I have the ability to choose where I land if you gather my meaning. I arrived on the beach and saw no one. It is not me those men were after."

He nodded. "Well, 'twould seem our attackers today were parasites who wished nothing but to do me harm at somebody's direction. You being with me placed ye in danger and I apologize for that, lass."

"Braxton's men didn't know who they were?"

"Nay, no one recognized them, but we have sent word to the McDonnel clan to see if any men are missing. They were wearing their tartans." He gestured to her food once more. "Ye must eat, lass. You've had a shock to the system and food will help ye rest easier tonight."

Kenzie settled into her food, and Ben was content to sit and watch over her as she did so. Surprisingly, the silence was pleasant, not at all similar to when he and Aline had been alone. Then, Ben had always tried to be busy, to show purpose or explain what was happening with the estate. But with Kenzie, there was no pressure to fill the silence with meaningless words. He was quite content to just sit and watch her, enjoy her presence and nothing more.

She pushed the bowl away and laid down her spoon. "Thank you for bringing my dinner up to me. I feel better for eating it."

"I knew ye would." Ben picked up the tray and placed it on the table beside the bed. "I'll leave ye now to get some rest."

"Ben," she said, climbing out of bed and coming to stand before him.

He looked down, meeting her gaze. "Yes."

She smiled a little and then pulled him into a hug. Ben froze, not expecting such a gesture, but then the suppleness and warmth of Kenzie seeped into his soul, and Ben's arms encircled her back, pulling her close.

She smelt of rosemary, delicate and sweet.

"Thank you for saving me today. I'll be forever grateful, and I promise, if I can ever return the favor, I shall." She looked up at him, her eyes fierce with promise. "I will save your life if it's in my power to do so."

A cold shiver ran down his spine, and he pulled away, laughing a little to hide his unease. The lass's words sounded more like a premonition than a promise. "You dinna need to make such promises. From what Gwen's told me, you've already saved my life, and so I think that makes us even, yes? And as a man of honor, I'll always protect those in my care."

"Even so, as my thanks, it's my promise."

Kenzie yawned, and he helped her get back into bed. Ben blew out the candle and stoked her fire before leaving her room. His steps slowed as he walked to his own chamber, his mind on the men who had attacked them. Who had they been? If Kenzie didn't have cause for concern, then their words on the cliff today were true…

Someone wanted him dead, so much so that money had been offered in exchange for his life.

It wouldn't be the first time such a bounty had been offered…but still, since his marriage, he'd not sought out conflict. If anything, he'd become a man who looked for ways other than using his sword to stop conflict. 'Twas not right that he'd be targeted now, years after his last melee with a rival clan.

He must return home, and as soon as possible. His son could be their next target, and should anything happen to Alasdair, he'd never forgive himself, nor could he live with such grief. It was time to return to Castle Ross and be the laird he'd been born to be.

CHAPTER 6

A few days later, Kenzie strode into the Great Hall and found all the tables and chairs set to the side of the room, servants busy laying out platters of food, while others arranged pretty flowers atop the tables.

"Is something happening, Gwen?" Kenzie asked, coming up to her ancestor and helping her push a table to the side.

"Aye, a wedding. My maid, who's been with me since we were both girls, is getting married today. I canna believe we'll both be married and soon, no doubt, Gracie will be with a child of her own. I'm very happy for her."

"You sound it." Kenzie looked about the room, the smell of pine permeating the air. "Is there anything I can do to help?"

"I think we're almost ready, lass, but we're about to walk to the church, if ye wanted to join us. We'll be having the small celebration here afterwards."

"I'd love to come. I've never seen a medieval wedding before."

Gwen stopped what she was doing and met her gaze. "Is that what they call this time?"

"Yes. Well, we have a few names for the past. Viking age, the Middle ages covers the time in Europe from 5th—15th century, also called the Dark Ages, the Renaissance, and then we had the Early Modern period, such as the Golden Age, Elizabethan, and Jacobean.

"This is fascinating. Were there more?" Gwen leaned on the table, her attention riveted on Kenzie.

"Yes, then came the Georgian and Regency, Napoleonic and Victorian times, and the Industrial Revolution. I live in the post-Cold War era, which is the time after 1991."

Gwen shook her head, her eyes alight with awe. "I had no idea. How wonderful to know such things." She turned back to her work. "It makes me quite jealous."

"May I ask you something, Gwen? It's a question that has been plaguing me for some time…ever since I helped Abby go back in time."

"Of course." Gwen called a servant to take over what she was doing and walked Kenzie to the fire, where they could talk in reasonable privacy. "What's troubling ye?"

"When Abby arrived at Castle Druiminn she mentioned that you were able to see the future, and that was how you decided that she would be perfect for your brother."

Gwen smiled. "I do have the 'sight,' which is what I call it, and as much as it vexed my brother at the time, I knew the moment I saw Abby that she was made for him, but she just happened to be born in the wrong time."

Kenzie sighed, remembering how heartbroken Abby had been that she'd never see the love of her life again. How wonderful to be so in love, to crave someone with every ounce of your being and give up everything to be with him forever. "Did you have to learn the sight, or did it come naturally to ye?"

"Ah, I see, you wish to learn more of what ye can do? Is that what ye're asking me, lass?"

"I am, I suppose." She bit her lip, wondering how to ask her next question and afraid of the answer at the same time. "Do ye use your abilities to tweak the future?"

"That's forbidden, my dear. An unwritten rule, if you will. I used my sight to simply offer someone a chance for a different path than the one they were walking. I've never used my ability to see what was to come and then try and alter my life to cheat destiny. Some things, my dear, are best left to fate."

"I understand," Kenzie said, as she heard male voices entering the hall. Braxton strode into the room, along with Ben who had young Madeline on his shoulders. He threw the little girl up in the air as he got her down. Her tinkling laugh filled the room before she ran off toward her waiting Nurse. Both men stood before the fire at the opposite end of the room, their backs to them, seemingly unaware of their presence.

"I can see by ye study of the laird that ye like Ben." Gwen took Kenzie's hand, it was warm and comforting. "Ye can tell me, lass. I won't judge ye."

"I do like him, but not in the way you may think." Kenzie met Gwen's gaze. "I think I judged him too harshly when we first met. I should've trusted your opinion of him and seen past my annoyance at a man who was not only drunk, but extremely ill."

Gwen laughed. "Aye, he was that, but Ben has always been a rascal." She squeezed her hand and headed back toward the servants. "But if you like him more than you are admitting, that would be fine, too, my dear. Your life is your own."

Kenzie looked back to where Ben was standing. A shiver stole through her when their gazes locked. The pit of her stomach twisted in the most delightful way, and she swallowed, unable to look away. He was dressed in dark trews and jacket, an emerald green waistcoat that was done up to the base of his neck. Both the men had mud splattered on their lower legs, having been riding—probably looking for more outlaws such as had tried to kill them last week.

Gwen shrieked and strode quickly over to them "What are ye doing! Ye need to go change. Now. The wedding is about to start and ye're as dirty as pigs in a sty."

Kenzie chuckled as both men, shamefaced, headed toward the stairs to change. Kenzie followed Gwen outside and looked around while waiting. The front of the house was riddled with cart tracks that had marked the muddy ground. In the distance, Kenzie could see the small square church that looked much like a house, the only feature indicating that it was a house of God, and not a barn or outbuilding, was the steeple on its roof.

The building certainly wasn't standing in her time, so at some point it must've burned or fallen down. She would look into that when she returned home.

Two very large trees stood by the road that led away from the house, and Kenzie wondered when they had been cut down, as they hadn't survived the passing of time either. The stable looked reasonably similar, although the thatched roof was now slate tile. Kenzie headed across the yard and noted where the vegetable garden was situated was lawn in the twenty-first century and housed a pretty little rose arbor that looked over the sea.

"The house is different, is it not? Tell me about it."

Kenzie jumped a little at Ben's deep baritone. She'd not heard him sneak up on her and it only enforced that she was really quite vulnerable in this time. She had no fighting skills, no ability to get away or idea of where she was going. The forest around the estate was a lot denser than she was used to, and overall, everything was just... different. It was any wonder Gwen had asked her to keep close by and do as they said at all times.

"Some things are different, like trees, plants, and roads, but otherwise, it's eerily similar. At times, I feel like someone's hired my house, and I've stepped on to their movie set."

Ben frowned. "I dinna understand yer meaning, lass." He clasped her hand and wrapped it about his arm before leading her toward the church. "But tell me about it."

"In my time, there are things called movies. If they were making a movie here, it would be an historical film. You know what actors on a stage do, right? Well, think about what they do on stage, but their actions and words are captured in a way to view at a later time or place. That's what a movie is." Kenzie laughed at Ben's blank stare. "Oh my gosh, I can see you have no idea what I just said, explaining what a movie is, is extremely hard."

He smiled. "I think this movie that ye talk of will have to remain one of life's mysteries."

The thought of mysteries reminded Kenzie of Ben's demise in only a few months. She bit her lip, hating the fact that she held such knowledge. Gwen was right, sometimes things were best left to fate. "You asked me after our attack if I had any enemies, but I want to discuss further if you do. Have you had a chance to think over who may have wanted you dead."

"I have enemies." he stated matter of factly. "Aye, lass, too many to count, but to attack me in the way in which those men did was foolhardy. They were not an organized, well-trained army, but men desperate for coin. We have not yet heard back from the McDonnels, but I dinna believe the men to be of that clan. I have sent out word to the few clans I trust to let me know should they hear of anyone who wishes me or mine harm. Whoever my current enemy is, I shall know it soon enough."

"So, you don't know of anyone who wishes you harm? There must be someone or those men wouldn't have said what they did."

Ben pulled her to a stop, turning Kenzie to look at him. She had to tilt her neck to meet his gaze. His lack of care in finding out who wanted him dead wasn't helpful. Since he'd returned to health, and their conversations had increased, Kenzie liked him a little more each day, and hated the thought of his impending demise.

"Since none of the men who attacked us will be returning to their hired foe, I foresee no immediate danger. I will continue to kill anyone who wishes me harm until my foe comes to finish the job himself. I just hope it is a worthy battle."

"Are you not scared of dying? I'm terrified of it." Just the thought of a sword cutting in her two was enough to send Kenzie into a cold sweat. And after the ferocious, blood-thirsty bastards who had come after them the other day, it had proven to her that this time was dangerous, fierce, and for the most part, lawless.

They walked on, and she ignored the visceral reaction that occurred whenever he pulled her close or touched her in some small way. "Death is a part of life and we all shall meet that fate. I have no fear of what is to come. I assume it will be something like sleep, but permanent." He grinned.

Kenzie chuckled at the use of his words. "I imagine you're right, which, when you state it as such, isn't so scary at all. We sleep every night and are not afraid of that."

"Do ye sleep at night when ye go to bed? If ye state ye do, it shall ruin the fantasy I have of ye when ye go to your room."

Kenzie smacked his arm, laughing. "Do not start flirting with me, Laird Ross. You'll get nowhere fast."

"Really." It wasn't a question, and Kenzie ignored the fact that he was staring at her. "I beg to differ," he said, after a time.

Wow. Wow. Wow. "I'm not attracted to you in that way, and I'm only starting to like you. Do not push our friendship." *Liar.*

Many nights she'd lain awake, wanting him with a fierceness that was maddening. It was the oddest thing, since she didn't really know the man, but then, for women in her time, it wasn't so out of the ordinary to act upon desire. The thought of his hands caressing her skin, clasping her hips, or holding her face in his palms as he kissed her, drove her mad. Kenzie had finally accepted that she wanted him. Wanted to sample his fine body before she went home.

"I would lay good money down that you, my sweet Kenzie, are lying your delectable undergarments off. Should I pull ye behind those trees just beside the church and kiss ye senseless, this denied attraction ye boast about would crumble like chalk."

Never before had Kenzie been in a situation where she wanted a man to do exactly as he was threatening, while also praying he would not. Should Ben kiss her, even chastely, it would be hard to halt what she desperately desired. But she wasn't staying in this time and this man beside her only had months to live. If she couldn't stop his death, there was no future here. None.

"I don't give you leave to kiss me and as a gentleman I know you'll honor my wishes."

"I'm no gentleman." His whispered words against her ear sent butterflies to take flight in her stomach. Damn it. Damn everything. Why did this man have to be so intoxicating? Why couldn't he have stayed the barbarian who only saw her as a piece of meat who could give him pleasure? If only he'd go back to that obnoxious being, her denial of him would be a lot easier. Not this man, a man who appreciated a joke or lighthearted tease. One of the most attractive features any man could have was a sense of humor, and to find the big, bad Black Ben had one wasn't something Kenzie had expected.

"Yes, you are," she said, calling his bluff and pulling him toward the church. "Or you would've done it already."

"Now ye really are poking a lion, lass."

They came up to the small, rectangular church that sported dirt floors and coarse, wooden pews. The alter was stone; no ornate marble or granite sat at the head of the church, just candles to light the space.

Kenzie found Gwen and sat beside her, noting that Ben sat on the pew behind them. A kitchen maid sat beside Ben with more excitement than Kenzie wanted to see. The girl's chatter as they waited for the bride and groom bordered on pathetic, and Kenzie focused on the priest instead of musing over why a woman talking to Ben aggravated her so much.

Oh, who am I kidding? It is bloody obvious why I don't want anyone talking to Ben. I want him all for myself.

"Remember, my dear, your life is your own."

"What do you mean by that?" Gwen threw her a knowing look and Kenzie narrowed her eyes, not liking her ancestor's insight. It was bad enough that Kenzie even liked a man born hundreds of years before her, without it being obvious to others.

"Like I said, if ye like him, ye shouldn't let time or place play a role in that. What's life if it's not to be enjoyed?"

"And you think I would enjoy him?"

Gwen laughed. "Yes, very much so."

Thankfully, the bride and groom arrived and saved Kenzie from any further uncomfortable conversation with Gwen. The woman's words had scorched her cheeks. Disregarding how red her face must be, she turned with the congregation to watch the couple walk toward the priest. The bride wore a blue gown that would've been unremarkable had it not been cut to flatter the woman's figure, which made it very pretty. Her groom wore the Macleod tartan and clean shirt, making him look very respectable and handsome. They were a striking pair and, based on the sweet looks they were giving each other, very much in love.

The service wasn't as long as some of the weddings Kenzie had been to before. The priest said some words in Gaelic that she couldn't understand, followed by a piece of tartan being wrapped about the couple's hands, tying them together in union, and they kissed to seal their fate.

A little while later, in the great hall, Kenzie listened to a band of musicians playing a harp and fiddle. The music was lively, practically begging celebrants to get up and dance. The happy couple, too, took part in the festivities, and Kenzie noted that most of the people present were house servants and yard staff.

All seemed to be enjoy drinking, dancing with each other, and laughing at inane jokes and stories. Laughter, above all else, rang through the hall and it was lovely.

"Are ye enjoying yourself, lass? Ye seem quite taken with our celebration of the holy sanctimony that ye call marriage."

"It's a great party and the couple look so in love. I should imagine there are a lot of marriages that aren't as lucky."

"Ye're right about that." The somber tone of Ben's reply gave Kenzie pause. Had his marriage been an unhappy one? She thought not, but maybe she was wrong. Kenzie understood what it was like to be a child of an unhappy marriage, and it was certainly worse if you were stuck in an unhappy union and unable to get out.

Ben sipped from his wine, his eyes no longer as clear and bright as they usually were. The party had been going on for some hours now, and it seemed as if he was enjoying himself a little too much now that he was almost back to full health.

"I understand you were married. Will you tell me a little about her? Only if you wish to, of course." For weeks, Kenzie had wanted to know who Ben had married. What had this mysterious Aline been like? Was she nice? Beautiful? Tall or short? And how had she managed to get this big, hulking Scot to succumb to vows?

Ben's attention didn't waver from the dancing couples before them. He was quiet for so long that Kenzie wondered if he was going to answer, when he said, "What's to say, other than the lass married me under false pretenses, and I ruined her life."

Kenzie coughed, stunned. Not entirely, anyway. "She bore you a child. I'm sure Aline didn't think that you ruined her life." And to Kenzie, now that she'd come to know Ben a little, she couldn't find much not to like. He was strong, loyal, cared for those around him...

"When ye friend Abby came back, Aedan was engaged to Aline. I tricked the lass into running away with me. To marry me under the pretense that I loved her and that she'd be happier and better off at Castle Ross."

"Did you come to love her?" Kenzie asked, unsure why his answer was important to her. Couples married all the time under the guise of affection, and although it may not be present when the vows were first spoken, it didn't mean that they weren't present at all during the union. Love could grow, blossom out of the most unstable foundation.

"Aye, I cared for her a great deal and she, too, me. And then she died."

"I'm sure...I'm certain she wouldn't hold a grudge toward you for her death. You cannot think that she does."

"Aye, 'tis exactly what I think, and it's something that I have to live with each and every day."

Ben walked off, leaving her to watch the dancing couples alone. He headed toward the stairs at the opposite end of the hall. She sighed, feeling for the man. Maybe her asking about his past had been wrong. Aline's death and speaking of their time together was still too raw for the laird to face, which was understandable. His wife hadn't been gone a year.

The night wore on and Kenzie left the celebration to continue without her. Some guests lay strewn across the floor beside the hall fires, while others drank at tables and laughed about numerous tales and adventures. Bidding Gwen and Braxton good night, Kenzie headed upstairs.

The sound of giggling coming from the first-floor landing made her pause. She continued on slowly, hoping she wasn't about to walk in on a couple enjoying the dark solitude the floor granted and came face-to-face with Ben. He sat in a window alcove, the silver light of the moon kissing his bare chest while the maid she'd seen earlier at the church petted and giggled into his neck.

Kenzie stopped short, and she shut her mouth with a snap, hoping like hell that what her eyes were seeing wasn't actually happening. And to think she'd been sorry for the man. She shook her head. What an idiot she was.

They finally noticed her presence. The smug glance from the giggling maid made Kenzie's blood boil. "Apologies for interrupting. I'll just continue on and leave you to it, shall I." She threw Ben a scathing glance and received one in return. How dare he be annoyed with *her*! She wasn't the one who had recently been almost-crying about a dead wife and now found it appropriate to fornicate with a maid in a window.

Making it to her room, Kenzie slammed her door, a pathetic, youthful reaction that she regretted immediately. The last thing Kenzie wanted Ben to think was that she cared what he did. Who he slept with. Who he kissed. As far as she was concerned, he could do whatever he wanted. After all, he only had another six months to live, he best get as many lays in as possible.

Shame washed over her at such a thought, and she ripped off her dress, kicking it across the floor toward the wardrobe. She pulled on a clean shift she slept in and stoked her fire.

Venting her frustrations out on the charred wood with the poker, she soon had the red coals licking the kindling. "Not bad for a city girl, if I do say so myself."

The door to her room opened with such force the handle smashed into the wall before it slammed closed again.

"What the hell do you think you're doing? Get out." Kenzie didn't move, but just turned back to the fire, looking anywhere but toward the door where the Scot she was determined to hate stood.

"I just thought since ye slammed ye door closed, I should slam the door open."

"Oh, aren't you the joker." Kenzie turned to face Ben. His shirt was back on, well, gaping open at the neck and allowing her to see his nicely formed chest and his bulging muscles. Not to mention he'd rolled up his sleeves, and her first thought was, *this man is aware of what he does to women, and he uses his prowess to his advantage.* "But now you can leave. Like I asked."

"Ye seemed a little upset, lass. I thought 'twas best that I checked on ye."

"Upset?" She paused, crossing her arms over her chest. "Over what?"

"Me and the servant lass that ye walked in on." He stalked toward her, and Kenzie had the overwhelming urge to run. Seeing him again only confirmed his words. Yes, she was angry and damn it, jealous as well. So jealous that a woman was enjoying him, laughing with him, touching him, and it wasn't her.

"Whatever, Ben. I'm sure given the size of your ego, you wouldn't believe my denial, so I won't waste my breath." The air in the room seemed to evaporate as he stood before her. She could smell the alcohol on his breath, but also something else simmering in his dark gaze. Desire.

"Do ye deny it?" He watched her, his gaze intent and full of promise. What the promise would comprise was anyone's guess, but Kenzie had a fair idea what she wanted it to lead to. It wasn't like she'd never kissed a man before, and this one certainly looked like he wanted to kiss her.

But should she allow such intimacy? She wasn't staying, and he was doomed to die if she couldn't change history. Any emotional connection she could form toward this man would only end in pain and heartache. A kiss just wasn't worth the angst. Not to mention, she'd just caught him in the arms of another woman. She wasn't that desperate.

"Did ye enjoy your servant?" Kenzie said, mocking him with his Scottish brogue. Unfortunately, her attempt at a Scottish accent only seemed to please him.

"Not as much as I enjoyed yer voice just then." He reached out and clasped her chin, lifting her face to look at him. "Ye're so beautiful."

The butterflies in Kenzie's stomach went into overdrive, and she took a calming breath. "Your flattery will get you nowhere. And you're drunk, so nothing you say can be held as truth."

"Och, but this might." Like a moth to a flame, Kenzie couldn't pull away as she watched Ben lower his lips to hers.

This is bad. Very, very bad. I should stop him...

"Oh my. Apologies, my dear. Had I known you had company I would never have burst in so."

Kenzie jumped back and tripped over the chair behind her, landing with a thump on her ass. The heat on her cheeks burned hotter than the flames behind her, and she couldn't meet Gwen's eyes. "No, I apologize. I'm not sure what I was doing actually..."

"Well, I could tell ye what you were about to do, if ye were confused." Ben threw her a cocky grin and walked to the door. "Pleasant dreams, lass," he said, closing the door behind him.

Kenzie bit her lip, knowing only too well her dreams wouldn't be pleasant but frustrating instead. "I'm so sorry, Gwen. I'm not sure what came over me. I have no idea what the hell I was thinking."

"The Laird of Ross looked like he was about to kiss ye, my dear. Care to tell me what's happening between the pair of ye?" Gwen helped Kenzie to stand and then sat in one of the chairs before the hearth, gesturing for Kenzie to do the same.

She did, sitting and staring at the flames, anywhere other than Gwen. "It's my fault. I got jealous seeing Ben with another woman." She sighed, flopping back into her chair. "How ludicrous is that? Anyone would think I was a child the way I'm acting."

"I know ye are not a child, lass."

"I'm a woman who runs her own business," she said. "This very house is rented out for weddings and events. And a bed and breakfast for those who wish to sleep within its walls. I allow people to come through here and see the wonderful history it holds. I'm about to expand my holdings and commence restoration of an estate south of here and do the same thing. I'm not a child, but the way I reacted in seeing Ben with that servant made me want to throw a tantrum like a spoiled little brat who didn't get her own way."

"Ben was doing what?" Gwen asked, her eyes wide with shock.

"They weren't doing anything truly scandalous," Kenzie said quickly, to dispel her ancestor's horror, "but he did have a maid sitting on his lap and seemed to be enjoying being a typical male when a woman shows the slightest interest."

Gwen's eyes narrowed, but other than that, Kenzie found it hard to read the woman and what she thought of what the Laird of Ross was up to under her roof.

"I can see how the rascal can get under ye skin. He truly is a sweet man beneath all that armor he wears. And when you see the real Ben, there are few who wouldn't be persuaded to fall for his spell."

"You didn't." The words blurted from Kenzie, and in some small way, she supposed she wanted to know more about them, what had happened that stopped a marriage between the pair.

"I came to realize my feelings for Ben were only mediocre, at best. He was like a brother to me, a friend." Gwen stared into the fire, lost in her own thoughts. "When I met Braxton, I knew my life would never be the same again. My heart stopped at the sight of him, and I realized it wouldn't beat again until he was mine."

Tears prickled Kenzie's eyes at Gwen's profession of love for husband. "I don't think I've ever heard anything more beautiful in my life."

"Well, I hope ye do, my dear, and from the man you choose to give your heart to." Gwen leaned forward, suddenly serious. "Ye are to tell me if I need to prepare Braxton for an attachment between you and Ben."

"Why would you need to prepare him? Does Braxton not like Ben?" Kenzie touched her temple, a little light-headed at the thought that Ben was unwelcome here. Was there something Gwen wasn't telling her? She'd thought they got along well. Was there some underlying jealousy on Braxton's behalf in regard to Gwen?

"Och, he likes Ben well enough, but not enough for his descendant." She smiled. "But if ye think a relationship with Ben would make ye happy, then we'll support ye, for however long you're here."

"I only planned on staying a few months, and I'm not looking for a relationship with Ben. But there is something that I need to talk to you about, and I'm not sure how you'll take it." *Most probably not well.* With Ben being like a brother to Gwen, knowing what Kenzie was about to disclose would break her heart, if not send her into a panic. It wasn't easy to say.

"You can tell me anything. I'll never judge ye."

"Even when what I'm about to tell you proves that I've been less than honest with you? And what I'm about to say will cause you worry, and that in itself is not something I ever want to do to you or Braxton." And she didn't. Even as short as her stay had been, she'd come to love her family as much as if she'd been born to them and known them her whole life.

"Now ye do have me worried. I suggest ye spit it out, lass."

Kenzie searched for the right words to tell Gwen the truth. "There is another reason that I came back in time to see you. Of course, my main reason was to meet you and Braxton and, if you chose, to learn from you in regard to our mutual abilities."

"And the second reason?"

"Well, that's a little more complicated." She took a deep breath and decided she would just say it and be done with it. "I've come back to try and find out who killed the Laird of Ross. Black Ben as you all know him."

Gwen stood, her face ashen. "What are ye saying, lass. Ben is killed? And when? When is this to happen?"

"I'm sorry. I know this news is terrible and not something you wish to hear, but it's the truth. It's already written in history's pages. Sometime this May, the laird meets his fate."

"Well, we'll just have to change the text on those pages." Gwen paced to the bed and back, a deep frown line between her brows. "Tell me everything ye know of the situation. Mayhap I can help."

Kenzie didn't think the time appropriate to remind Gwen that they weren't technically allowed to change the past, but she held her tongue. "History states there's an ambush at Castle Ross that happens three months from now. There's a battle of some kind—over what was never recorded, for I don't believe people knew, and Ben is presumably killed. It's one of Scotland's unsolved mysteries. No one knows what happened to his lad after the altercation, either. The castle was burned to the ground and remains a ruin to this day. Well," Kenzie said, correcting what she'd said, "in my time." Kenzie hated seeing Gwen so rattled, but, if anyone could help her twist history, it was Gwen. "There are, of course, different scenarios about why it happened, but nothing has ever been proven."

"What are the scenarios?"

"That out of the grief of losing his wife, he took his own life, and that of the child." An awful thought that Kenzie didn't even want to contemplate. And after meeting Ben, it was a scenario that she no longer believed happened. Ben, for all his scandalous traits, loved children from what she'd seen of him around the estate. The thought that he could harm his own child just wasn't possible. It just wasn't in him to do such a thing.

"No, I don't believe that one," Gwen said, pacing some more. "What else?"

"That he handed the child over to his wife's family and disappeared. Burned down his estate to make it seem like he was murdered or had died during the fire. Left Scotland indefinitely."

Gwen met her gaze. "And what do you think happened."

Kenzie sat, having agonized over this very question for nigh on two years. "That he was murdered by his wife's family, and the child taken to be raised under the tutelage of Clan Grant. That's what I think happened, and I'll know for sure by May."

Gwen halted her pacing. "You are not going to Castle Ross with Ben. I forbid it. You could be killed and then what of our family? Our line will end with you. I can't allow that to happen."

It was a possibility that Kenzie had thought of herself. Of course, she had. This was medieval Scotland. Anything was possible, and death lurked around most corners, waiting for the unsuspecting to cloak its death shroud upon them. But she wouldn't allow it to happen to her. There was one thing she had that no one else other than the woman standing before her had. Witchcraft.

"I can leave at a moment's notice; disappear in a blink of an eye. Should I get into trouble, I promise you, Gwen, that I'll leave. But I must know what happens to the renowned Black Ben. His story has fascinated me since I was a little girl. Did you know there's a painting that hangs in this very house, of him? It was painted after he died, and so I always assumed you had it done as a way of remembering him."

Gwen bit her lip. "I canna let ye go. It would be wrong of me to be so lax in your wellbeing. Had I known you were here as a means to solve or change an historical event. Something, lass, that we should not do, I might add,

I would've sent ye home myself. In fact, I ought to do it now."

"I'll only come back," Kenzie said, crossing her arms. "I need to know the truth, and I know it's against the rules, but I will try and halt his demise if at all possible."

"You care for him."

It wasn't a question, and Kenzie sighed. She'd not meant to care for the rough, bad-mouthed, Scottish heathen, but she did. Somewhere between vexing and teasing her mercilessly, he'd managed to spark a yearning in her that she'd never felt for anyone else. And no matter how much she might state otherwise, Kenzie was aware that should he kiss her, it would not end there…

Not that she was going to tell Gwen such a thing. Not yet, at least. "Everyone likes Black Ben, and although we didn't get along at first, I can stomach him well enough. So, in a small way, I care for him, of course, but not in the way you may think." *Liar, liar, pants on fire!* She did care for him, terribly so, to the point that it scared her. From the instant she'd seen his portrait, tall and strong, standing in a field of heather with a castle in the background, she'd wondered about the man. Who he was? What had he been like?

That he was easy on the eye didn't hurt, either. Locks as dark as the night sky, and a small tilt of his lips that hinted at his mischievous character. She had been drawn to him immediately. And once she'd learned of the mystery surrounding his death, it had been almost an obsession of hers to find out what had happened to the Laird of Ross.

"Before you all hie off to Castle Ross and get your-selves killed, there is something we should try first. Mayhap, if we ask Ben to send for his son, just that small change in this time may alter what will take place in the future."

It was something she'd not thought of and certainly something they ought to give a go. Hope burst through her at the thought and again she had to remind herself that Black Ben was a frenemy, nothing more. "That's a fantastic idea. Do you think Ben will be willing to send for his son?"

At the sound of thunder, Gwen went to the window and looked out over the ocean and the impending storm. "I can ask. I'll make up some excuse as to why we wish to meet his boy. He may refuse at first, but if I know Ben, and I do very well, he'll continue to think of the proposal for some days afterward, and it is only then that he will decide yes or no to my request."

Kenzie stood and came over to stand next to her ancestor. "You must do it tomorrow. No delaying. The sooner we remove his boy from that estate, the better."

"I agree." Gwen sighed. "History is written, Kenzie. It will be hard to change what is already inscribed in the pages of time. We may delay or alter Ben's demise, but some way, somehow, his death will occur."

Kenzie shivered. "You changed history by bringing Abby back in time and my sending her back kept her here. Why will this plan not work?"

"Because, Ben is from this time. This is his life, and it has already occurred, been lived. I brought Abby back and altered a life that was not complete." Gwen frowned, taking her hand. "Do you understand what I'm trying to say?"

Kenzie nodded, unfortunately understanding only too well what Gwen meant. "Well, we have to alter history. It has to work. He has his boy who needs him, tenant families, and his clan that relies on him for their survival." She walked over to the small table that held a jug and bowl along with a tumbler of mead and poured herself a cup. "We can try," she said, taking a sip. "That's all we can do and hope for the best."

Gwen nodded. "Try we must and we'll see. Now," she said, walking to the bed and pulling down the top woolen blanket. "It's late and ye should get some rest. We have a big day ahead of us tomorrow."

Kenzie came over and hugged Gwen quickly. "Thank you for trying to help."

"Always," Gwen said, kissing Kenzie's cheek before leaving.

She lay down under the fur blankets and pulled it up over her. The tapestries swayed a little with the drafts throughout the room, and she thought of Ben. No matter how annoying the man was, she cared for him, the small amount that it was, but nonetheless, she did, and she would hate for him to die so young.

No one deserved to be murdered, and when Kenzie had read of his disappearance it was what she'd always thought had happened to him. Foul play had occurred, and with any luck, their plan to bring Ben's son to Gwen and Braxton's estate might alter the past enough to ensure he survived.

And if that plan didn't work, well, she would just have to think up another one.

CHAPTER 7

enzie sat beside Gwen in the library, Braxton standing behind them, while Ben stood before the fire, hips spread, and arms folded over a muscular chest, barely hidden by the shirt that he wore.

She swallowed. Was he doing some kind of exercise regime that she didn't know about? Maybe he'd been helping with the chores about the estate and had buffed up that way, but wow, he was big.

And looking pretty nice to the eye. Too nice in fact. Kenzie caught Ben's gaze and her stomach tightened at the raw hunger she read in his eyes. How was it he could look at a woman in such a way and think no one would notice? She cast Gwen a glance and was met with a raised brow. Kenzie sat up, clasping her hands in her lap, and fought to control her wayward mind.

"Are ye going to ask me what it is ye want? As much as I love standing before ye all and being the object of Kenzie's interest, I do wish to go for a ride."

"I beg your pardon," Kenzie said, her face flaming.

"What?" Ben asked, a devilish grin lifting his lips,

which only reminded Kenzie how damn gorgeous he was. "You weren't looking at me?"

"No, I was not," she stated, beyond mortified at being called out.

Braxton cleared his throat. "Since you're still not well enough to travel back to Castle Ross, we thought ye may wish to bring Alasdair here, to stay with us while you recuperate from ye illness."

Ben ran a hand through his hair, leaving it on end. "Oh aye, is that all? I thought ye were about to berate me for kissing Kenzie last eve."

"You kissed Kenzie?" Braxton rounded the settee, and Gwen stood quickly, clasping her husband's arm.

"It was hardly a kiss, Ben. More like a chaste peck," Kenzie said, shaking her head.

"I'm inclined to think of it as a taste of better things to come."

"'Tis nothing to worry about, Braxton. Do not forget that Kenzie is an adult and able to make her own choices, even if ye may not agree with them."

Braxton glowered at Ben, who merely grinned in return. "I don't agree with that choice."

Kenzie didn't miss the flicker of pain that crossed Ben's visage, before he laughed it off. "Dinna get bothered by it, Braxton, my old friend. It was only a little kiss and nothing remarkable. I'll not be pursuing Kenzie if that is ye concern. I'm merely teasing."

Kenzie stood there, stunned into silence. Had he really just said her kiss was unremarkable? What the hell! "Well, I wasn't going to be sharing any more kisses anyway, so it doesn't bother me at all, should you not pursue anything further with me."

Ben's eyes narrowed on her, his gaze dipping to her

lips. She glared back, ridiculously affronted. Not that she cared one bit that he didn't like her in that way. Even if his kiss teased at something so much better… Actually, really great if she was being honest, but she wouldn't give him the pleasure of seeing how annoyed his rebuttal made her.

"So, will ye bring Alasdair back here? We'd so love to meet your boy." Gwen let go of Braxton and joined Ben at the hearth, taking his hand. "It'll be good for him to be here, to be around a clan that will love him as much as his own."

Ben's features softened at Gwen's words and an odd unnerving feeling settled in the pit of Kenzie's stomach. Was she jealous of Gwen? Just the thought of such a thing was unreasonable. Gwen was happily married to Braxton and that was an end to it. She was merely being kind and persuasive to an old friend. And Kenzie was being an idiot.

"It's settled then," Braxton said, walking over to the desk and pulling out a piece of parchment and laying it on the dark wooden surface. "Write to ye clan and have the boy sent here immediately. We'll hold a feast, celebrating the birth of the future Laird of Ross." Braxton turned to Gwen. "Mayhap ye brother would wish to attend. I'm sure Abby would welcome a visit to see the new estate and with Kenzie being here, 'tis an extra boon."

Gwen clapped her hands, her face wreathed in smiles. "Och, it sounds a fabulous idea, Braxton. We should have thought of it sooner."

Kenzie smiled at their joy and stole a look at Ben who also seemed pleased by the idea but maybe a little more guarded than her ancestors were. Ben walked over to the desk and sat, writing out the missive as Braxton and Gwen discussed details of the feast and what other families they would invite.

With nothing else to do, Kenzie sat on the settee, watching the flames in the grate lick at the wood. The sound of the reed pen scratching over the parchment filled the room after Gwen and Braxton left them alone in the library. If she were back home in her own time, she would flick on the television and watch a movie or something, anything to chase the boredom away. And yet how could anyone be bored here? It was like living in her own period movie. With real-life warriors and grand estates, families that held great power surrounded by those who probably wished for some of that power themselves.

"Why do they call you Black Ben?" In all her study of the man it had never been explained why he was nick-named thus. She turned in her chair to see him folding the missive and putting it aside.

"My hair."

Not for the first time, she noticed his dark locks. In fact, Ben had the features of a Spaniard more than a Scotsman, but still it was odd that his name was solely due to his hair color. "Truly? That's it?"

He laughed and joined her on the chair, Kenzie shuffled over a little, not wanting him to get any ideas now that they were alone since he didn't find her kisses remarkable…

"Aye, that's it. I was always recognizable at any skirmish or clan gathering due to my hair. Someone, I forget who, named me Black Ben, and it stuck. I'm also the best longbow shot in all of Scotland, and possibly England, as well, but 'tis my hair that I'm known by.

Without thinking, Kenzie reached out and touched his dark locks, the color a deep shade of ebony and as black as the night sky. He was forbidden to her, a man she shouldn't dally with. A Scottish legend with a mysterious story. He'd always fascinated her and here he was before her, looking at her as if he wished to devour her whole.

Kenzie tightened her grip on his hair, pulling him toward her. Ben mumbled something in Gaelic she couldn't understand before yanking her against his chest and kissing her with a force that left her breathless.

Their teeth smashed together before he bit her bottom lip, soothing it immediately with his tongue. It was so dirty and hot, Kenzie was totally out of her depth. Yes, she'd kissed men before, quite a few, in fact, but never anybody like this. Ben's kisses left her reeling for purchase on ground as slippery as the snow atop the Highland mountains.

"Are ye sure you should be kissing me, lass? Will not Braxton disapprove?"

"I don't require anyone to give me permission to kiss who I want. And maybe you shouldn't be kissing me, since I'm so unremarkable."

He took her lips again and this time a moan pushed past her lips. With her busy life, she'd missed out on the pleasure of kissing.

"I lied. Ye are more than remarkable, lass." Ben winked, and desire flowed through her at his words. Silly for a modern woman to worry about what this Highlander from the seventeenth century thought, but for some strange reason, Kenzie wanted him to like her.

She kissed him hard, taking everything he was willing to give her while they were alone.

"Ye should let me kiss ye every day."

Kenzie couldn't agree more. One could drown in his stormy blue eyes. "Maybe I will." *Of course I will!*

He grinned. "Aye, ye will."

A servant carrying a bucket came into the room and stumbled to a stop. Unable to meet the servant's eye,

Kenzie jumped up and stepped away. Ben, on the other hand, simply lounged back in the chair, as if being caught in such a position by household staff was a common occurrence.

Kenzie wasn't sure if she should be worried by that fact or take her cue from him. But, this wasn't her home, it was Gwen and Braxton's, and she ought to be more respecting of them and their lifestyle.

Without a word, Kenzie left the room, walking straight to her own. If she were to stay in this time, she needed to stay away from Ben, at least in the sexual way. No matter how invigorating his kisses were, he wasn't for her to play with.

~

*B*en watched Kenzie leave the room until she was out of sight. The servant left, too, which was just as well, or he would've been tempted to glare at the lass for interrupting what had been turning into a delightful afternoon.

For weeks he'd been without the comfort only a woman could bring, but as much as it chafed to admit it, after meeting Kenzie, he hadn't wanted anyone else to warm his bed. He wanted her, and it was damn frustrating.

Kenzie was not the kind of lass who'd want to stay in this time. Nor would she do well as a lady of a great house such as his own. The time here was not for the faint of heart, and the day-to-day life in a castle was not easy. There was the staff to run, and ensure his clansmen were kept fed and housed. Tally the books and keep the home up. Aline had done a superb job as his wife, but the lass had been brought up to do such things. Kenzie, on the other hand, had not.

A rap at the door was followed by another servant who held out a missive. "This just arrived, Laird Ross."

Ben thanked the lad and broke the seal, scanning the letter quickly. It was from his manservant and friend who was looking after his lands in his absence. His mention of Aline's father visiting, and the prolonged time he'd spent with Ben's son made the hair on the back of his neck rise.

What was the man trying to tell him by visiting his lad when he himself was away? Unease trickled down his spine, and he stood, striding quickly toward the foyer. He ran into Braxton on his way to find his servant to ready his departure without delay.

"Is all well, Ben?" Braxton asked, halting his steps.

"Aline's father has been at Castle Ross. I must return. His visit during my absence is a warning I'm not likely to ignore. I must go." He stepped away, but Braxton pulled him to a stop.

"Now? But we were about to celebrate the arrival of Kenzie and your son. Surely, if you brought ye boy to stay here with us, there is naught that Clan Grant can do."

It was true, Braxton and Gwen lived under the protection of Clan Macleod. 'Twould be a fool indeed who tried to cause trouble here, but Castle Ross was isolated, and with his son there alone with only the servants as protection, Ben had left him in a vulnerable position. There was also little chance of Clan Grant allowing the lad to travel here in the first place. Not if they wished Alasdair to stay with them; they would not see him anywhere but where he was right now.

He swore, running a hand through his hair. He'd been a selfish bastard for leaving the boy not long after his birth.

No matter how far he traveled from his lands, the memory of Aline and her unbearable sweetness while she'd lain dying wrecked his mind even now.

It was his fault she'd died. To prove to her that his marrying her was due to his affection, the more time he spent with her, the more he actually came to like the lass, and somehow, in the time that they were married, he had come to care for her deeply.

"I cannot risk my son or lands. I must go."

"Aye," Braxton said, clasping him on his shoulder. "I'll see that ye servant is notified and you're on ye way by daybreak."

"No, I must leave now." He started toward the stairs. "I'll have a cart sent to gather the remainder of my possessions, which are few, but I'll go by horseback tonight. If I can trouble ye for one of ye best fighting men, I would be greatly appreciative."

"Anything," Braxton said without hesitation. "I'll have James sent for. He's my best swordsman."

Ben thanked him and started up the stairs. He stopped after two steps and turned to face Braxton. "Will yet tell Kenzie and Gwen of my parting? I dinna want to say goodbye. I've never been vera good at it." His goodbye with Aline had left him with many unsaid words. How he was sorry that he'd married her under false pretenses. That he feared she'd guessed his deception but tried to make the best of a situation that wasn't what she'd hoped for. That he'd made her have his son, which, in turn, had killed her. Goodbyes were never easy, and Ben now avoided them like the pox.

Understanding dawned in Braxton's eyes. "I can do that for ye. I'll also have ye horse ready to depart within the next half hour."

"Thank ye, Braxton. You're a good man." One of the best, in fact. It was no surprise why Aedan Macleod had allowed the man to marry his sister.

It didn't take Ben long to put the few articles he'd traveled with together into a sack. Going about the room and checking he had everything that he needed for the journey home; he doubted a cart would be required, after all. He left the room and strode down the hall, slowing his steps as he passed Kenzie's quarters. No feminine chatter came from behind the door and he wondered if she were in there, reading or looking out over the estate's lands. Was she lying on her bed, dreaming of him...?

He cursed himself as a damn fool for acting like a green lad. It was not like he'd never met a lass before who'd made the blood in his veins burn. So soon after the death of his wife, he didn't need to become embroiled with some meddling woman from the future who had a tongue as sharp as his blade. There were a few lasses at his own estate that would scratch the itch that annoyed him daily. He would seek them out as soon as he returned home.

Another lie. He would do no such thing.

But first he had to deal with his deceased wife's clan and make perfectly clear that they had better keep off his lands unless he was present. Ben could understand that after the death of Aline they harbored anger and resentment toward him, but he could not allow them to take what was his.

CHAPTER 8

$\mathcal{A}$t dinner, Kenzie sat stunned as Braxton told both her and Gwen of Ben's departure that afternoon. She'd been sitting in her room, trepidation making the book she'd held in her hands shake when she'd heard Ben stride down the hall. It must have been the time that he was going. That he was leaving to return to Castle Ross had not been what she'd expected to hear. A small part of her had hoped he'd stride into her room and quench the thirst she had for him. After what had happened in the library, she thought he might take charge, burst into her room, and seduce her.

Apparently not.

It was an odd reaction to have since Kenzie had never liked overbearing men. Maybe it was because she'd inherited a Scottish estate and had taken over the running and care of it when she was of age. She'd been brought up to be independent and often did what needed to be done herself. She had never relied on any others for support. Of course, she had been happy if it was offered, but it had not been needed, necessarily.

So, to want Ben to take charge of her body, throw her onto her bed, play her like a fine instrument until she sang, wasn't the norm.

"Why did you not try and stop him? Aedan and Abby will be here later today. And now there is no point in bringing them all this way." A small frown line marred Gwen's brow and it was a frustration and disappointment Kenzie understood.

"You wanted me to keep Black Ben, one of the most fearsome Scots this side of Edinburgh here against his will? I dinna have a death wish, wife."

Gwen huffed out an annoyed breath. "I thought he was bringing his son here."

"Yes, well I suppose he wished to return home to ensure that not only was his son well, but also that Castle Ross does not come into jeopardy by Clan Grant. You know they never approved of Aline marrying him, and they're seeking out justified revenge, in their opinion if I know anything about them."

Kenzie hadn't thought it was as bad as all that, but perhaps she was allowing her twenty-first-century mind not to rationalize too much and not see just how hard and dangerous this time was for others.

"Do you think Clan Grant will strike at Ben?" Knowing that in only three months Ben would be killed, Kenzie couldn't help but think that this was perhaps the start of the Black Ben mystery that historians had wondered about. Clan Grant held a grudge, so it could be that laird who had a price on Ben's head.

"I have to follow him, Gwen. You know why." Kenzie didn't want to say any more as Braxton wasn't aware of Ben's fate, but perhaps it was only a matter of time, if his accusing glance at Gwen was any indication.

"I promised Kenzie not to say anything, but under the circumstances, I'm sure she will understand," Gwen said, setting down her napkin.

Kenzie wasn't too sure about that...

Gwen explained to Braxton what she had told her only weeks ago and watched with growing alarm as her ancestor's visage took on a horrified look.

"I must notify Aedan of this. As soon as he arrives and you," Braxton said, his attention snapping to her, "must explain everything that ye know of Black Ben's death. We cannot allow what history has deemed his fate to happen. He deserves better than that."

When Kenzie had first met Ben, she couldn't think of a more fitting outcome for the man. But now, the Highlander may be a little rough around the edges, but he did genuinely care for her family, and his death was not justified. Men married women without love all the time. It was not a crime worthy of death. Clan Grant might never believe that the marriage was a happy one, but Kenzie would disagree. Ben had certainly found Aline attractive, and Kenzie was sure that he had made her as happy as he could. They may not have loved each other, but they did care for each other a great deal, and that is more than many could boast.

It was no one's fault that Aline had passed away during childbirth. Unfortunately, that happened, even in her own time.

They sat in the grand hall, the large fire burning and throwing heat about the cathedral-type room. Some of the clan sat on trestle tables before them, eating and talking, all of them unaware of Kenzie's troubles.

The doors to the front of the house burst open, and in strode a rider who looked saddle worn and tired. He gazed about the room and then started toward them, handing a missive to Braxton before Gwen handed him some coin, and he was gone as quick as he came. The clansmen present stopped eating and cast speculative glances their way.

"Who's the missive from, my dear," Gwen asked, taking a roll of bread and dipping it into the stew.

"Aedan. Abby isn't well, and they're unable to come." He paused, folding the missive again. "'Tis probably for the best. I shall travel to Druiminn Castle and speak to them in person. You'll come, too, Gwen. If what Kenzie knows of Ben's future is true, having you at Druiminn will be safer, should I have to accompany Aedan to Castle Ross."

"You think Aedan will travel to Ben's home, knowing what we do?" It shouldn't surprise Kenzie that he would, as it was exactly what she herself wanted to do. Ben was his oldest friend and ally. The man had married Aline so Aedan could marry Abby. If they did arrive with reinforcements, it might be enough to tweak Ben's past and his death would never occur. Hope bloomed in her chest.

"Aedan will go, and so, too, will my husband, but take care, Braxton. Kenzie knows very little in relation to Ben's death. He just seems to disappear. So, whoever his enemy is, he's cunning and most likely someone Ben knows but does not suspect. Mayhap 'tis someone none of ye would."

Kenzie stood, the crunch of her chair across the flagstone floor echoed loud within the room. "I'm going, too, and I'll pack tonight." She held up her hand when Braxton stood and crossed his arms.

"Stop, Braxton. I'm going, and there is nothing you can do to stop me. As much as I love you both very much, I have to go. It was one of my main reasons for traveling back. And anyway," she said, shrugging, "you and Aedan will soon be at Castle Ross. There is nothing for me to fear."

Braxton looked less than convinced, but Gwen smiled, pulling her husband to sit back down. "I will have a horse prepared for departure first thing in the morning and send some armed men with ye. You'll be safe, my dear, but be warned, 'tis a five-day horse ride to Castle Ross. Are ye sure you're up to it? If you're not used to such long distances on horseback, it can become quite uncomfortable."

Kenzie waved her concerns away, absolutely positive that this was the right choice. Five days on horseback shouldn't be so bad. As long as the horse didn't get spooked and bolt, everything would be great. "I'll be fine. I promise. Five-day horse ride will be fine. With all the renovations I've done in my life, I think it's safe to say I've done worse."

～

She had not done worse. In fact, the pain in her legs and her bottom could very well be the worst hurt she'd ever experienced in her life. The first day of travel had gone well, and though when she'd jumped down from her mare to eat it had taken a few steps and stretching to feel herself again, it hadn't been so bad.

But by end of day two, her inner thighs had started to rub against the saddle, even though she'd worn trews under her dress. Not only that, her bottom was so numb that she wondered if it had fallen off.

And no matter how much she rubbed it, or walked about when they stopped, nothing helped. It also didn't help that the few armed men that accompanied her seemed quite amused by her unfortunate circumstances. Kenzie was positive they'd taken the long way round to Castle Ross and were spending less time on breaks. No doubt taking pleasure from her pain.

Damn Highlanders.

By day five, the outer lands of Castle Ross could not come soon enough. They rested the horses beside a slow flowing river, and Kenzie took the opportunity to wash her face and freshen up as much as she could. The thought of a warm soaking bath made her get the men going sooner than they probably wanted, but Kenzie had had enough. If she ever sat on another horse it would be too soon. If only she had her car, she would've been at Castle Ross within a few hours.

Her first glimpse of Castle Ross was nothing like she expected. It sat on a picturesque outcrop of land beside a loch. One single road led toward the castle, and the greenest land circled the building like a protective screen from the waters below. Kenzie pulled her horse to a stop, taking in the castle's magnificence. In her own time, she'd only seen the ruins of this great home. To see it in its full glory—chimneys with smoke puffing out, windows twinkling in the afternoon sun, people milling about outside, going about their jobs—was amazing.

As they came closer, the structure became more imposing. She had always tried to imagine the castle as it once was, but with only a few walls remaining, and even those broken and crumbling with age, it was hard to tell just how large the home had once been.

Seeing it now was awe-inspiring. Castle Ross was, in one word, stunning.

"They've seen us," one of her guards shouted.

Kenzie tore her gaze from the many turrets and windows of the castle, to the men who had come out from the entrance gate and were blocking their way.

They rode up to them, and seeing that her guards dismounted, Kenzie did the same, trying to stem the niggling bite of fear that trembled in her stomach that they might be seen as a threat. All would be well once they understood she was a friend of Laird Ross.

"What's ye business with the Laird Ross this day?"

An imposing guard, with shoulders the size of a heavyweight boxer, stepped in front of the other men, crossing his arms over his chest. Kenzie couldn't stop looking at the size of his muscles until one of her own men cleared his throat.

"I'm a relative of Gwendolyn Macleod and friend to Laird Ross. I've traveled here to speak with your laird."

"Ye're English." The question was more like a statement that left a bitter taste in the man's mouth.

Kenzie raised her chin, not about to let this man treat her with disrespect. "And Scottish, not that it is any concern of yours. Now, if you please, would you inform your laird of my arrival and let him choose if where I grew up affects our friendship."

The man's gaze narrowed on her, but a flicker of respect entered his brown orbs and some of Kenzie's trepidation dissipated.

"If you'll follow me, I'll take ye to our laird."

When all of them started to follow, the guard stopped, pointing at her men. "Just the lady. Ye men stay here until our laird deems it safe."

Kenzie turned to face her guards. "These are Gwendolyn MacLeod and Sir Braxton's men. They are not a threat."

"Even so, our laird will be the decider on that."

She frowned, not wanting to leave the men who'd kept her safe for the past five days out in the cold. "I shall not be long. This is just precautionary, I'm sure. As soon as I see the laird, I'll have you brought inside."

"Right ye are, miss," her guard said, nodding slightly, but clasping the helm of his sword in silent warning to any who might wish to do her harm. Kenzie smiled, thankful that men she'd only known a few days could be so loyal as to give up their lives for her. Not that it was necessary here, as the Laird of Ross would soon welcome them. But this time was fraught with danger, and one who owned such large, profitable holdings could not be complacent.

They started toward the castle and the arched doorway. The guards stepped to the side and allowed her to enter the castle proper. Goose bumps rose on her skin at the temperature change, somehow inside the castle walls it was colder, and she pulled her shawl closer about her shoulders.

The entrance opened into a large anteroom with no real function, from what Kenzie could tell, before going through a door adjacent to the front one the room gave way to the great hall. Wooden tables ran the length of the room—one of which housed two padded seats that was undoubtedly where the laird and his wife would break their fast—and on both sides of the space, two large fires burned with ferocity.

Kenzie stood transfixed, taking in all that was before her. In her time, all of this was rubble, nothing but layers of stone that had long fallen into total disrepair. The fireplace still stood, but other than that, that was it.

"You may wait near the fire," the guard said, pointing toward it as if she couldn't see it right in front of her.

Kenzie nodded, not really worried where she waited, so long as she got to stay in this room and memorize everything so when she returned to her time, she could ensure Castle Ross was restored to its exact former glory.

She strolled over to the table where the laird would eat at meal times and ran her hand over the top of the dark wooden chair engraved with scrolls and different patterns. An embroidered cushion that sported a hunting scene was its only luxury. The embroidery was very well done, and Kenzie wondered if Aline had stitched it for their comfort.

The sound of a banging door made her jump, and she recognized the footsteps without turning about. "Good evening, Ben," she said, feeling the presence of him as he came to stand behind her.

His hands came down on her shoulders and he turned her to face him. Kenzie had to look up to meet his eyes, and a shiver of expectation ran through her as his gaze was warm and welcoming.

"What are ye doing here, lass? I didn't expect to see ye again."

He let his hands drop to his sides, and she missed the contact as soon as it was gone. How was it possible that in less than a week she had missed the rogue? From the moment he'd returned to his estate, Kenzie had known she would follow him if only to try and save him from his own fate. To say goodbye.

"My parents' marriage wasn't a happy one and I didn't want to return to my time regretting any of my choices here. My mother regrets most of her choices in life, probably all but me, and I don't want to live like that. I had to see you again."

A slight, wicked smile lifted his lips, and Kenzie's legs jiggled like jelly. "And what would seeing me again achieve, lass?" He stepped closer still, and without thought, she reached out, clasping his hip, the tartan kilt rough against her palms.

"It would mean I would achieve saying goodbye to you. You disappeared without coming to see me, so we may wish each other well."

"I dinna think ye would care if we wished each other well. We dinna part on the best terms the last time I saw ye. If I recall we were in disagreement about the kiss."

"I hardly think it was a disagreement."

He stepped closer, giving her a lazy smile.

Should she let him tease her into kissing him? Right now, Kenzie wanted nothing more than to show him he was not the only one who could taunt and tease. But by doing so opened up a whole can of worms where emotions could start to come into play and feelings that could result in pain.

"I should imagine you've kissed many women." History certainly stated Black Ben had a woman in every port and inland town, prior to his marriage, at least. Kenzie hated reading about such things, knowing so many women had enjoyed the man before her, but maybe with any luck it was all false. It was something certainly to hope for.

"I have, but no one that mattered since Aline passed away."

"Gwen said she found you the night before you arrived at her home in a tavern, and your business there was obvious, if you know what I mean."

"Nay, what do ye mean, lass," he asked, meekly.

Kenzie almost scoffed. There wasn't a meek bone in his body. "The rumors that followed you to Gwen and Braxton's home suggested you'd been whoring your way around Scotland since Aline's death."

"Aye, I may have been, but ye cannot believe everything ye hear. And I'm here now, with you."

"*Hmm*," Kenzie said, sitting herself down on a chair close to the fire. "I have some of Braxton's men outside the walls. Will you let them in? I'm sure they're hungry and in need of a good night's sleep."

"When the guards came and told me of your arrival, I sent them word to allow the men to enter. Cook will have some fare taken out to them since we've already eaten this evening."

Her stomach chose that exact time to rumble. "Would it be any trouble if I could also have something to eat? I've not eaten since lunch."

Ben yelled out to a man who stood silently at the end of the room. "Have some of tonight's dinner brought up for our guest, and have a room prepared. She'll be staying for a time."

She met his gaze and her toes curled and her body thrummed from the look. They were alone here now. Gwen and Braxton were miles away and not around to interrupt…

"You have a beautiful castle. I've visited it, you know, in my time."

"Ye have?" Ben's seemed genuinely delighted by the notion. "And 'tis it as grand as it is right now? Are my descendants still ruling the area?"

Thankfully, the food arrived for it allowed Kenzie to prepare her answer. She placed an apple and a pear on her plate along with some flat bread and pheasant. What could she say to Ben that wouldn't give away what was to happen to him in a few months? Had she been in his position, she would want to know the truth, no matter how painful. "Castle Ross, unfortunately, is not as grand, and your family is no longer in charge of it. But it has a new owner now, who is determined to make it as magnificent as it once was. I have no doubt she will succeed."

He sat forward, the line between his brow as deep as a ravine. "My family no longer have Castle Ross?" He gestured with his hands. "How can that be? Why?"

"A lot of castles and great estates were lost to the great families who owned them after the first World War that took place in 1918 to 1922. They placed taxes on estates that were never there before, and after such a bloody war, where a lot of families lost their heirs and the workers who helped keep the estates running were killed in action, a lot of the homes were sold or demolished." It wasn't what had happened to Ben's family or Castle Ross, but it was the truth for so many others, and Kenzie wasn't ready to tell Ben that he lost his home in his own time due to an unknown entity that she had yet to figure out. This way was better and hopefully, would ease the hurt he no doubt was feeling about the revelation. "I'm sorry, Ben. I know it's not what anyone would wish to hear."

"What is this World War you talk of?"

How could she explain this to him and make sense? "It's a large-scale war involving many powerful countries around the world. This war spanned multiple locations with wide-spread battles." He looked bewildered.

He slumped on to a nearby chair, running his hand across his stubbled jaw. "This is upsetting."

"History is cruel, and this is not something that you were ever to know. Had I not arrived and told you, it would not be a concern of yours."

"Aye," he said throwing her that devilishly gorgeous lazy smile that made her ache. "I see yer point."

Kenzie ate some pheasant, using her fingers to pick up

the bird since she couldn't find a knife. She watched Ben while she chewed. He was lost in thought and staring at the fire. She didn't like seeing him look so sad, but she could understand why he was quiet, so she let him be while she finished her food.

"Tell me of one of your fondest memories growing up here. I'm sure this castle has lots of history and tales that its walls could tell."

He met her gaze, nodding. "'Tis true, it has many stories. One of my fondest was hiding from my Nurse. Upstairs near the nursery there is a hidden room between the two rooms. Not many of the staff know of it, and whenever I wished to skip my reading or writing lessons, I'd hide in there. I could hear them running about, calling out my name, and eventually, I'd come out and sit back at my desk as if I'd been there the whole time."

Kenzie laughed. She could just imagine the young laird being a little shit when he was younger. "It seems your ability to be naughty hasn't changed."

He threw her a look of pure wickedness and her stomach clenched.

"Where's the fun in being good?"

Not willing to open that can of worms, Kenzie placed her empty plate down. "I hope you don't mind me coming to stay. As I said, I've always wanted to see Castle Ross, and since I'm here now, I thought it a good idea to visit."

"I dinna mind in the least. I look forward to having ye stay here with me."

"Gwen mentioned that Clan Grant were here. Are they still?"

"Nay, they were gone by the time I arrived home, but my steward mentioned that Evan Grant, the future laird, was only too willing to yell and order around my clansmen while he was here. Not that they obeyed, mind. My men would know better than to betray me in such a way, but I wonder at what Evan meant by such actions. 'Tis certainly an act of betrayal. I would never presume to do such a thing in his keep."

Aline's family seemed to be troublesome and the more Kenzie heard of them the more she was inclined to believe it was them who would attack and kill Ben. He may not believe anyone was out to get him, but they were. History said so, and the Grants were showing many signs of antagonism toward Ben. She would have to convince him to be wary of them.

Ben sipped his ale and his gaze caught hers over the top of the mug. He placed the cup down and leaned forward in his chair. "Let us talk of other things. I dinna want to waste my breath on the Grants."

"What would you like to discuss instead?" Kenzie asked, warily.

"I would like to discuss this feeling that I have toward ye that I get each and every time you're near."

Kenzie would like to do more than talk about the 'feeling' but would it be too forward if she made the first move? This period in history said *no* to acting in such a way, but she doubted Ben would care overly much. She got up and went to stand before the fire.

"I won't play coy and say that I don't know what you're talking about, because I do." Boy, did she ever. She'd been drawn to the man ever since she was a young girl and she'd seen the painting of him. She'd always wondered what he'd been like, who he'd loved, and what had happened to him. "Maybe we could try that kiss again?" she said, hoping he'd agree.

Shock registered on his face before the hunger that

made her own blood sing took hold. He stood and came toward her. Unable to wait a minute longer, Kenzie reached up and pulled him down for a kiss.

Their lips met, and her heart was in serious trouble. For all the roughness about Ben, his lips were as soft as butter. His hands clasped her face, and he deepened the kiss, the invasion of his tongue not wet and sloppy like so many other men she'd kissed, but sweet and seductive. Kissing was always enjoyable, but this kaleidoscope of emotions, the rioting feelings that he evoked in her, left her grasping for purchase and unlike anything she'd ever felt before.

Kenzie threw herself into the kiss, no longer satisfied with doing what was safe, or what was expected. Tonight, she would allow herself to be swept up by a man who challenged, infuriated, and fascinated her all at once.

She lifted herself up on her toes, wrapping her arms about his neck. Ben did the same, but in a more languorous way, sliding his hands down her throat and arms and then her hips, pulling her hard against him. Within Ben's arms, everything was different. It was as if her senses were on overdrive and out of control.

His hands flexed against her hips as he ground against her. She gasped, feeling the bulging excitement behind his kilt. He was big. She hoped she'd not bitten off more than she could chew.

"Do ye want me to stop, lass?" He pulled back a fraction, his lust-laden gaze burning with unsated need. "I shall leave ye, should ye wish it. But if we continue this way, I'm not sure I'll ever let ye leave my arms again."

Oh my… This man said all the right words. It was if she was living a real-life romance novel, where the heroine found her soulmate in a different century. Not that they were soulmates—they fought and disagreed on too many things, but still… His deep Scottish brogue was seriously sexy. "I don't want you to stop."

He growled and hoisted her into his arms, kissing her with a fervor that left her breathless. His determined strides ate up the distance from the great hall to the stone staircase. Was he taking her to his room? *Oh, yes, please.*

Kenzie didn't break the kiss, not ever wanting to stop kissing this man. There was something about him that drew her even before she'd known him in person. It was an oddity she'd never understood. Perhaps they'd been destined to meet all along and be just as they were now, clasped together and about to have some hot and heavy sex.

Making his room, he kicked the door shut, and Kenzie giggled. It was so barbarian of him. He placed her on her feet, and she started to undo the laces at the front of her dress. He watched her in silence. Each time her gown gaped a little more, his gaze turned darker.

With a swoosh, her gown pooled at her feet, and she stood before him in nothing but her shift. Thankfully, beneath her feet was a bearskin rug and a roaring fire behind her that threw out plenty of warmth. "Are you going to take off your kilt, Ben" she asked, running her hand down his back and over his perfectly formed ass.

"Why don't ye do it for me."

Kenzie grinned and untied the sporran about his waist, before unpinning his kilt. It, too, fell heavy upon the floor and left him standing in nothing but his birthday suit. Kenzie expelled a satisfied sigh at the sight of Ben naked. Now he was hers to do with as she pleased. Not a shred of embarrassment marked his visage, and she marveled at his confidence. "You're more of an expert at this type of thing. What did you want to do next, my liege?"

Ben lifted her up as if she weighed nothing at all, and she wrapped her legs about his hips, gasping as his member nestled against her sex. She'd never been this close to a man that she wanted so much before. His hardness and pricking of hair against her tickled and teased.

Yearning for more, she undulated against his cock and heard his muffled curse against her ear. She wanted to ride him, lose control, and be anything but a lady in his arms.

"Ye're so sweet, lass." His hand moved up her leg to clasp her bottom, squeezing her flesh and rubbing it in turn. "I want ye so much."

She clasped his unshaven jaw, making him meet her gaze. "I want you, too. More than I've ever wanted anyone in my life, but there's something you should know."

He frowned, taking in her features. "What is it?"

"I don't want you to think I'm sleeping with you to gain a husband because I'm not. No offense, but I'm not staying, so I'm hoping you'll look at this interaction as a bit of fun—an enjoyable way to pass the time while I'm still here."

He chuckled, picking her up again and walking toward the bed. "Are ye trying to tell me in the nicest way possible that ye're not looking to have me as ye husband? That ye just want me to tup ye so well that your time passes pleasantly?"

He laid her on the bed, and a shiver of excitement ran through her. "That's exactly what I'm saying." Kenzie reached down and stroked his cock, unable to fathom she was about to sleep with a Highland warrior. Ben leaned over her, a tower of muscle and dark beauty, and somewhere deep inside, Kenzie knew her life would never be the same again.

~

*B*en watched a full-body flush disperse across perfect, unblemished skin, and he wanted to kiss every inch that the rose bloom marked. Kenzie was so beautiful and smart that she literally left him in awe.

That her viperish, no-nonsense tongue didn't put up with any of his shit was also quite a turn-on.

She shuffled back on his animal-skin-covered bed, and he followed her, running his hand along one flawless foot all the way to her hip, where he reached around and kneaded one perfectly sized ass globe.

"Will it vex ye to know that since ye attended me that first night, I've wanted to tup ye? Have ye just as you are right now. Naked and mine to do with as I please."

Her breasts were a perfect handful, and he ran a finger over the peaks, watching as the skin on her nipples pulled tight and darkened in color. Kenzie's breathing became ragged, which was only fair, as Ben's own body was on fire and not the least in control.

This woman did odd things to him, made him yearn for things that he'd never thought to have again. He reminded himself this was a little fun. A bit of tupping between two adults who wanted no other responsibilities with it. Never again would he place another woman in jeopardy by making her pregnant. No matter what the healer said, Ben couldn't help but wonder if giving birth was the sole reason behind Aline's untimely death. Not a tumor…

Tonight, he would take this lass, but he wouldn't spill his seed within her. Never again would he be so reckless.

She reached up and linked her fingers behind his neck, the trust in her eyes making his body ache with need. "If we're being honest with each other I, too, need to tell you that on that first night, before you opened your mouth and ruined all my fantasies, I wanted you, too. You were so untouchable and rugged, I thought my heart would burst free from my chest, you made it beat so hard."

Pleasure rocked through Ben at her words. She had wanted him? The truth of her statement made him desire her even more. Writhing and screaming his name against his ear, feeling her body convulse around his cock when she came.

Damn, he needed her like he needed air.

"I'm glad to hear it, lass," he said, taking her lips, showing her without words how much he wanted her. Needed her even. She kissed him back, taking his mouth with vigor. Her hips pushed up against his hard sex, teasing him as much as herself with the friction.

"I want you Ben. Now."

He growled and sitting up, kneeled between her legs. Again, the delightful blush rose on her skin, but she would color a lot more before this night was over. He grinned at the thought.

He pulled her legs up and ran a finger down the inner side of her thigh, all the way to the apex of her legs where she glistened with arousal. It took all of his control not to take her as quick and fast as he wanted. But no, not tonight. Somehow, in some way, he'd earned her trust enough that she was willing to give herself to him. He wanted to be the man, like no other, in giving her pleasure.

He would not mess it up or rush what he wanted

Kenzie to remember forever. Take a little piece of his soul to the future with her and measure all her lovers against his standard.

Slowly, he ran his finger across her patch of curls, sliding it between her folds, enjoying the view of Kenzie biting her lip and squirming beneath his touch.

He delved further and found her entrance hot and tight, too tight to be able to take him straight away. Ben pushed into her heat, watching her as he teased her wider, deeper with each stroke.

"What are you doing to me?" She sighed, reaching for him.

He met her gaze and was glad to see the lust that echoed his own reflected in her emerald eyes. "Has it been a while since ye slept with a man, lass? I dinna want to hurt ye." She nodded, moaning when he stroked the pleasure point, before sliding again into her welcoming heat.

"I'm so ready. Truly ready right now, Ben." She licked her lips, and seeing her delightful pink tongue made his cock tighten. The need running through his veins was too much, and Ben took himself into his own hand, stroking his cock, while fucking her with his fingers.

It was too good. Too right. Kenzie reached up and helped him. He had to have her. Now. He came down over her, and excitement and trepidation met his gaze.

"All will be well, lass. I'm sure ye won't have any trouble accommodating me once I finish teasing ye. I want to give ye pleasure and nothing more."

"*Hmm.* Sounds perfect." Kenzie wrapped her legs about his hips, her mons pressing against his cock. He slid against her, teasing them more. He was near to losing himself like a lad who'd just found out what his cock could do.

"I'm sorry, lass," he said and sheathed himself fully within her. She swore, and he fought not to smile at the expletive she uttered. How different she was from anyone he'd ever known before. And not afraid to bare her soul to him and enjoy what he offered.

Ben cautioned himself to take care. He didn't need to feel any more than he already did for the lass. Anything further would only leave him bereft when she left.

He slowed his strokes, giving her time to adjust to his size, which unfortunately for Kenzie, was quite a large cock to take for any woman. She slowly relaxed in his hold, grinned when her feet slid up to sit atop his ass.

She sighed; her gaze, full of wonder, met his. "We seem to fit well." She grinned, biting her bottom lip.

At her subdued chuckle, Ben pushed into her further, wanting Kenzie to come around him, shatter and break against his cock. An overwhelming sensation that the woman beneath him threatened his life, but in a good way, consumed him. He didn't want to prepare her for anyone else, have her measure all her lovers after him against his ability.

Damn it, Ben didn't even want to imagine her leaving and getting on with her life with someone else. Allowing other men to make love to her, touch and kiss her as he wished to do. Over and over again if she'd allow it.

Which, if the scraping of her nails on his shoulders were any indication, she did.

Forever…echoed in his mind, and he sliced it away. Whatever this was between him and Kenzie, whatever it was that drew them like a moth to flame was only fleeting. A flash in time for them to enjoy each other's company. Forever was not a word he would associate with the lass and their future.

He took her more forcefully, and she moaned, her hands splaying against his back. Sweat trickled down his brow, as he pushed in further. His balls tightened, his body desperate for the pleasure he would take from her when they came.

She called out his name, and he was desperate to make her say it again; their joining became almost frantic. Not a whisper of space separated them, and he clasped her, fucked her hard and fast, knowing that with each stroke, the closer they both climbed to that peak that would topple them over into an abyss of satisfaction.

"Oh, Ben," she gasped, the breath of her words making the hairs on his neck spike. "Don't you dare stop. It feels so good."

"I'm not going to stop, lass. Not until ye shatter into a million pieces."

Their gazes locked, and her mouth opened as if to say something else, before she threw her head back, his name the only word she released into the room. He rode her until all her pleasure was spent and he'd drawn out as much of her orgasm as he could.

Ben pushed, once, twice but didn't dare take his plea-sure any further, and he pulled out to stroke his cock and spill his seed over her heaving stomach. There was some-thing innately dirty, but exciting, at marking a woman in such a way. He took a nearby rag and wiped her stomach clean before Kenzie rolled over to lay in his arms when he flopped beside her.

"That was the best," she said, flinging her arm over his waist and closing her eyes. "I enjoyed that immensely."

Ben frowned, not wanting to imagine her in the throes of pleasure with anyone but himself. He ran a hand over her back, pulling her close. "Not all men give their women such enjoyment. Why, the next imbecile ye sleep with may be a dud, and not even know which hole to put his cock into."

She chuckled against his chest and placed a light kiss over his heart. "With such a good teacher as I've had tonight, I'm sure I can bestow my learning onto them, enough to make even you proud."

Ben grunted a noncommittal reply. He wanted to murder the bastard who would even think to touch his Kenzie. Was she trying to drive him mad with such thoughts of others in her bed? Something told him she was. "Do not test me, lass. Ye may not like what happens when ye do." Or she'd like it too much and want more of the same. Which was quite fine with him.

"Really?" she said, looking up and meeting his gaze. "And what would your punishment be?"

Wild thoughts about taking her again, not just in this bed, but wherever they found themselves alone, bombarded his mind. Kenzie had been affectionate and active in his bed; to the core of his very soul, he believed that she would enjoy whatever he proposed. "Would ye like to find out?"

The glide of her hand drifted down his abdomen and settled against his already hardening cock. She slid a finger down its length, and he clenched his jaw, wanting her to wrap her fingers about his girth and stroke.

"I would," she said, doing what he wanted. Could this lass read his mind?

Ben rolled her onto her back, kissing her deeply, before showing her exactly what happened to twenty-first-century women who teased Highland lords.

*K*enzie woke up with a start, the sun's bright rays slicing into the room through the windows that housed multiple panes of square glass. She sat up, feeling Ben's gaze on her without even looking at him. Not that she wasn't aware of his lovely, pleasing, sprawled body beside her, because she was. Terribly aware.

"What are ye doing, lass? I hope ye don't regret ye decision of last eve." He rolled on to his back and stretched, reminding her of a well-satisfied cat. She lost herself in the sight of him, the memory of what he'd done to her, more than once the night before, making her blush.

"I had a nightmare." One that she couldn't tell Ben about for it was about him and the fate that beheld him. Of faceless men who seized the castle, killing everyone with no regard and chasing down Ben, slicing him from behind, where he fell face down, his eyes sightless toward where she stood watching it all. She shivered and threw back the blankets to get out of bed.

Ben reached over, pulling her back toward him. His arm may as well have been a steel vice for her effort to remove it. He kissed her shoulder, and the delectable nerves that only he brought forth fluttered in her belly. "You're safe, Kenzie. I'm not sure what ye dream was about, but I'll protect ye with my own life if it comes to that. Ye have nothing to fear here when you're with me."

"I know I am. It was just a dream, I'll forget it soon enough." *Liar…* She snuggled up against his chest. If only she could stay situated such, life would be perfect. With the animal skins surrounding them and the hard planes of muscle that held her close, Kenzie fought not to feel more than she ought toward the Highlander. She was here to find out and possibly stop who threatened his life. To learn all she could about Castle Ross's layout for the restoration that awaited her in her time. And to perhaps have a lot of hot sex in-between. Nothing more.

Yeah right. I am delusional if I think that is all I am here for.

Sleeping together was a mistake, there was no doubt about that, but emotions and feelings couldn't be allowed to grow. No deep, gut-wrenching ones that broke your heart when something bad happened. They could be friends only. Friends with benefits.

"Why did ye travel here? Really?" His tone was serious, and she wondered if he suspected her of anything.

Kenzie had two choices, tell him the truth or half-truth. She opted for the latter. "To be with you before I return home. I want to get to know more about you, your son, and your home. Your life here at Castle Ross. If you'll allow me to stay that is."

He mulled over her words before he met her gaze. "I'm glad ye came, and I'm only too willing to let ye warm my bed for the weeks that you'll be here."

"You don't mind me coming uninvited? Halfway here, I wasn't sure if it was the best plan. And with your child still being a baby, I didn't want to be a burden."

"You've already improved my sleeping arrangements." He kissed her quickly before rolling off the bed and walking over to the fire, standing before it as naked as the day he was born. *Man, his butt is nice.* "And I want ye to meet Alasdair. I've not been home long myself, and I'm amazed at how grown he is."

Kenzie followed him to the fire and wrapped her arms about his waist from behind. "You sounded sad when you said that. Are ye worried about having spent so much time away from Alasdair when he was only a few weeks old?" It was a reasonable assumption. Not that Kenzie would ever have done such a thing, but she wasn't Ben. He'd just lost his wife during what should've been one of the happiest times of his life. It was no wonder he ran away and sought to forget all his problems. People handled situations differently, and she needed to remember that."

"He has forgotten me, but I intend to remedy that. I'll soon have him knowing exactly who his father is and who loves him most in the world."

Kenzie squeezed him a little harder. "I know you will and he's a baby. He'll soon know you again." She looked up at him. "Will you let me meet him?"

Ben turned and wrapped his arms about her, his dark, unruly hair making him seem more rugged and untamed than ever before. But it didn't matter how dangerous he looked, under his armor the man had a heart of gold. One that worried his boy had forgotten him and no longer needed his father, just the servants who'd taken care of him.

"Of course, ye can, lass. I'll introduce ye after we break our fast."

CHAPTER 9

*a*fter they had broken their fast in the great hall, Kenzie followed Ben up to the third story of the castle where Aline had set up a nursery for Alasdair. The room was as large as Kenzie's and just as cozy. Thick animal skins covered the floor and a large fire burned in the grate. This room had narrower windows, which looked out toward the woodland. Tapestries hung from three of the walls, cocooning the room even more. Aline had done a beautiful job with the stone-cold space that most castles were renowned for, and a twinge of sadness pricked Kenzie that she'd not lived to enjoy her child.

A wet-nurse sat with Alasdair in her lap, feeding the six-month-old when they entered. The little boy, with a light fluttering of dark curls atop his head, seemed to have fallen asleep while eating and took turns suckling before sleeping again. It was the cutest thing Kenzie had ever seen.

The nurse stood and placed the boy into the cot before righting her cloths. She bobbed a curtsy to Ben. "My liege, may I be of some assistance to ye?"

Ben looked into the cot, reaching out to push the locks of hair off the boy's forehead. "I want to introduce ye to Kenzie, a relative to Sir Braxton and Gwendolyn Macleod. She's staying with us for a few months and may attend on Alasdair whenever she wishes."

The older woman's eyes grew wide at the mention of her impending stay, and Kenzie lifted her chin, not willing to allow anyone to look down on her for doing something that was right and what she wanted more than anything. Being here with Ben was the second-best choice she'd made since traveling back to medieval Scotland, other than meeting Gwen and Braxton. They may think her fast, a woman of loose morals, but she didn't care. Let them talk. It was nothing to her.

The woman nodded. "Very good, my lord. Did ye wish to visit with the wee Alasdair now? I can come back after I take the bairn's clothes down for washing."

"That would be welcome. Thank you, Ginny."

Once the woman was gone, perhaps even now racing downstairs to tell everyone that the laird was showing the baby to a woman who wasn't his wife, Kenzie walked up to the cot.

The small boy lay sound asleep, his hair similar to Ben's in color and impending curls. He also had similar-shaped eyes, and the nose was exactly the same. As for the boy's mouth, it was plumper than Ben's, and no doubt came from his mama. The thought that Ben made beautiful babies flittered through Kenzie's mind.

She shook off thoughts of children with the Highlander. They were not useful or helpful at all. "He's beautiful, Ben. I can see why you were in a rush to come home. And if you don't mind, I'd love to help you take care of him, help you to get to know him before I leave."

He smiled, with a look of pure adoration and love toward the boy. "I didn't know how much I had missed the lad until I saw him again. He was barely weeks old when I left. An action I will regret always, but he's not gone backward since my departure. If anything, he has only grown stronger. He'll be a great warrior one day."

The little baby flinched at something in his dreams, and Kenzie smiled, unable to stop herself from reaching out and touching his soft-as-silk baby cheek. "He's been cared for well. Your staff are a credit to you."

"Aye, they are. But I'm filled with shame that it was not only this babe that brought me home but another threat. One that I've not told ye of."

Kenzie already knew of the threat, but she let him tell her himself. If Ben was willing to discuss his life with her, allow her to help him, discuss things that could possibly be troubling him, then she would welcome being his support.

"What was the reason?" she asked.

"Aline's father, the Laird of Clan Grant visited here while I was away. Her father and Evan, Aline's brother, made their displeasure at our marriage known from the time of our elopement. In fact, they came here after our marriage and demanded she return with them and forget the error of her ways." A grin tweaked his lips, and he met Kenzie's gaze. "She did not. In fact, she gave them a well-deserved set-down and eventually, they came around. Although they've never liked me, and vice versa, I will admit, but we respected each other while around Aline."

Kenzie could just imagine how Highland Scots of this time took the news when their daughters and sons married without consent. Marriages of this time were made usually to form alliances, strengthen clans, and ensure more power in different locales about the land.

"From what I've heard, they really wanted Aline to marry Laird Macleod. Did you ever think there was much love between Aline and Aedan? From what Gwen has told me, if he'd married her, it would've been out of duty and the keep's need. Not because he wished to."

"Aye, the marriage would've been a disaster had it gone ahead, and thanks to me and my seductive charms, Aedan was able to marry the woman he loved."

"Abby is lovely."

"She is that, and Aedan is a besotted fool when it comes to his twenty-first-century wife. She is kind and honest and mayhap just as smart as you."

Kenzie chuckled. "How hard was it for you to admit such a thing? Something tells me getting a compliment out of you isn't the easiest thing."

"'Tis not," he said, pulling the blanket up on his son's chest when it slipped. "But I'll make an exception with you, for it's true." His carefree visage twisted to concern.

"Clan Grant are up to something, and I have to find out what. They stayed here for some time. It doesn't bode well, and I can't help but feel they're warning me to be on guard."

"You think the Laird Grant will cause problems for you, even though you're the father of their grandson? You may have married Aline under false pretenses, but it certainly didn't continue along that same vein. Why do you think he's still angry at you?" The more Kenzie heard of Clan Grant the more she was positive it was them who rid Scotland of the famous Laird of Ross. It certainly seemed to point toward them, but one really couldn't be sure in medieval Scotland. Anything was possible, she supposed.

"While I will admit to never being close with the Grants, we were certainly never at odds over anything. I can only assume his residual anger toward me is solely due to Aline's death. They blame me."

"Well, they shouldn't blame you. Anyone can die in childbirth. Hell, women in my time are still passing away, unfortunately. Terrible things happen, and there's nothing we can do about it. Life is what it is." Ben didn't reply, just stared down at his boy.

"Should we let him sleep? I can come back later and have a hold. Maybe we could bring Alasdair downstairs to spend some time with us in the great hall. I'm sure some of your clansmen would enjoy seeing him, too."

The door to the chamber opened and in walked the wet-nurse, holding a bundle of what looked like freshly laundered clothing. "Did ye wish me to come back, my Laird?"

Ben tucked his son in some more and took Kenzie's hand, holding it in his own. Kenzie noted the nurse's gaze latch onto the embrace, but the woman masked whatever thoughts she had over the contact.

"Nay, we'll let Alasdair sleep, but when he wakes and is fed, please have him brought down to the hall. I will spend some time with him there."

"Very good, m'lord." The woman bobbed another quick curtsy before going about her duties.

With one last look at his boy, Ben pulled Kenzie from the room, making their way downstairs. "Did ye wish for a tour about the castle and grounds, lass? Alasdair will be asleep for a while, so we have time."

"I'd love a tour. I didn't get to see much of it when I first arrived." Other than Ben's bedroom, and by the knowing smile on his face he understood the meaning behind her words.

"Well, this is the third floor, houses the nursery, Alasdair's wet-nurse, my head housekeeper, and manservant. In the attic space live the other maids, if they don't still live with their family or husbands in the village—a short walk from here."

"We didn't pass a village. I didn't know one was so close." Kenzie wondered what town it was, and then it came to her. "You mean Dornie. I would love to see what it looks like in this time. Not that it's a bustling city in mine, but I would like to see what its origins were like."

"We shall go there. I promise ye." They went down one level and onto the floor that housed Ben's and her bedchamber. "This level is for guests, and myself, of course. There are twelve rooms in total—most with the same layout. Although mine has a secret entrance that I'll show ye one day. Just in case."

Kenzie didn't like the sound of that but could understand his need to show her. "Let's hope that I'll never have to use it."

They walked along the corridor toward their rooms. He stopped before a narrow cupboard that sat against the wall. Opening its front door, he squatted and pushed at the back of the cupboard where a small twang was heard before the back swung open and showed the entrance into a stone room beyond.

"This is where I used to hide from my tutor."

Kenzie knelt and looked into the dark space. Did you have candles in there? It looks awfully dark."

"Aye, candles and animal skins. I can assure ye, it's still habitable should the need arise."

He closed the doors quickly as a servant came up the stairs. "Now, to the ground floor." Like most castles, each floor was connected by a stone spiral staircase. The ground floor held the massive great hall, an entrance chamber with no purpose other than to stop the cold going straight into the great hall during the winter months. The kitchens were off one end of the great hall, while the other housed another ante room that was Ben's private office, or solar, as he called it.

"Should we go outside? You could show me about the castle proper, and we'll leave the town and outlying areas for another day." It was marvelous to walk about Ben's home and let him tell her stories of his childhood, all that happened within the heavily fortified walls.

"My mother had been considered one of Scotland's most beautiful women, not noble by birth, but born into a farming family who'd made their fortune in cattle. A money source I still trade in to this day. Mother had been the sole inheritor of all her father's holdings. Making her an heiress. She was an only child, ye see.

"And your father. What of his background?"

"My father was already the laird by the time he'd met mother. He'd been besotted from the day they met, and the marriage was hasty."

Kenzie laughed, understanding why that would be, if Ben's father had similar looks and temperament to his son. She found it hard to be around Ben and not have one part of her brain constantly wondering when she could get him alone.

Walking along the side of the castle they came upon a vegetable garden where linen sheets billowed on a line. At the very back of the castle the yard was flat and well maintained, with low grasses that looked similar to lawn, but native. Kenzie walked up to the wall at the edge of the garden and looked down to the rocky shoreline below. The beach was sandy and possibly safe enough to swim. This part of Ross would be a little more troublesome to access if anyone wanted to invade via the sea.

It would probably end terribly, with the boat smashed to smithereens against the stones.

"I love the ocean. It's so vast and deep. Did you know that the highest mountains on earth are below sea level?"

Ben threw her a puzzled look. "Ye tease. 'Tis impossible, lass."

She leaned against the wall, pulling her shawl a little closer around her. The wind off the ocean was cold. "It's true. Can you imagine how deep some parts would be? How dark? It's kind of scary when you think about it. A whole other world we know nothing about."

He laughed, and she smiled, her enjoyment at hearing his deep masculine chuckle warming her blood. "You think I'm mad now, don't you?"

"Nay, not mad. Mayhap a lot wiser as to the wonders of this world than I am, but that's to be expected when one is from the future." He pulled her against him, heedless of anyone who saw them. "What else do ye know?"

Kenzie wrapped her arms about his waist. "Let me see…there's lots of things, like, all the land masses of this world have been found and are populated. We have planes that allow us to fly around the world. From here, for instance, I could travel to America, what you would know as the English colonies in seven hours or so. Bees can smell fear. Scotland just voted to remain part of England."

At her last statement Ben held her away, his face a mask of shock and outrage. "That cannot be true. A true Scot would never do such a thing."

"They did, but times are different in the future. Scotland relies on a lot of income from England for support. Most industries have closed or moved elsewhere. Some think Scotland wouldn't be able to survive on its own, and so they voted to stay part of the United Kingdom." She stepped back into his embrace, rubbing his back when he still didn't reply. In fact, Ben looked like he could be ill.

"It breaks my heart to know that."

Kenzie could understand how it would. It had broken her own a little when the country had voted to stay. But that was the word of the people, and what the majority had wanted. "You must know that Scotland is a lot different from this time. It's no longer so harsh to make a living. The divide between the wealthy and poor has lessened, for the better, I think. The country relies heavily on tourism, people visiting it for its beauty and history. It still is a wonderful place."

"But it is not free." Sadness tinged his voice and Kenzie regretted telling him of his homeland's current political situation.

"I didn't tell you to upset you, Ben. I think, if you were to see my Scotland, you'd like it. It's hard not to."

He didn't reply, just turned them toward the castle and back indoors. "We've wanted our freedom for so long. Hell, my own ancestors fought and died for that cause. How could our descendants vote to stay? It makes no sense."

The distraught look on his face broke her heart, and she hated that she'd even brought the subject up. What had she been thinking? She needed to keep her mouth shut from now on.

A guard walked briskly toward them when they came into the great hall, and Kenzie's attention snapped to the large sword that bounced against his leg. The tall, muscular man looked her up and down, and Kenzie had the oddest feeling that he knew she didn't belong.

"Riders, my liege, coming from the southwest. It looks to be Clan Grant."

A chill ran down Kenzie's spine, and like a flick of switch, Ben stilled, his body tensing under her hold.

Close the gate, and we'll see what they want when they arrive."

"They have a wagon traveling with them," the guard said, stepping back, bowing a little.

Ben swore and met her gaze. "Then it's not a war party, but something else." He kissed her cheek and strode away, pausing at the door. "Stay here, Kenzie. I'll be back soon to let ye know what is happening."

Kenzie watched him until he was out of sight and then went and stood before one of the two fires, which burned in the room. Clan Grant was here? This wasn't good, and if they were the clan behind Ben's demise, it was even worse than she thought. Had her arrival at Castle Ross brought forward his death in some way? Had she already changed history by doing something as miniscule as sleeping with him? She chewed her bottom lip, her mind awash with what their arrival could mean, not just for Ben but the people who relied on him.

Not to mention the little boy who lay upstairs, more than ever needing his father to remain alive to keep him safe from those who ruled by tyranny and fear.

❧

*B*en went up to the gatehouse and looked over the wall toward the forest beyond. The arriving party had long disappeared under the green foliage on their way to Castle Ross, and Ben wondered why they were back. *What do they want from me?*

Clipped footsteps sounded, and he looked to his side and noted his good friend and clansman, Bruce.

"It's Clan Grant that's coming, and they have a woman with them. I believe it may be Aline's only sister, Athol. A lot of luggage accompanies her. She travels with her brother, Evan. The Laird of Grant is not present."

What does this mean? Ben rubbed his jaw, hearing the rattle of the carriage on the dirt road before he saw it. "Keep the gate closed, but we'll go and greet them with six of our best swordsmen. I do not trust them that this isn't just a ruse to allow them inside before they attack. The Grants have never been known as peacemakers."

They were, in fact, known for their backstabbing of their fellow clansmen, if it meant they gained more power, money, or land. Oh ay, they had been civil at Laird Macleod's, but that was when the Laird of Grant had thought an alliance was assured. A marriage between two clans.

But when Ben had run away with Aline, Clan Grant had shown its true colors and had demanded Macleod have Ben hunted down and hanged, drawn and quartered.

The carriage came into view, and Ben went outside the castle walls to greet the Grants. Evan arrived first; his stoic gaze, all hard angles, reminded Ben of why this clan couldn't be trusted. Not toward him, at least.

Evan Grant bowed a little atop the horse. "Laird Ross, Ben, 'tis good to see ye again. It's been too long."

Ben ground his teeth. Not long enough. "I wasn't expecting ye. What brings ye to my castle doors?" *And what do ye bastards want?* They had not bothered to come to farewell Aline, and so, to show themselves now made the dormant anger Ben had for them simmer.

"I've come here, along with my sister, to offer our

apologies and ask for forgiveness for the trouble that's always been between us since ye married Aline. We were wrong in treating ye with so little respect, and so we've come to stay for a time, if ye agree. Father would like Athol to be of help to ye and little Alasdair." Evan dismounted the horse just as the carriage rocked to a halt.

The clansmen about Ben shifted and clasped their swords. Evan raised his hands in submission. "We dinna come here to start a clan war. Father wished for us to work together, strengthen our alliances just as we should. We're family, after all."

Ben narrowed his eyes. "Family, ye say. Well, that is to be seen, but I will welcome ye to my home, offer ye food and a bed, but do not cross me, Evan. Ye sister may have been my wife, and the grandchild of ye father may lie asleep within the walls. But that doesn't mean I will not slit ye throat should ye be here on any other ruse than friendship."

Evan shook his head. "No ruse, I assure ye." He walked back toward the carriage and opened the door, helping his sister, who Ben had never met before, from the vehicle.

As the woman stepped down, the blood drained from his face and left him ill at ease. His clansmen Bruce swore, and Ben could well understand why. Athol was the spitting image of her deceased sister. He took in her every feature and couldn't see a difference. *What kind of madness is this?*

Evan walked her toward them, and Ben noted the strong determination in the woman's gaze, which was identical to what Aline's had been. "This is my sister, Athol Grant, the much younger sister of Aline." Evan met Athol's gaze. "This is the Laird of Ross, or Black Ben, as a lot of the Highlanders know him as. He was Aline's husband."

"I understand the mechanics of family, Evan. I do not need ye to teach me, thank ye very much." Athol curtsied and met Ben's gaze, ice blue eyes staring back at him, and he couldn't quite catch his breath.

"May I call you Ben, too? Or would ye prefer brother, or my liege?" The flirtatious glance made Ben pause.

"Ben will do well enough." He gestured them toward the castle gates. "Open the gates and allow them enter," he yelled out to his men. The creaking of the wooden doors sounded loud in the quiet afternoon.

He walked them into the yard and toward the castle itself. "I'll have rooms prepared for ye, and if ye wish, you can go upstairs and refresh yourselves before dinner this evening." He walked them toward the great hall, and seeing Kenzie sitting before the fire brought a smile to his mouth.

She looked pensive, and when she glanced at him, a small frown line marred her brow. He went to her, not caring if the party who'd just arrived followed him or not. "I'll explain everything as soon as we're alone," he said, before the others came to stand with them.

"And who is this?" Athol said, smiling at Kenzie with genuine kindness. Mayhap the lass wasn't similar to Aline in that sense. His wife, God rest her soul, had been quick to judge, disliked anyone she met, and took some time to warm up to them. Athol may have been cut from the same tartan, but perhaps wasn't so quick to dislike and distrust. He mayhap had judged her too quickly.

"This is my guest, Kenzie, from Sir Braxton and Gwendolyn Macleod. She's a distant relative to Laird Macleod and Gwendolyn, his sister."

Evan narrowed his eyes on Kenzie and Ben watched

him, not about to let the Scot insult her in any way. Not when both of them were guests under his roof.

"A Macleod. What are ye doing here, lass? Did ye travel here with other Macleods or are ye on your own?"

Kenzie's face turned a delightful pink, and Ben clasped the hilt of his sword, an action that he was pleased Evan noted. Good. He wanted him to take heed. "I invited her to stay after we met at Sir Braxton and Gwendolyn's estate. I hope ye don't have a problem with that." Not that Ben cared what the Grant thought or said, but he wouldn't have him treating Kenzie with anything other than respect.

"None at all, 'tis your home. You may do as ye like." Evan smiled a little at Kenzie and it looked more like a snarl. "Are ye married, lass? You look of an age that ye should be."

Kenzie laughed and covered it with a cough. "No, I'm not, my lord. And I'm not looking to be anytime soon."

Athol stepped forward, kissing one of Kenzie's cheeks. "'Tis lovely to meet ye, Kenzie. Our family have long been allies of Clan Macleod and it's very nice to meet one at last. I couldn't attend the Highland games, alas, with Aline, where she met the Laird Ross. I was too young, ye see. Not of age."

"And what brings you to Castle Ross?" Kenzie asked.

"Our father was very distraught, as Ben knows only too well, after Aline passed away. He held Ben to blame, ye see," Athol said, coming over to Ben and taking his arm. "But he wishes to wrong that right, and so, here ye find us today."

He looked down at the dark-haired lass and across to Kenzie whose gaze was fixated on where Athol's hand sat against his arm.

"Father has come to his senses about the whole situation. And as I'm Aline's sister, 'tis only right that I came to Castle Ross to look after the wee babe. For as long as Laird Ross will have me, I'm willing to stay and help him raise his boy, just as I know my sister would want me to had she had the choice."

"So, you're going to be staying for months, years even?" Kenzie threw Ben an alarmed glance, and he frowned, unsure himself what was unfolding before him.

"Ye don't need to stay, for Alasdair is growing strong and is healthy. But, of course, ye are welcome here for a visit, but I wouldn't dare take ye from your family for too long. Or a future with a husband of ye own choice."

"Ye are not taking me from anything, Ben, and we owe it to ye after how father reacted after Aline's death." Athol smiled up at him, and the breath in his lungs froze. She was so like Aline it was terrifying.

Had he not known and buried Aline himself, he would swear she was standing beside him right now. It wasn't a situation he'd ever planned or thought to eventuate, and Ben wasn't sure how he felt toward the woman beside him. It was confusing, to say the least.

Ben summoned a servant. "Are the rooms ready for the Grants?"

The young maid nodded. "Yes, they are. If ye would follow me."

"We shall see you both at dinner." Athol smiled and again Ben couldn't fathom how similar the sisters were. It was like looking at a ghost.

CHAPTER 10

After Evan and Athol had departed their company, Ben had been called away with his clansmen about some matter regarding the fish stock and storage, and Kenzie was left to entertain herself.

She'd gone back outside and explored the castle a little more before heading back indoors and having a quick wash before dinner. The castle was quiet when she left her room, although when she made the staircase, she could hear the muffled sound of a baby crying.

Going up to the third floor, Kenzie made her way toward Alasdair's room and walked in to find him awake and kicking at his blankets. The wet-nurse was nowhere to be seen. He was the most adorable little cherub she'd ever seen, and without thought, she picked him up, putting him over her shoulder and patting his back.

"You're so adorable, aren't you, little man. And why are you awake? Did you not want to sleep?" Kenzie sat down on the rocking chair beside the crib and rocked him until he calmed down.

She ran her hand over his bottom, and the dampness

of the cloths that were acting as a nappy told her what was wrong. Seeing the small table that the nurse had called a changing table, Kenzie took Alasdair over to it and laid him down.

He suckled his thumb, kicking his legs, obviously annoyed at whatever was soiling his nappy. Kenzie untied the cloth and prepared herself for whatever was in there and cautiously looked, relieved to see it was only wet. She smiled at her own silliness. She'd never done this before.

Kenzie rubbed Alasdair's belly, cooing at him while she reached over to the side of the table and grabbed a wet cloth that sat in a bowl of water. Cleverly, it sat above a burning candle, which kept the liquid warm enough not to startle the baby when she wiped it over his bottom.

He watched her, his trust and innocence making her heart turn over in her chest. What a little darling. And Kenzie couldn't help but feel sorry for the lad that he'd never know his mama.

Kenzie allowed the air to dry his bottom, before seeing a pile of folded nappies on the table. She placed one under him, and tried to remember how it was tied, muddling her way through it enough that she was sure the wet-nurse would be happy.

"Ye like children." A voice said from the doorway.

Kenzie finished dressing Alasdair and picked him up, placing him over her shoulder once more. "I do, although I've never had any of my own. But he's the sweetest boy."

Athol came up to her and peeked at the baby. "He looks like Aline more than Ben, but I suppose that may change in time." She walked over to the window and stared out at the growing dusk.

"Did you want to hold him?" Kenzie asked, rocking

him a little when he started to fuss. He was probably hungry for his next feed.

"No, 'tis not something that, I, as a lady, need to do. We have servants for that."

Kenzie met her gaze and read the disdain that stared back at her through cold, blue orbs. "Aren't you here to help the laird raise his son? And if you are wouldn't that entail holding the child at some point?"

"I will help raise him, but I'll not be his nurse. When I said I will help raise him, I merely meant to give him guidance and teach him about what is expected of him and what the clans, both Ross and Grant, expect of him in the coming years. Nothing more."

Alasdair settled in Kenzie's arms, and she stole a peek at his sweet little face, smiling when she saw that he'd fallen asleep. "But surely, if you aspire to have a child one day yourself, you'd wish to hold your own baby. How could you not want to hold this sweet bundle of love, if only to practice?"

Athol snorted, which, considering her status as a lady, wasn't at all ladylike. But something told Kenzie that the woman before her said one thing in front of those who would be influenced by her but then did quite another.

"When I marry, I will have children, as is my duty as a wife, but that is all, for that is what is expected of me." Athol walked over to the change table and ran her hand across the wood, her expression one of boredom.

"I'm sorry Athol, but that sounds very cold." Kenzie wanted to say more, but she chose not to. All of them were guests of Ben's, and she didn't want to start an argument with a woman who came from a clan that wasn't the most placid in Scotland.

Athol shrugged, not seeming to care what Kenzie said.

A sound at the door made Kenzie start and expecting the wet-nurse she turned only to see Ben leaning on the door-frame. His smile left Kenzie breathless and for a time she wasn't able to form any words.

"You're a natural," he said, coming up to her and kissing his son's head. The gesture was extremely intimate, and Kenzie didn't miss the annoyance that crossed Athol's face.

"I was just telling Kenzie what a sweet boy ye have. May I hold him, Ben? Kenzie wasn't sure if I should or not since I've never done so before."

"I never—"

"Pass him to me," Athol said, holding out her arms. "Or should I sit. Mayhap sitting would be best," she said, moving to the chair and making herself comfortable.

"Do ye mind, lass?" Ben asked, rubbing his son's back.

Kenzie adjusted her hold on Alasdair but reluctantly handed him to Athol, who, interestingly, was more than willing to hold the baby, now that Ben was in the room. The change of heart wasn't missed on her, and it only solidified what Kenzie had wondered about before. Athol was conniving and said things that would help her own cause. She had no wish to hold the child, and seeing the little boy now squirming left Kenzie with a sense of triumph.

As expected, the baby became uncomfortable with the woman holding him uneasily. She did look awkward. Even Ben looked pained. The wet-nurse entered and offered to take the babe, who Athol was only too happy to relinquish.

"I suppose it's time for dinner. May I walk with you down to the great hall, Ben?"

Ben nodded and looked to Kenzie. "Are ye coming, lass?

About to join them, Kenzie paused when Athol waved her away. "Kenzie will be down shortly. You said you wished to relieve yourself first before the meal." Athol threw her a consoling look. "Mayhap you should see the castle healer if you're having pains in the stomach."

Mortified, Kenzie's face suffused with heat, and she snapped her mouth shut before she told this high-and-mighty *lady* what she could do with her smart mouth. What the hell was Athol's problem?

"Are ye well, Kenzie? Did ye want me to send the healer up to ye room?" Ben let go of Athol's arm, and it warmed her blood to see annoyance on Athol's face. What an awful person she was to lie, and right before her without a flicker of guilt.

"I'm fine, but I do wish to freshen up."

Ben nodded and left with Athol without so much as a glance back at her. Kenzie glared at the now vacant doorway. *Okay, Athol, if this is how you want to play the game, all's fair in love and war.*

∾

*D*inner that evening was odd. Ben sat between Athol and Kenzie and normally, being placed between two such beautiful women would've warmed his blood, but this evening it was like sitting between two warring clans.

Something had changed since the Grant's arrival earlier today, for now Kenzie and Athol didn't seem to agree or get along about anything at all. Not about the food or drink. What Kenzie liked, Athol disliked, and she even went so far as to give the serving lass a good scolding that her disappointment was to be repeated to the cook once she returned to the kitchens.

The fish was too dry or the mead too sweet. The fire that burned behind them was too hot, or Kenzie's gown, which Ben thought most attractive, was too revealing for a woman. Athol even went so far as to hint that Kenzie was a woman of little morals. The comment was not lost on some of his servants, who seemed to agree with the Grant's comment if their snickering smiles were anything to go by. He wouldn't stand for it, not from anyone.

Ben had had enough. "Athol, while it pleases me that you're visiting me and your nephew at Castle Ross, do not be forgetting that Kenzie is also my guest, and no matter what ye opinion of her gown is, there is no reason to be so cutting in ye remarks."

Athol's eyes grew round as the bowls on the table, and her brother glared at him. He'd promised that he'd not allow anyone to slight Kenzie. Not even his family-related-by-marriage, and he would keep that promise.

"Forgive me, Laird Ross. I mean no offense. But I couldn't help but wonder if Kenzie knows that gowns such as she's wearing are of an older style, and women now wear less revealing necklines. I was merely trying to help the woman, who clearly has no means of righting such a wrong."

"How very kind of you," Kenzie said, sarcasm heavy in her tone. Seemingly something that was completely missed by Athol. "Maybe you could sew my gowns to be as prudish as your own."

Athol gaped and slammed her goblet down, spilling a little of the contents on the table. "I was merely being helpful. No need to be prickly simply because I am gowned more appropriately than yourself."

Ben clapped his hands, gaining the clan's attention. "Let us have some music and dancing."

"What a wonderful idea," Kenzie said, pushing back her chair and walking down into the center of the hall. She sided up beside Bruce, one of Ben's best fighting men, and curtsied before him.

Ben ground his teeth as he watched her ask Bruce to dance. The sight of his lass being held close in another's arms hollowed him out inside. Athol laid her hand against his arm and it did little except annoy him that he'd have to divert his attention away from Kenzie who now danced and laughed with his clansman.

"Would ye dance with me, Ben. I know Aline would wish for us to enjoy each other's company."

Something about the lass's words left him on edge, and he shook his head. "Another time, lass. I'd prefer to watch this evening's entertainments. You go ahead and find yourself a partner. I'm sure with ye pretty face there are many who would wish to dance with ye."

Just not himself.

Bruce finished his dance with Kenzie, and she was soon swept up into another of his clansman's arms. Bruce came and sat beside him, taking a long swig of his drink before throwing him an amused glance. "Kenzie is a lot of fun. I like the lass."

"Aye," he mumbled, annoyed at himself more than his friend for acting like a jealous ass, which he was. He should be happy the lass was enjoying his home, getting along with his clansmen and women. Her time here should be one of enjoyment, if he could make it so, and therefore, his jealously over Kenzie having a good time was not necessary. "Aye, my friend," Ben said, slapping Bruce on the back and smiling at Kenzie. "We're fortunate to have her as a guest."

"And what about…" Bruce gestured toward Athol who was also taking part in the impromptu dancing before them.

Ben sighed. "She's like looking at a ghost. With her here, I feel like Aline is watching me." Wanting him back, although he could never look at Athol in the way the lass might wish.

"Ye do realize what the Grants being here means, do ye not?"

"It doesn't mean anything. As they said, they're merely wishing to fix a wrong they did against me." Not that Ben believed that at all. He'd seen how Athol looked at him when she thought no one was watching. Her small touches weren't something he wished for. She was his wife's sister, a woman that he'd, of course, care for, but never in the way in which the lass wanted.

"Ye don't actually believe that, do ye?" Bruce threw him an amused glance before refilling his tumbler of mead. "The Grants want something from ye, and I think they mean to marry ye off to their surviving daughter, which, if ye were looking for another wife, would make sense."

"Dinna say that. Ye know better than anyone that I'm not looking to marry again."

"So, the thought has not entered ye mind with the lovely Kenzie? I know, should I be in your position right now, I'd seriously consider it."

Ben narrowed his eyes at the sight of his clansmen's appreciative inspection of Kenzie, before he reminded himself he wasn't jealous. Fool. Never was there a man more so than he was right now. "Kenzie will be returning home soon—without a hand fasting to me."

"'Tis a shame, I think the lass would do well here, and by the way she keeps looking at ye, I'm guessing she'd like to stay as well."

Ben looked up and caught Kenzie's attention. She was standing beside Clan Grant's men, but not conversing with any of them. That she was a beautiful woman was obvious, and a pang of regret pierced Ben that she couldn't be his forever.

Someone else's, in another time and place, that he couldn't even watch and appreciate from afar. He poured more mead into his tumbler.

"Mayhap I should look to Aline's sister and marry again. My son would be well cared for by having a woman so like his own mother. The same values would be bestowed upon Alasdair that Aline would've taught him."

Bruce raised his brow. "Ye said yourself ye didn't wish to marry again, and there are plenty of women who would warm ye bed without so much as a backward glance when the pleasure was over. Ye have yer heir. Leave it at that."

Ben rubbed a hand over his face. His clansman was right, yet, if he did marry Athol, at least that would secure his keep and lands from possible clan war. Not that he suspected the Grants of wanting to do him harm, but Laird Grant not accompanying his son and daughter here did leave him wondering if their truce, the burying of ill will, was really so.

"Tomorrow I'll be helping with the preparations for Beltane. Have the horses prepared, as I'll take Kenzie with me out to collect the wood for the fires."

"The berry trees are showing that they'll be abundant in fruit this year. It'll mean a harsh winter."

"Aye, but we have a good many cattle ready, and in the coming months, we'll send them south to Stirling for sale.

'Tis time that I started to act as the laird that I am and ensure Castle Ross and the tenants who rely on this keep are kept safe and well during the harsher months to come. We shall celebrate Beltane, hope that the crops will be plentiful, and all will be well with the people here."

Ben caught Kenzie slipping out the doors that led to the front of the keep and he stood, downing his drink. "I leave ye in charge. I'll be back anon." Bruce didn't say anything, but Ben wasn't stupid enough not to know his clansman had seen Kenzie leave the great hall.

No one followed her, and yet that still didn't make it safe for her. Castle Ross wasn't impenetrable, and he couldn't guarantee her safety, even with his own clansmen if they'd imbibed too much drink. She was an unmarried woman and there were some who'd think she was too forward and fast for staying here without a husband. Kenzie would be an easy target and he could not allow that.

He found her at the side of the castle that looked out over the sea. The stars shone brightly down upon her and with her light gown she looked like a ghostly apparition, her gown billowing out behind her like mist.

Ben came up behind her and wrapped his arms about her waist, breathing deep the smell of roses that wafted from her hair. Kenzie always smelled so good, as fresh as a summer day. "What are ye doing out here, lass. 'Tis not safe."

"I think I've had too much to drink, and I needed the fresh air. The mead tonight seems stronger than it was previous evenings."

He frowned. "Do ye feel ill? Can I get ye something to eat, perhaps? That may settle ye stomach."

"No," she said, turning in his arms and wrapping hers about his waist.

Being like this together, holding the woman who'd captured his attention from the second he laid eyes on her, was right. And yet, not. She wasn't staying. Wasn't of this time and would never be his.

"Athol hates me, and she wants you, so of course I have to hate her back." She grinned up at him, and he laughed.

"Aye, I think ye may be right. And even though an alliance with her family would save me from clan war, I'll not be doing what she wants. I have an heir. I dinna need a wife. I also have a bonny lass who's warming my bed, so I'm quite content."

"I don't trust any of them. Keep your wits about you, Ben. They're trouble. I can feel it."

He loved that she didn't shy away from telling him what she thought. Was not scared of his reaction, simply trusted that he would never hurt her, even if what she said could be cutting or worrying.

"I'll be on my guard, lass. I promise ye that."

She yawned. "I think I will go up to bed and get some rest. I'm sure I'll feel better tomorrow."

Ben leaned down and kissed her gently, he didn't try and deepen the embrace, he wasn't a mongrel, and his lass wasn't feeling well, but still, tasting her again, having her pliant, sweet body against his left him wanting her with a savagery he'd never experienced before.

Mayhap he had finally lost his mind or another organ that he wasn't entirely sure he wanted to give away.

"Come," he said, pulling her toward the castle. "I'll take ye to your room, for tomorrow, I need ye well rested. I have a surprise for ye."

Kenzie's emerald eyes lit up and twinkled in the starlight. "What is it? You have to tell me."

Ben laughed, pulling her closer to his side. Damn, he would never tire of seeing her smile. "Nay, lass, you'll have to wait until tomorrow, and then all will be revealed.

Her pout made him pull her into a notch on the outer castle walls and kiss her. Deeper this time, with more intent than he intended, but with Kenzie he didn't have any control. Was wont to lose it whenever around her. Maddening wench.

"Maybe you should tuck me in, my liege." Her teasing grin made his cock twitch.

He shook his head, taking her hand and pulling her through the castle doors. "Nay, I may be known in your time as a hardened warrior, but even I will not take advantage of a woman who's not feeling well. Ye need your sleep, lass, and even though I shall take ye up on the offer of tucking ye in, I will be leaving shortly thereafter."

Kenzie shrugged. "Spoilsport."

Ben didn't know what the word meant, but he took a wild guess. "Tomorrow evening, lass, and I promise I'll do more than tuck ye in."

"*Hmm.*" She grinned, her hand sliding over the back of his kilt and across his ass. "I'm going to hold you to it."

So would he.

CHAPTER 11

*T*he following morning, Kenzie met Ben out the front of the keep. The horses were saddled and waiting, along with her Highlander who sat atop a mighty dark beast she'd not seen before.

"Wow, your horse is high. How many hands is he."

Ben's mouth gaped, and his eyes widened in alarm. "Ye have trews on, lass. Mayhap ye forgot ye skirt?"

Kenzie jumped up on her horse with the help of a stable hand and adjusted her seat. When the maid had told her this morning that she was to go riding, there was no way she was going to go in the monstrous gown the woman had laid out for her. Since Athol had said her gowns were old-fashioned and not appropriate, new gowns had magically appeared in her wardrobe. She smiled; no doubt it had been Ben who'd sent them to her.

She assumed they'd been Aline's, and so she'd accepted the gifts, knowing that it had probably not been easy for Ben to let her use the dresses. Aline was a little smaller in the breast department than herself, so Kenzie had been wearing a woolen scarf with a lot of the dresses if only to give her some modesty. No one wanted to see her breasts pop out over the top.

"I haven't forgotten it," she said, grinning at his outraged face. She moved her mount closer to him and lifted his chin with her finger, shutting his mouth. "Do ye not like my trews, my liege?"

Ben's eyes darkened with intent, and she could swear she heard a growl emanate from him. "Ye know I do."

Kenzie ran her hand over his thigh, clasping his knee. "Good then, because I like you in your skirt."

"'Tis a kilt, lass."

She smiled. "I know it is; I'm just teasing you."

Ben kicked his mount and called for her to follow. They rode into the surrounding forest, away from the sea on which the keep sat, until they came across an area where some trees had been felled. Ben dismounted and came over to help her.

He slid her down the front of him, letting her feel every ripple of hardened muscle. Maddening. "Now who's teasing?"

Ben looked around. Kenzie did likewise and noted clansmen were busy tying the horses and going to collect tools such as saws and axes. He pressed her against the side of her horse and kissed her, took her lips desperately. Kenzie pushed against him, taking all that he gave, and wondered what had brought on his sudden urge.

Not that he had to have an excuse, for Kenzie would kiss him anytime and anywhere he pleased, but still… "What brought that on?" she asked, when he finally stepped back.

He ran a finger down her cheek, staring at her with an intensity that startled her. Kenzie reined in her somersaulting emotions. It would be so very easy to fall totally in love with this Highlander.

"I thought ye looked in need of a thorough kissing." His brogue was thick and laden with desire.

"You can kiss me anytime you like." And he could, especially if he continued to look at her as if she was the whole world. She cleared her throat. "So, what are we doing here? This looks like you have work for me to do."

He gestured to the trees. "'Tis Beltane tomorrow and today we collect the wood for the fires." He pulled her toward the trees. "Ye are going to help me fell a tree with this saw. Not a large one, so dinna be scared, but just a small one that I'm sure ye will be able to handle."

Kenzie turned and watched the other clansmen at work. The cutting down of the larger trees looked hard, and even in the fresh morning air, sweat poured off their brows. Others worked axes into the fallen trees, cutting the limbs into smaller lengths and placing them onto waiting carts. "How many trees will you cut down for Beltane?"

"We gather the smaller limbs that fall off through the year, so we dinna normally cut down more than ten trees and we scatter the cutting so as not to leave one place in the forest bare of growth."

Good idea. Kenzie took the saw and walked it over to the small tree that Ben stood beside. "So, we're to cut this one down?"

"Looks as good as any other." He lifted his side of the saw and, working in unison they started to cut down the tree. It didn't take long for it to fall, since it was ridiculously small compared to some of the others, but at least Kenzie had contributed a little to Beltane.

Ben shouted out for some of the clansmen nearby to come and put the wood on the cart. Kenzie looked about the grove. It was a beautiful place, smelled of wooded undergrowth with a sprinkling of pine. Although she couldn't spy any of those types of trees.

"What's that sound?" she asked, turning her head toward what she thought might be running water."

"The workers, lass," Ben said, lifting some smaller branches and placing them on the cart. As they worked, the day became warmer, not hot by any means, but comfortable, considering they were in Scotland.

Kenzie helped where she could, but eventually she sat on an old, rotting log and watched as Ben worked with the men, getting what they needed for Beltane. In her time, people just lit bonfires and used the old ancient pagan tradition as a reason to get drunk and have fun with friends.

To see Beltane in this time would be something. From the earnestness of it all, medieval Scotland certainly took the night a lot more seriously than people did in her time.

One of the workers came back with wet hair and Kenzie stood. "Ben, that man looks like he's had a swim. There is water nearby, isn't there? I thought I could hear water running."

He stopped what he was doing, running a hand through his hair and pushing it off his face. Her heart flip-flopped at the sight of him—rumpled, sweaty, marks of dirt across his face where he'd wiped at the dripping sweat. "Oh ay, sorry, lass. Yes, there's a stream and small waterfall a little way through those trees there," he said, pointing over her shoulder. "If ye follow the animal path, you'll come to it."

"Will it be safe for me to go and have a look?"

"Aye, just yell if ye need anything."

Kenzie nodded and started off in the direction Ben

told her. The path was easy to see and well-used by the animals. The sound of rushing water became louder, and she gasped when she came to the pretty hidden spot.

The stream was narrow, and dark, mostly likely deep. She stood, looking down into the stone, moss, and soil walls of the little river. The waterfall flowed over the side into the pool beneath.

It was fast moving, white water bubbling up, but so inviting. Kenzie climbed down the side, taking care not to fall in but with the moss and damp ground underfoot it was precarious. Reaching the water's edge, she pulled off her boots and stockings and slipped her feet into the water. It was cold, but not cold enough to be uncomfortable were you to swim in it.

She heard Ben call out her name, and she replied in turn, waiting for him to peer down at her from atop the river's bank.

"What are ye doing down there, lass. Can ye swim?"

"I can swim." She gestured for him to join her. "Come down here, and feel the water. It's so refreshing."

"Aye, do ye mean freezing enough that it would turn more than my lips blue should I fall in?"

Kenzie laughed. "Never fear, my liege. I shall warm you up again."

The devilish glint in his eyes sent pleasure coiling between her legs. He came and sat beside her, leaning on his knees as he watched the water. "Are ye feeling better today, lass? I forgot to ask when we started out this morning."

"I feel a lot better, thank you." Kenzie shut her eyes and faced the sun, the warmth warming her all over. Not to mention the man beside her who warmed her from the inside out. To use a modern colloquialism, she had it bad.

"Have you ever swam here?"

"Aye, I used to bring Aline here, and we'd swim. 'Tis a private spot and peaceful."

"Is this part of your land?" Kenzie thought about her time and how so much had changed. The forest they now sat in was a quarter of what it was now. Over the years, the trees had been felled for farmland. And never, in all her surveys of the land at Castle Ross had she come across this waterfall. It made her wonder if it was even there anymore, or if farming further north had changed the flow of the streams and it was no longer anything but a dry quarry.

"Yes, and once the celebrations of Beltane are finished tomorrow, I shall take ye about the property and show ye the farm, have ye meet the tenant farmers and such. I'd like ye to know all there is about Castle Ross before ye leave."

Kenzie bit her lip, hating the thought of going anywhere that this strapping, Highlander beside her wasn't. She would miss him, even though she was still getting to know him.

Standing, and taking care not to fall into the river, she pushed down his knees and straddled his legs, wrapping her arms about his neck. "I want to know all there is to know about you as well."

"I need to make it up to them for leaving them alone these past months. With the preparations of Beltane underway, I'm hoping to make the celebration one they'll no forget and mayhap one which they forgive their laird for being dumb-skulled.

"You were mourning, Ben. Of all things, people of this harsh time understand that emotion best, I think." There was so much death in this time, not just from clan skirmishes but also disease. The hygiene here was nonexistent, and it was surprising that anyone survived at all. Why, just the other day, Kenzie had seen a servant empty a chamber pot out the window of her room and then throw a small bit of bread that she'd not finished into her mouth. Not so much as a washing of hands in-between the two things.

She wiggled a little closer to him and bit her lip at the obvious bulge. "I missed you last night." Kenzie kissed the lobe of his ear, biting lightly before kissing his neck. His unshaved jaw rasped against her lips, and the need for him, the want inside her, doubled. "Will you come to me tonight, my liege?"

He clasped her ass and pushed her against him. She leaned forward and stole a kiss. "Why wait until tonight."

Kenzie grinned, having not thought of that, but, in trews it wouldn't be as easy as it would've been had she worn a dress. "What if ye men catch us? I'm in pants. It's not like I can just shuffle my dress back down and hide what we're about."

His fingers clenched against her trews before sliding one of his hands and clasping her sex at the front. Kenzie gasped, having not expected that.

His eyes darkened. "Ye make me want ye so much, lass."

"The feeling's mutual," she said, stifling a moan when he played with her through her pants. "God, I want you," she said, breathless. Her climax was quick, and she wrapped her arms about his neck and enjoyed what his touch did to her.

She slumped against him, and it was some time before she gathered her wits. She kissed him and reveled in his lustful gaze. "Now I need to swim to cool off."

Ben helped her stand before, silently, he untied his

sporran and kilt, lifting his shirt over his head and throwing it on the grassy bank. Then with a grin, he jumped feet first into the water.

He came up gasping. "'Tis freezing, lass. Come in," he said, laughing.

Kenzie was already undressing before she too jumped in, coming up beside him. "You're not wrong about that!" she laughed, wrapping her arms about Ben's neck. He walked her to the side of the stream and pushed her against the bank. Kenzie wrapped her legs about his hips and grinned. "What are you going to do with me now?" she teased.

He slid inside her, and she moaned, throwing her head back against the grass. "That feels so good, Ben." He fit her like a glove, knew what she enjoyed and what she liked. Was able to pleasure her with very little effort at all.

Ben gave little regard to being gentle and took her desperately. Not that she minded being fucked, for this was exactly what he was doing and doing it so well that she wanted more, so much more.

"When I saw ye in your trews this morn, I've been thinking of nothing but how to rid ye of them." He kissed her hard, and she pulled him tighter against her, the coiling of pleasure getting tighter and tighter before he moaned and came hard, pumping into her with little care.

It was delicious.

They stayed like that for a time, before Ben stilled in her arms. He pulled out, his face devoid of color. "Wash yeself, lass." He ran a hand through his hair. "Quickly now. Do as I say."

"What are ye talking about. Why?" Kenzie did as he asked. What with the thunderous look on his face she'd not do anything else, but what was going on? "What's wrong, Ben?"

He reached between her legs and helped clean her, and she pushed him away. "Stop. What are you doing?" Kenzie cleaned herself some more before it hit her what he was doing and why. "You came inside me. Is that what this is about?"

"Damn it," he swore, glaring off toward the rivers bank. "I'm sorry, lass. 'Twas a mistake that I'll not repeat again." He mumbled something inaudible, before looking at her with such a lost expression her heart went out to him. "I've put ye at risk."

"Ben, it's unlikely I'll fall pregnant. As a modern woman from the twenty-first century, I know when the fertile time of my cycle is, and it was two or more weeks ago. You're panicking for nothing." Kenzie finished washing herself and stepped from the water, leaving Ben staring after her. She shook out her clothes and started to fight getting into her pants since she was still wet. "You're worrying about nothing."

"Ye will not have my children."

The words stung, and she quickly slid on her shirt and coat. "Thanks for ruining what was otherwise a memorable experience." Kenzie scrambled up the river's edge and heard Ben exit the water hard on her heels. He caught up to her on the top of the bank.

"I have my heir, I'm not looking to have any more. If ye think I'm angry at ye, lass I'm not. I'm angry at myself for losing my control, my wits, when I'm around ye."

His words went some way in placating her, but it wasn't enough. Not quite. "Why is it that you're not going to have any more children? You're young, why not marry again and have a whole army of Alasdairs in your nursery."

Ben stopped some feet from her, and the look on his face was one of horror. What was going on?

"I'll not marry again. Ever. So, if ye wish to seduce me again, ye must ensure I release out of ye, you must remind me of my duty."

Kenzie laughed, the sound mocking. "Seriously?" She stepped up to him, nose to nose. "If I seduce you again and you forget to pull yourself out before coming, I will be the last person on earth who'll remind you of your *duty*," she said, spitting the word at him. "And you needn't worry that I'll fall pregnant and make you marry me. You know full well I'm not staying and won't tie ye down. The famous Black Ben can continue sowing his wild oats all over Scotland like you have been."

He gaped at her, and Kenzie regretted her words immediately. She took a calming breath.

"I have my reasons for not wanting any more children, lass. I needn't tell you or anyone what they are, and I dinna need ye judging me about my choices."

Ben's accent was thick as his temper grew, but damn it, they'd made a mistake. His absurd reaction to it wasn't necessary. "Maybe I should return to Gwen and Braxton's home and leave you be. But just a word of warning, Laird of Ross. Ye may wish to send Athol back home with her brother before you're married off to her without ye consent."

He ground his teeth, and she turned on her heel and made for the grove where the echoing sound of men and woodcutters could be heard. Ben clasped her arm, ripping her about to face him.

"Mayhap ye should."

His words were like a slap across the face. Kenzie ripped her arm from his grasp and glared at him. "I'm going back to the castle. Don't follow me." She did as she threatened, blinking away the prick of tears as she made it back to her horse. What was Ben's problem? His overreaction to what they'd done was irrational. It was almost as if he was terrified of her becoming pregnant.

She shook her head. Maybe when they'd calmed down, he would tell her his reasons, but until then, he needed to stay exactly where he was. Well away from her.

CHAPTER 12

*B*en stood beside the largest bonfire that burned
before the gates of Castle Ross. The flames
towered into the sky, and he was pleased that this Beltane
had been successful so far. Everyone seemed to be enjoying
themselves, all but one woman who sat on a stool, talking
to Bruce. Kenzie was obviously not her bubbly, happy self.
It was his fault, and he hated himself for it.

Yesterday, he'd acted like a brute, demanding she wash
herself all because he'd lost control. Forced her to wash his
seed away. Terrified that she would have his child.

Worse was the realization that the image of Kenzie
round with his baby inside of her, left him both panicked
yet with so much longing that for the last day he'd kept his
distance from her. He'd come to realize that was exactly
what he wanted.

Her…and everything I can have with her.

Tonight, he would explain his fear, and he hoped that it
would be enough for her to forgive him his idiocy.

Athol sidled up beside him and clasped his arm, her
breast rubbing indecently against his arm. He looked back

173

at Kenzie and noted her narrowed glare aimed at him, before she turned toward Bruce and gave him her back.

He ground his teeth. Maddening woman!

"Would ye dance with me, Ben? Tonight, has been such a great celebration, but I dinna want it to be over without having one turn about the fire with ye."

The clansmen surrounding him cheered him on, and conceding, Ben pulled her into a jig about the bonfire. With Athol in his arms, laughing up at him, he was almost transported back to last year's Beltane. When Aline was alive, pregnant but still wanting to enjoy the festivities like everyone else.

Athol was so like her, but not so much in temperament. During the time Ben had been married to Aline, she had mellowed, grown kinder and more understanding of those about her. Athol had not. If anything, Ben had the impression the lass was spoiled and used to getting her own way.

He looked down at the lass and didn't mistake the asking in her eyes for more. The dance changed, and he passed her onto another clansman while he took the arm of his cook. The rotund woman laughed at having him as a partner and Ben laughed too, for the first time that night.

The dance went on, and when he turned to take his final partner's hand, pleasure almost brought him to his knees. Kenzie.

"Ye look beautiful this eve, lass. A gift given to us through time."

"Now you're flattering me, Ben?" Her tone sounded bored and dread coiled in his gut. He pulled her out of the dance and walked her a little out of the light and away from his clansmen.

"I owe ye an apology for handling ye roughly yesterday

in the water, making ye wash yourself as if the thought of ye having my child repulsed me."

Her emerald eyes met his and he fought not to pull her into his arms and kiss her. Show her just how sorry he was for acting the medieval ass.

"Are ye repulsed by the thought of me pregnant with your baby?"

"Nay, never that. Ye know that Aline died after having Alasdair. Well, the reason behind her death was not only because of the child but a tumor in her womb. The clan healer believed it at first to be another child, but during the birth it became known that it was not. She bled to death in my arms. I will not risk another woman for the sake of offspring."

Kenzie sighed. "Life is a risk, Ben. Living in this time, you, of all people, should know this. You cannot save everyone. It's not possible."

She was right, and yet the guilt of tupping Aline each and every night in order to have a child still tormented him. He'd not had a care for her health, having not thought he'd lose her solely due to having a baby. But his tupping had been her death sentence, and he couldn't forgive himself for that. No matter what Aline had said on her deathbed or what Kenzie said now. His wife was dead, and it was his fault.

"Just so you know, there is no threat to me in regard to having your child. No doubt you're aware that women bleed once a month. Well, let's just say my once-a-month has started."

He would be lying if he said he didn't feel an over-whelming sense of relief. Ben said a silent thank you to God and pushed a flyaway lock of her hair behind her ear. "I'm sorry for yesterday, lass. Say ye forgive me."

She half-smiled up at him, and for the first time since their fight, it was as if the sun shone in the middle of the night. "I'm sorry, too."

"I want to kiss ye so much, lass," he said, leaning down and whispering the words against her ear.

"Why don't you then?" She raised her brow, tempting him beyond thought or reason.

"There ye are, my liege. Brother has already returned to the castle, and I have no one to escort me." Athol took Ben's arm, and Kenzie stepped away, giving him space.

"I see Bruce is headed back, but I am not just yet, lass." Ben yelled out to Bruce who turned and came toward them. He ignored the annoyed glare Athol threw up at him.

"Take Lady Athol up to the keep, Bruce, and ensure she reaches her room safely. I'm not returning yet."

Bruce nodded, gesturing for Athol to walk beside him, which she did reluctantly while throwing dirks at Kenzie.

Once alone with the few clansmen still celebrating Beltane, Ben poured them both a tumbler of ale and handed one to Kenzie. "Here's hoping the crops will be blessed and plentiful," he said, a loud cheer coming up from his men and tenants.

"Here here," Kenzie said, clapping her cup against his. "And here's to the Laird of Ross. Shall he prosper, be free of war, and live a long and happy life," Kenzie said for only him to hear.

Without thought, Ben leaned down and kissed her, not caring who saw or what they thought. He'd wanted to kiss her all day, beg her forgiveness and grovel, if need be.

Kenzie wrapped her arms about his neck and deepened the kiss, and for a time, he lost all thought. Och, what a sweet, smart lass was wont to do to a man and he'd not always have this woman in his arms. So best to make the most of it while he could.

~

The following morning, after bathing, Kenzie broke her fast in the great hall, sending up a silent prayer of thanks that she'd had the forethought to bring tampons and sanitary pads with her to seventeenth century Scotland.

She bade Bruce good morning, along with a few of the other clansmen she'd come to know over the last few weeks, before taking her seat up on the dais. Ben wasn't seated there, and she frowned, wondering where he was.

Her solitude was short-lived before Athol came and sat beside her, her smug smile leaving Kenzie on edge.

"Good morning, lass. I hope ye slept well."

The urbane conversation didn't fool Kenzie, but she would play along for a little while and see what Athol had to say for herself. "I did, thank you. Beltane was wonderful but tiring, as I'm sure you agree."

"Oh, ay, I agree, and when ye're sleeping with the laird, it's even more tiring, isn't it, lass? But I wouldn't know about that, since I'm not the one who's sullied her reputation and is now known as the castle whore."

"What?" Kenzie coughed, almost choking on her food. "Why would you say such a thing?"

"'Tis true, is it not? My brother informed me himself that he saw ye last evening, pawing the laird at the bonfire. Kissing Ben with such vigor that he'd not been able to breathe. Not to mention, my maid said she saw you on the night of your arrival all but throwing yourself at the laird."

Kenzie shook her head, heat suffusing her face. "He

could breathe well enough." How dare this woman chastise her. "I wasn't aware you were betrothed to the laird and he therefore cannot kiss other women."

Athol gestured to a servant, holding up her cup and waving it about until it was filled. "You're no woman, only a whore—who I'll soon get rid of. My father is on his way, and he'll make the laird see the error of his ways. If ye think to marry Ben, ye can think again. I'll not have a woman of loose morals raising my nephew and teaching him her own dreadful ideals."

Kenzie snorted. "For starters, kissing the laird doesn't make me a whore. Secondly, if I'm kissing the laird, one should assume I have the ear of the laird, and perhaps you should temper your hatred of me. Thirdly, I don't wish to marry Ben. I like Ben, don't get me wrong, but I'm young and not looking for a husband." Just the thought of marrying at her age was too crazy to contemplate. Not to mention the fact that she would be returning to the twenty-first century soon, and poor little Athol's worry was for nothing. Not that Kenzie could tell her that.

Kenzie looked about the room. Many eyes, mostly the women folk who sat at table or served to break everyone's fast, were on her. Their attention snapping away as soon as Kenzie noticed their interest. She swallowed her unease. Did they really think her a whore? A trollop without family? The thought was not comforting.

"And ye think I should believe such lies. Do ye think me a simpleton?"

Kenzie shrugged. "If the shoe fits."

"What is that supposed to mean?" Athol asked, slamming her cup down and gaining the attention of those seated before them.

"Only that I do think you're a simpleton. I also think

you're a bitch who needs to stay out of my business. If the Laird of Ross wishes to have you for his wife, I'm sure he'll ask. Until then, if I want to kiss him, and," she said, leaning forward, "more than that, I will." Kenzie stood and left, walking toward the door that led outside.

A walk along the shore was what she needed to get away from this castle and, most especially, the nasty little Athol Grant. Worse of all was that Athol was right in a lot of ways. Maybe she'd been too forward, too public with her interest in Ben. She would have to temper it when in public. The last thing she wanted was to cause trouble or shame to Gwen and Braxton.

The beach curved and ran in front of the small town that Kenzie had noticed on her first day here. She walked along the stony shore, alone with her thoughts. Her most worrying one at present, was when should she return home. Already, she'd been at Castle Ross for a month. How much longer should she stay? Her whole reason for traveling back to seventeenth century Scotland had been to meet Gwen and the Laird of Ross and study the design of the castle and the outlying buildings. She'd done that.

Kenzie smiled. But she was also here to find out what had happened to Black Ben. What or who was it that had erased him from history and took his life, well before his old age?

She picked up a flat rock and faced the ocean, throwing it and watching as her attempt to make it skim across the top of the water failed. At Gwen and Braxton's estate the enemy had made its presence known, had hit at Ben when he'd least expected it.

But at his own keep, there had been no sign of anyone trying to hurt him. No threats via his person or letter. Nothing. So, what had changed? If her memory served her correctly, it was late May that the Laird of Ross disappeared from the pages of history. A ghost that was never heard of again.

So, where were they? Or, were they already here...

The sounds of shouting caught her attention, and she looked back toward the castle, watching as a group of riders came up to the gate and dismounted. Was it Clan Grant? Athol had said at breakfast that her father was coming, but today! Surely not. Or, hopefully not.

Kenzie sat on the shore and let the lulling sounds of the lapping waves soothe her. Castle Ross had certainly been blessed with its position, such as it was.

Even with the beautiful location, it was written in history that an ugly situation was going to unfold here in the next few weeks. But who was behind Ben's demise? After the many weeks of being near the laird, Kenzie's stomach twisted at the thought that his life would be snuffed out. That his son, the sweet, adorable Alasdair would also disappear. As much as she'd thought the Grants were behind his death, could they kill their own grandchild? She didn't think so, no matter how much they'd hated Aline's attachment to the laird.

The castle had burned to the ground. Had the child been lost that way? The problem with unsolved Scottish mysteries was that no one knew. And if anyone did, they had never told a soul.

She sighed. Damn it, she didn't want anything to happen to Ben or his boy. No one in their right mind would wish such a fate against another human being. So could she allow history to follow that course?

No.

There was no way in hell she'd allow history to repeat itself. She would stop anyone who thought to injure the laird and his child and damn the consequences. Ben deserved to live the remainder of his days here at Castle Ross, bringing up his boy and allowing the lad to inherit the castle as was his birthright.

No unknown, murdering bastard would win. Kenzie would make sure of that.

"Are ye alright, lass? Can I help ye with anything?"

Kenzie turned to see an elderly woman hobbling toward her on the rocky shore, and she stood, going toward her instead, lest she fall over and break a hip. Which in this time could mean certain death.

Coming up to the woman, she clasped her hand in welcome. "I'm Kenzie. I'm staying up at Castle Ross. It's a pleasure to meet you."

The older woman's eyes brightened at her words. "Oh, at the castle, aye. I'm the healer in these parts and know the laird well. I birthed the little bairn, did ye know."

"I did know that," Kenzie said, walking with the woman back toward the village. "The laird was very lucky to have you that night, considering what happened afterward." Kenzie didn't say anymore, as it was obvious to what she was referring, and the sadness that entered the healer's eyes confirmed she was aware of what Kenzie meant.

"Aye, very sad. And it pains me that the laird left these parts for a time in trying to heal his heart. He may not have loved Lady Aline, but he cared for her a great deal."

They walked into the small village. The homes, all different sizes with varying degrees of weathered thatched roofs, stretched out in front of them. Kenzie took the older woman's arm. "Which one is your home? I'll walk you back, if you like."

"Oh, I'd like that very much, thank ye, Kenzie."

Kenzie smiled, and they walked a little way on the rough dirt track that ran before the cottages facing the sea. "Have you lived here all your life?" she asked, curious. This was a person who knew Ben better than anyone else around.

"I was born here, as were my parents. My ma was a healer and taught me all that she'd learned. When the laird came home with a wife, I knew a child would follow soon. And thank the Lord, I was right."

"Alasdair is the sweetest boy, and he's growing and thriving well. Not that I'm much of an expert on children, but he certainly seems content."

"As he should be." The old woman stopped before a cottage, one of the smallest along the whole line of cottages, and pushed open the door. A rough wooden floor lay inside. A fire burned in the grate, and a pot of something that smelled like ham and onions, a delicious combination, sat over the fire, cooking.

"You have a lovely home." The place was filled with herbs and small bottles that sat on most available surfaces, but it was tidy and clean. A single chair sat before the hearth, and a small animal rug was the only luxury Kenzie could see.

"Thank ye, lass. I do love it as it's mine and no one else's." The old woman groaned as she sat, gesturing to Kenzie to join her at the fire. "Tell me, has the laird's spirits lifted since he returned home? I should call on him, but I haven't seen him since the night of Aline's death, and well, I canna help but think the laird is angry at me."

"Oh no, I'm sure you're mistaken." Not that Ben had said anything to her, and Kenzie supposed he could blame the old woman in some way, but surely common sense would prevail, and Ben could see Aline's death hadn't been the healer's fault.

No one could've known a tumor was growing in Aline's uterus. This was the seventeenth century, for crying out loud; they didn't even have toilet paper.

"You should come up to the castle one day and let go of your worry over the laird not welcoming you back. I'm sure he's perfectly fine in his heart."

The older woman's eyes narrowed as she contemplated Kenzie's words. "Ye aren't from Scotland, lass. In fact, I dinna feel yer from England either. You're a long way away from home, yes?"

Kenzie nodded. "Yes, a long way, but I will be returning home soon."

"There's talk in the village that the laird admires ye more than any lass in a very long time. Even Aline, God rest her soul, wasn't loved as a wife should be. But, as that love was not returned from her either, it matters little."

"You believe Laird Ross didn't love his wife?" Curiosity and an absurd hankering to hear someone say that Ben didn't love Aline, consumed Kenzie. To think that he could care deeply for anyone else, never open his heart again due to the loss of his wife left Kenzie more out of sorts than she liked to admit.

"Nay, not that I was aware. And it was mutual, but alas, unions such as theirs are common enough, and they made the best of the situation. I will tell ye this though, lass, Laird Ross and Lady Aline were very close, and looked out for one another. Mayhap in time they would've fallen in love, but alas, 'tis not something we'll ever know."

"I suppose you're right." Small children ran in front of the cottage windows and reminded Kenzie that she should probably return to the castle before Ben worried about her whereabouts.

She stood. "If I may, I do have a question for you, since we've run into each other and I'm in need of a healer."

"Anything lass. What is it that I can help ye with?"

"I've not been feeling very well this last week. I'm not sure if it's the food, which I'm still getting used to, or because of my monthly courses. If you understand what I mean."

"Oh, of course, lass." The older woman waddled over to a shelf beside the fireplace and searched through the many bottled ointments and tonics there. "Ah, here 'tis." The healer came back to her side, holding out a small bottle. "This is wormwood and is used to settle the stomach. Use it before ye meal, and it should help ye. If not, come back and see me."

"Thank you, that's very kind." Kenzie slid it into her pocket and clasped the lady's hand. "I hope we meet again."

"I'm sure we shall, Kenzie."

She smiled and left, ducking a little so she didn't knock her head on the small doorframe. She walked back along the beach toward the castle. Riders rode out the gate and Kenzie stopped to see where they were going, and when the first rider started toward the village, the dark unruly hair and savage scowl gave away who was heading in her direction.

She stopped and watched as Ben noticed her, his shoulders slumping. Was he relieved or aggravated to see her? From the deadly glare he was bestowing on her as he came closer on his mount, Kenzie assumed the latter.

"Hi," she said as he jumped down from his horse and stood before her with hands on hips and fists clenched.

"Where have ye been, woman? Nary a word as to where ye were going, and I'm left to worry about ye whereabouts, thinking the worst has happened and ye dead somewhere."

"As you can see, I'm not dead." She walked up to him and wrapped her arms about his waist, completely forgetting her decision to stop showing affection in public. "I saw that you had new visitors and didn't think you'd miss me too much. I'm sorry if I scared you."

He continued to stare, and she tightened her grip. "I'm quite alive and warm, maybe you'd like to hug me back?" She threw him a mischievous grin, and he relaxed a little in her arms.

"I dinna know where ye were." He paused. "Where were ye, lass?"

"With the healer in the village."

He frowned. Was it because she'd met the woman who was with Aline on the night she died or if he was concerned for her health.

"Are ye sick, lass?"

"Not now, but I have been feeling queasy. She's given me something."

He took her hand and placed it on his arm as he walked them back toward his horse. "I'll have someone speak to the cooks and make sure ye food is tasted before ye eat it. I'm not sure what ye're used to eating in your time, but mayhap, 'tis just that yer not used to our way of preparing and cooking our food."

Kenzie laughed, having thought as much herself. "The healer has given me some medicine, which will hopefully help. I'm sure it's something similar to Bali Belly."

"Bali Belly?" The word on Ben's lips sounded odd, and Kenzie smiled. "It's a term I learned when traveling in Bali a couple of years ago. It's a tropical country, and people who visit there often become sick after drinking their water or eating their food. I became a little ill there, as well, so I'm sure my stomach is just protesting like it did when I was in Bali."

They came to Ben's horse, and he hoisted her up, following soon after. The weight of him behind her, his strong arms coming about her waist to clasp the reins did odd things, lovely things, to her body.

"News arrived while you were gone as well. It seems Abby has fallen ill after the birth of her child and Gwen and Braxton have travelled there to nurse her. They've asked that you return to Castle Druiminn prior to May. Gwen was most insistent."

Kenzie understood the date and why Gwen wanted her out of here by then, but she wasn't going anywhere. Not yet at least. "Is Abby going to be okay?"

"Aye, Gwen wrote that she improves daily, but the planned visit by Aedan and Braxton will not go ahead. You may read the missive when we return, but Gwen was most sorry that they are unable to attend at this time."

He called out to his men to follow him and he turned the horse, kicking it into a canter. Kenzie snuggled back into his chest, sighing when one strong, warm arm wrapped about her waist, holding her snug. This news from Gwen wasn't welcome. It meant that they were on their own here, no back-up when it came to whoever attacked Ben and Castle Ross.

"We're going to start seeding tomorrow. I shall not see ye until late in the evening. Will ye be well at the castle, do ye think?"

Ben's question pulled her from her thoughts. "Can I help? I'd so love to see how it's done and it would give me a chance to be with you. I'll only be bored at the castle. Please, tell me I can come." She did not wish to be stuck indoors with Athol. The woman had ceased hiding her loathing of Kenzie and was often plain rude. "We could take a basket, have a picnic for lunch. We could have the wet nurse bring out Alasdair for an hour or two. Give him some fresh air and sunlight."

"He could sicken if he's taken outdoors at such a young age. I dinna think that's a good idea."

Kenzie smiled. "You're wrong, Ben. Fresh air and sunlight is good for everyone, including babies. As long as he's kept warm, fresh air will do him good."

Ben seemed to think on her suggestion before he said, "What's a picnic?"

"A basket of food that we'd share together."

The lightest kiss touched her neck. A shiver ran down her spine and Kenzie couldn't wait to get Ben alone. He may come across as a hard, medieval Highland warrior to some people, but to Kenzie, he was so much more than that. The man had a heart, one that she was terribly close to falling for. A man who was fiercely loyal and loving toward his son, and clansmen, and women. The thought that someone wanted him dead and would succeed with their plan within a matter of weeks made her stomach twist.

"After dinner this evening, I want to talk to you about something that I think you need to know about," Kenzie said, deciding that it was time Ben knew the truth.

"Ye cannot tell me now?"

Kenzie could feel Ben's inquisitive gaze on her, and she shook her head. "Not here. We need to be alone. It's something I think you'll question me about and I don't want anyone else to overhear."

"Ye will have my full attention, lass. I'll come to ye room." His hand idly ran over her stomach, and she bit her lip. "Mayhap you would allow me to warm ye bed afterward. I find my own sleeping quarters cold and not at all welcoming."

"Would that be wise with Clan Grant here? What if they catch us? You do know that Athol is aiming to marry you, don't you?" Kenzie didn't see the point of beating around the bush. If Ben hadn't seen the little minx's plans for himself then she would tell him. Not that Kenzie should be stopping him from marrying again—he ought to, no matter how much he said he was never going to have another wife. He was young, strong, a laird—it would be silly of him to remain a bachelor. Or, at least, a shame for anyone who would never get to know and love such a wonderful man.

And maybe, if he were to marry again, even to Athol —although the thought turned Kenzie's stomach—it would change his future. Twist what fate had in store for him and allow him to live out his days at Castle Ross, watch Alasdair grow into a man. Pass away as an old man with grandchildren surrounding him.

"They're housed in the opposite end of the castle and I'll not be seen. We're safe."

As they came closer to the castle Ben removed his hand and returned it to the rein. They walked through the gates to a commotion in the keep. Evan Grant and Bruce were having some sort of argument, which turned into a full-on fist fight.

Ben swore and jumped from the horse, running up to the two men who were rolling on the ground, the thump of fists into flesh loud in the otherwise quiet afternoon. Ben pulled them apart, no mean feat since both men were towers of muscular strength.

"What are ye doing?" he yelled at both of them, glaring at Bruce and then Evan. Both growled, snarling at each other like two savage dogs. Evan's nose bled, and he blew out the blood, only just missing Ben's leg.

The sight of blood, and the disgusting act, turned Kenzie's stomach, and she cringed. *Seriously, how revolting is that?* She attempted to get down off Ben's very tall horse, and the drop was higher than she anticipated, and she fell on her ass. Pulling her gown down over her knees, she stood, and all the men were looking at her.

Heat suffused her face, and she shrugged. "I'm still learning," she said, thankful when they turned their attention back on each other.

"What's the meaning behind this?" Ben asked, looking from one man to the other when both were quiet.

Bruce nodded toward Evan Grant. "Mayhap we should go into your solar, Ben. 'Twould not be appropriate out here."

Ben nodded. "Aye, fine then. Follow me, without," he said, pointing a finger at both men, "incident."

Kenzie watched them go and caught the gaze of an older gentleman she'd not seen before. A greying, bearded man who looked at her with distaste. A cold shiver ran down Kenzie's spine before he, too, turned and followed Ben and the others into the castle.

CHAPTER 13

*B*en stood behind his desk, watching as his clansman and Evan Grant wiped their bloody noses and cut brows. The Laird of Grant entered the room and stood behind his son, arms crossed and silent. "I want to know what this is about. And I want the truth."

"Evan Grant thought it would be appropriate to insult ye guest, Laird Ross. Not that I like to speak ill of a woman, but Lady Athol was also quite scathing in her remarks about Miss Kenzie."

Anger thrummed through his blood at the thought of Kenzie being degraded by anyone, especially other guests he'd made welcome at his keep. "Is that true?" He levelled his glare on Evan Grant and was pleased to see the man shift uncomfortably on his feet. Good, he wanted him to take pause, for he wouldn't stand for it.

"Yer man lies, but with the looks that Bruce has been sending yer pretty visitor, Kenzie 'tis any wonder he'd say such things. He wants her for himself, and if he can get ye to believe she's a whore, sleeps with any one of yer men, then you'll likely leave her be."

Bruce stormed across the room, and thankfully, the few guards he had standing at the back of the solar stopped the men from trying to kill each other again. "Ye lie, ye bastard. You're the one, along with yer sister, who said the Kenzie, was a strumpet, no doubt keeping many a bed warm and not only the laird's. That it was a disgrace for the lass to be here, anywhere near the future laird Alasdair, so tarnished is the woman's reputation."

Ben's eye twitched at the insult to Kenzie. "It would be unwise for Clan Grant to say such things about a woman who's a relative to Clan Macleod and close confidant to Gwendolyn Macleod."

Evan shook his head. "Why would we say such things? We have no reason. We're here as yer guests. You have my nephew upstairs—the future for both our clans. Our whole reason for coming to Castle Ross was to mend the rift between our two great houses. Why would we insult ye by saying such things? 'Tis not a sensible move."

Ben leaned over his desk, levelling both men with his thunderous gaze. "'Twould be unwise for what either of ye are saying to be true. Kenzie neither deserves to be ogled like a piece of meat by my men, nor does she deserve the censure and degradation by a clan that is here as my guest. And, if I hear of any such whisperings or see any slights in her direction, whoever that may be, they shall meet the end of my blade."

The Laird Grant stepped forward, clasping his son's shoulder when Even went to say something further. 'Twas lucky the laird had some sense when it came to his beloved boy.

"Apologies, Ben. While I'm unaware as to who speaks the truth, know that no further insult will be made, if my clan has, in fact, insulted the lass, Kenzie. 'Twill not happen again."

The Laird Grant pushed his son toward the door and left Ben and Bruce alone. Ben dismissed the guards. "Sit, Bruce," he said, taking his own seat behind the desk. "Explain. Now."

Bruce ran a hand over his jaw, wiping the blood that had pooled on his chin on his tunic. "I heard them with my own ears. Whispering in the great hall. I was busy with a kitchen maid near the alcove, not far from the fire, and I heard them as clear as I hear ye now. The kitchen lass heard their slander, too. I would not lie about such a thing. And I dinna look at Kenzie in that way. Ye know I like May and wish to marry her."

Ben hadn't known Bruce was as serious as he seemed to be toward the servant, and it cooled the hot and molten temper that had burned within him at the thought of his clansmen wishing to tup the woman he himself had become infatuated with. Actually, who he cared for more than any other, even Aline or Gwendolyn.

"I'm glad to hear it, Bruce, and of course yer words ring truer than those of Clan Grant's. Ye are my clansman, a brother to me, and I know when ye are telling the truth and when you're not. And Clan Grant are lying out of their asses."

"Aye, they are. The loathing they have for yer lass is palatable and I would be keeping a close watch on Kenzie for the time that she is staying here. I'd also not be turning my back on that clan. They make me uneasy and I dinna trust them."

Ben thought over Bruce's words. He'd never had reason to distrust his clansmen before and he wouldn't be starting now. He himself had caught the venom in Athol's eyes when it came to Kenzie, and if the lass thought to have him as her husband, then mayhap the family had taken on her view that Kenzie was an enemy that should be dealt with. Removed even.

"I thank ye for your words and support. I trust ye more than any other here, Bruce, and I'll not forget yer kindness nor your actions in defending Kenzie's honor. I thank ye for that. Say nothing to anyone but keep yer eyes open and ears to the ground, should any further whispers reach ye. I wish to know of them."

"Aye," Bruce said, standing. "Ye can count on that, Laird Ross. Now, if ye are in agreement, I shall take myself off to the kitchens and have May clean up my face. 'Tis stinging like a bastard."

Ben watched him leave and narrowed his eyes on the door. Something was afoot, and though Ben didn't know what that was, he would find out. And so help Clan Grant should they try anything stupid toward his people or himself. 'Twould not end well for them.

~

The next day, the sun burned off the dew, and the foggy morning lifted, leaving the beautiful green land with the promise of a lovely day. Ben, along with Kenzie, rode north to where his crops would be planted this year. The top paddocks had been left fallow the past year, rotated with the southern paddocks. Over the last month Ben had his field hands working the ground, removing weeds.

Men and women were already walking three oxen up and down the paddock, ploughing the land, turning the soil ready for planting.

Kenzie came to stand beside him; not even her work gown diminished her beauty. "You know, in my time we have great big farm machinery that does this for us. The days of walking an ox up and down for hours on end are long gone. Well, in developed countries, that is. In some third world areas the people still use such resources."

Ben looked out on his land, nodding to the few tenant farmers who waved in welcome. What was this farm machinery she spoke of? He couldn't imagine such things.

"A laird helping his tenant farmers to farm his land isn't normally what would happen, so I'm curious as to why you feel the need to be out here."

Ben sighed, hating the fact that by his own actions he felt the need to make it up to his people in any way he could. For letting them down the last year, being an absent landlord, a drunkard who had put his own pity before that of his people. His son.

"I need to show them that I'm here, present and willing to help to make Castle Ross a stronghold, a productive, safe place for my people. A home where my clansmen are well looked after, and their laird is willing to get off his ass and help those less fortunate."

"Well," she said, going over to the cart and picking up a small bag of grain. "I think today is a start along those lines." She walked out into the field, careful to follow the ruts the ox and plough had already turned out. "Are you coming?"

"Aye, lass." They followed the ox, dropping the seeds into the ground. By lunch, Kenzie looked tired and a little suntouched. "Come and have something to eat, lass. As ye suggested, I've had a basket of food delivered for ye, and we'll rest and eat."

Kenzie followed him toward a large ash tree and sighed

when she sat. "For a day that started off quite cool, it's turned out warm. Did you decide to have Alasdair come out or not?"

Ben watched as she swallowed some ale from a leather pouch, the little drip of drink that ran down her chin made him want to reach over and rub it away. Preferably with his mouth. "He had a little cough, so I thought it best he stays indoors today. But I'll take ye up on your idea, and we'll do something together another day."

She nodded, looking about. "This is nice," she said, taking some bread from the basket and placing a little ham into it. "I wanted to ask at breakfast, but with the Grants nearby I didn't, but why didn't you come to my room last night? I have something I want to talk to you about."

"Aye, I know, lass, and I apologize. The fight between Bruce and Evan Grant took longer than I thought it would to settle, and by the time I'd washed, it was late. I dinna wish to wake ye."

Kenzie wiggled over to sit next to him, the scent of flowers wafting from her hair, even after all the hard work she'd done. Was she always this perfect? Ben believed she might be.

"No matter what time it is, I'd welcome you."

Without thought Ben leaned forward and kissed her. She didn't hesitate, but leaned into his embrace, one hand wrapping about the nape of his neck and kissing him deeper. "Don't ever think that way again. My bed is cold when my Highlander isn't beside me."

"*Your Highlander?*" Her words brought him up with a mix of concern and delight. Yes, he was her Highlander, and she was his lass, but the time they had together would not be forever. Kenzie was returning to her century, and he was certainly not looking to marry again. The image of

Kenzie dying after giving birth to their child haunted his mind and he frowned. He'd lost Aline, put her into an early grave all because he'd wished for an heir. He would not risk Kenzie to simply gain a spare.

Ben sat back and looked out over the field, watching as the tenant farmers sat and ate their lunch a little way away. "What was it that ye wished to talk to me about, lass? Is it something ye can say here?"

If Kenzie noted his change of conversation or that he'd pulled back a little she didn't mention it, simply swallowed her bread and ham, meeting his gaze. "If I tell you what I know, you must promise me not to do anything, or react in any way that will cause alarm for your people."

A cold knot formed in his gut at her words. "What is it that ye know?"

"My trip back to this time wasn't solely to visit my ancestors, but also to learn a little more about you. I've been fascinated with the stories of Black Ben, the best longbow shot in Scotland. The tales written about you in my family's journal are almost famous."

Ben didn't think his life was worth such a tribute, but curious, he said, "Go on. What else, lass?"

Kenzie checked their surroundings and, satisfied no one was about, continued. "As you know, in my time, Clan Ross is no longer around. Of course, I'm sure there are Ross's about, but none here at your castle."

He frowned. "Aye, I remember ye sayin'"

"What I wasn't fully truthful about was when your line dies out, because it's with you, in your time, that the clan ends. You are known as one of Scotland's unsolved mysteries."

Shock ricocheted through him, and he stood, unsure what to do with such information. An unsolved mystery.

What the hell did that even mean? What happened to Alasdair? His son was only a baby. Surely, he'd not allowed anyone to harm the lad.

"Ye need to tell me all that ye know, and now." He ran a hand through his hair, anger thrumming through him. How long had Kenzie known? Well, he understood how long, since the day she arrived, and the fact she'd not told him of his future left a cold knot of anger in the pit of his stomach.

She should have told him.

"There isn't much to know. You're presumed killed, although there was never any confirmation of that, nor is your son seen again. When we were ambushed at Gwen's home I thought that the men behind your demise would show themselves again, but they haven't. There's been no threat at all, so something could have changed, but I don't want you to be hurt or Alasdair caught off guard. I'm telling you now in order for you to put in place some security measures to help stop whatever fate has in store for you."

"Ye cannot rewrite history, Kenzie. It is what it is." It could not be done, no matter how much he may wish to.

"When?" he asked, ignoring the flinch from Kenzie at his deadly tone. What did the lass expect? For him to be happy with such news? Welcome the knowledge that he would be dead before too long.

"Three weeks."

Ben skidded to a stop. "What!" That could not be true. Three weeks! He couldn't die or disappear in three weeks, and considering he'd had no intention of going anywhere again, the former must have happened to him.

He wouldn't let it happen.

"And ye tell me now!"

Kenzie stood and came over to him. "Please don't be angry with me. I couldn't tell you something like that. How could I tell you by the end of May 1605 you'd be gone? When I had no evidence, nothing to even point at to say, 'here—this is the cause?' You'd just think I was this crazy woman from the future."

Ben didn't reply. The lass made a little bit of sense, but... "I need to know of those things, so I might put in place armed men, increase my guards during both night and day to hold off any such attack. I can have men be aware and listen for any whispers of enemy talk. We're only weeks away from my supposed death and yer telling me this now."

He strode toward his horse, the need to get back to the castle, to Alasdair, bearing down on him. Nothing would happen to the lad, nor his home, or the people who took refuge there.

"Dinna follow me, lass," he said, ignoring Kenzie when she came up and clasped his leg as he tried to slip into the stirrup.

"I'm sorry, Ben. I wasn't supposed to care so much. I thought that by coming back I could keep myself removed from the people of this time, to not feel anything for what has already passed. But I can't. And I'm sorry I couldn't tell you before, but how do you tell someone such a thing without causing panic? All of what you're now feeling."

"Telling the truth can sometimes hurt, but better to know one's enemies and not be standing beside them waiting for a dirk in yer back."

"Ben," she said, pulling his reins and stopping him from leaving. "Please don't shut me out."

"What I want to know, lass, is were ye just going to stand in the keep and watch us all die. What was ye plan?

To return to Gwen and Braxton's before it occurred? I canna look at ye now."

~

*K*enzie blinked away the sting of tears as Ben galloped toward Castle Ross. She looked about and smiled at the few farmers who cast inquisitive glances her way. That they'd noticed her and Ben's argument was obvious by the uncomfortable looks they gave her in return.

She walked back over to where they had eaten lunch and packed up the small pack of food and drink before going over to where her horse was grazing and putting it into her saddle bag.

Lifting her leg, she managed to get her foot in the stirrup and get up on the saddle. Now, all she had to do was get back to the castle without getting lost. From here, she could just make out the roof of the structure, so she shouldn't have too much trouble, as long as no one tried to kill her along the way.

Medieval Scotland was a lot different to her own time. As she rode her horse, a placid mare who didn't like to exert herself too much, Kenzie thought over what Ben had said. That he was angry with her was expected, but she had never given thought to what she would have done if they were attacked when she was here.

Kenzie had just assumed…well she didn't know what she'd assumed, but it was stupid no matter what it was. She had come back to seventeenth century Scotland to find out what happened at Castle Ross and Ben on that fateful day in May. She would have to be here to see it.

And that in itself put her in danger. Not that she couldn't get herself out of this time in minutes, but still…

"Returning to the castle are ye, lass? Where's the laird?"

Kenzie started at the sound of Evan Grant as he pulled up alongside her. He was a big man, tall and as strong as Ben, but where pleasure coursed through her veins when near Ben, with Evan, her blood ran cold.

There was something about the man she did not trust or like. He was as off as food that was left out in the sun too long.

"He had to return before me."

Evan raised his brow, his gaze traveling over her salaciously. The inspection left her uncomfortable, and she frowned. "What brings you out and about? I didn't see you helping with the planting today."

"Was that where you were? Ye do know that ladies do not work in the fields like common farm hands. They're to breed our children and ensure our meals are hot, as well as our beds."

Kenzie laughed. It was either that or smack the man over the head with his own caveman club. "I see you think highly of women."

The oaf didn't pick up on her sarcasm and merely narrowed his eyes. "Not particularly. Although I do care for my sister and that is where you and I cross swords, in a manner of speaking."

"Oh. How so?" she asked, knowing her presence here had ruined all their plans. Or maybe it was her presence here that had ruined Ben. She started at the thought. Could it be her that caused his demise?

She wasn't sure, but with time travel, anything was possible. Perhaps she had returned to this time and was the reason behind Ben's death by whoever this unknown assailant was.

"Ye are a very fetching young lass, Kenzie. Are ye looking for a husband of ye own? I have not settled down as yet, and ye look the type who'd give me strong sons."

Kenzie choked on her own shock. She cast Evan a glance. He was deadly serious. Again, a chill raced down her spine, and she was sorry for whoever it was who ended up with him. Something told Kenzie that he would be a hard and possibly cruel husband.

"I'm not interested, sorry. I'll be returning home soon, in any case." Kenzie threw a half smile at him, trying to butter her reply, but he didn't fall for it and scowled.

"Yer too good for me then, is it, lass? Ye can warm the bed of the Laird of Ross, but not the future laird of Clan Grant? 'Tis insulting."

Kenzie glared at the man. How dare he be so crude and vile?

"It's also insulting that you'd say such a thing to me. If the Laird of Ross were here, would you be so honest in your opinions on what children I could birth you and how well I'd warm your bed?"

"'Twould be wise of ye to consider my offer. I think ye shall find that the laird and my sister will form an attachment, at some point, mayhap not as strong as the one between Ben and Aline, God rest her soul, but strong enough to tie the two families together once more. 'Tis only right that we have a voice in the upbringing of Alasdair."

His words gave Kenzie pause. "I thought that was why you were here now. To renew your friendship and blood ties without marriage. You've certainly not mentioned this desire to the laird as yet and you've been here some weeks now. Or is there a different reason for your stay at Castle Ross?"

To kill the laird when opportunity strikes?

"Nay, you're right, and we'd be sorely disappointed should someone come between our plans. Athol will take Aline's place, and you shall leave or marry me with very little fuss."

Kenzie's temper snapped. "Oh, I'm leaving soon enough, but I won't be marrying you, Evan Grant. I don't think we'd suit at all." If the man wanted a woman who'd cook, clean, and practically wipe his ass, she was most definitely not the woman for him.

"'Twould also be welcome if ye let Athol and Laird Ross spend some time with each other, without you as a distraction. I know the laird has taken a liking to ye, but if ye think you're any different from the many other whores who've graced his bed, ye are fooling yourself."

Jealousy coursed through her veins. Jealousy that was misplaced, since this thing, whatever this thing was between her and Ben was only short term. And damn the man, but he was right. Had she not come here, not just to this time, but to Castle Ross, Ben may have fallen for Athol, and they *may* have made some sort of future together.

Maybe it *was* her being here that killed him.

The thought filled her with dread, and she fought not to be sick. *What have I done?*

They arrived back at the castle together, not without a few odd looks from the guards at the gate or those who patrolled the battlements. Kenzie dismounted quickly and went inside to seek out Ben. She had to talk to him, make him forgive her, talk to her about what they could do to keep him alive. She hated the fact that he was angry with her.

But in all truth, she deserved it. She'd let him down.

Kenzie checked the solar but found it empty, along with the great hall. She took the stairs as quickly as she could, some of them not as high as the others, which made going up at a fast pace awkward.

The door to her room stood open, and walking past, Kenzie spied her maid sitting in the chair before the fire, mending the hem of the dress she'd managed to step on the day before.

Coming up to Ben's quarters, she knocked once, twice on the double wooden doors but heard no welcome response. Peeking inside she frowned when this room was empty also. Where was he?

The thought that maybe he'd not returned or had been hurt on his way back here had her turning and running down the corridor only to slam into a wall of muscle as she reached the top stairs step.

"*Oomph*," she said, reaching out to steady herself on his chest. He was a step or so below her and Ben was still as tall.

"What are ye running from, lass? Ye could've fallen and hurt yourself."

The chastisement after their earlier fight did nothing to lessen the panic clawing at her conscience. For the few weeks that they'd been here together, living as she would suspect a husband and wife would, she'd grown to care for this wonderful medieval man.

Never did she wish anything to happen to him. Once, he may have just been an image in a painting she'd wondered about. *Who was he? Was he ever happy? What was his life like? What happened to him?* But now? Now, the thought that he was only weeks from death left her raw and reeling.

She loved him.

"I'm looking for you. When I couldn't find you in your room, or anywhere in the castle, I worried that you'd been attacked on the road back to the castle."

He ran a hand through his ebony hair, leaving it standing on end. "I was looking for you, lass. I shouldn't have left ye on yer own. I left ye unprotected and I'm sorry for it."

Kenzie sighed. "We need to talk. Let's go to your room."

Ben nodded and strode up the passage, Kenzie beside him. How was it possible that just being beside him, feeling his strength and power, left her breathless and set her heart to pound? Ben was no longer "just a little fun" while she was visiting the past. In the short time she'd known him, he'd become one of the most important people in her life.

They entered his chamber and the key in the lock clicked loudly. Kenzie stood before the fire, wanting its warmth just in case what Ben was going to say left her cold.

"I was angry with ye. Actually," he said with a thinning of his lips, "I'm still angry with ye. I want to know why ye came back to my time? What did ye expect to achieve?"

Kenzie swallowed, choosing her words carefully. "I wanted to meet Gwen and Braxton, as you know. But I also wanted to meet you, if possible. I wanted to see Castle Ross, what it was like and how it worked before hundreds of years took its toll on the building."

"Not to mention a fire, if what ye say is true."

"Yes, that's right. In my time, Castle Ross is a ruin." Kenzie sat on the chair, folding her hands in her lap. "Ben, no one knows what happens to you or who did it. Originally, I came back to find out who it was, to solve the mystery that has haunted my family for generations. No one would believe me if I returned home with all the facts pertaining to your death and the destruction of this castle, but I had to know for myself. Maybe with research I could've solved your murder."

"And now?" He stood by the door, having not moved. His gaze was hard, hurt, and she hated that she'd done that to him.

"Now, I want to stop it from happening. The last thing I ever wished is for you to be hurt. For something to happen to Alasdair or your home you love so much. I didn't think." She swallowed, trying to find words. To voice her thoughts and feelings, some of which she'd never thought to say aloud.

"What. Didn't think *what*, lass?" His voice washed over her, commanding, but with a thread of need, of wanting to know what she thought.

"I never thought that I'd fall in love with you." Kenzie met his gaze. Never had she been so exposed. Her heart was before a pointy dagger and Ben could either remove the threat, save her, or pierce her stone dead.

What will he do?

~

*B*en had never thought to hear such words uttered to him. Aline certainly had never loved him, although they'd cared for each other a great deal. It was never this soul consuming joy that coursed through him at her words.

Once, he'd thought such emotions only made a man

weak, soft even, but not anymore. Having the love from such a strong-willed, intelligent, kind woman only made a man even more strong. "Come here, lass."

She all but ran across the room and threw herself into his arms. Having her against his chest was right, exactly where she should be. Ben breathed deep the scent of roses that wafted from her hair, kissing her temple.

"I'm sorry, lass."

She pulled back, the soft pad of her finger against his lips stopping his words. "No. I'm sorry. I should've been honest from the day we met, even if saying such a thing would be hard to hear. And there is something else that I've thought of that worries me, Ben."

He smoothed out the frown between her brows. "What else, Kenzie."

"There hasn't been any threat, and I'm worried that my being here has perhaps changed the course of that threat. Late May is when it happens, but what if it happens tomorrow? You're not prepared when you could've been. Maybe my being here is the reason you're killed. What if my coming back is actually what sparks your demise?"

Tears welled in her eyes and he pulled her against him, hating the pain in her eyes. "Lass, you're thinking too much, reading and worrying about things that are not in our control. If God almighty has me marked for a date late in May to meet him, then that is what will happen, and nothing ye say or do will alter that."

"We have to alter it. I cannot lose you."

Ben paused at her words, rocking her a little. "Kenzie, you're going to lose me either way. You're not staying."

She stilled in his arms, as if his words brought her back to sense. "I don't want to go back."

Her words, muffled against his shirt were almost

inaudible, but he heard them as if they were shouted across the room. "This isn't ye time, nor do I wish it to be. As much as I care for ye, want ye to stay. I'll not allow it. The world in which ye come from sounds as magical as you are. A place where 'tis easier to live, a place where ye have family and friends waiting for ye. Here ye have a man that loves ye as much as I fear you love him, but nothing else. 'Tis not enough."

Kenzie looked up at him, her eyes wide and as emerald as the grass on the Highland mountains. "You love me, too?"

Och, he loved her. Would miss her to the day he died with a fierceness beyond anything he'd ever known. How he would go on once she left was anyone's guess, and he would forever wonder if she'd return. Come and see him again. If he survived the attack in May that was due to happen. If history was indeed set in stone.

"Aye, I love ye. Too much to put into words."

"How will I live without you? I don't want to." A tear dropped down her cheek and he wiped it away with his thumb, cupping her face to look at him.

"'Tis a burden we'll both bear."

~

He kissed her then and Kenzie was lost. To be in his arms was where she belonged, and she couldn't face not living in a world where he did not. He was everything to her, and she couldn't lose him now. Not after she'd just found him.

Coming back to seventeenth century Scotland was not where she'd expected to find love. Nor had she been looking for it. She was young, she had a business to run, and a huge renovation project to look after. She had not thought that falling in love with a medieval Highlander would make her question her life, what was important to her. But Ben did that.

He made her question everything.

Ben stripped her of her gown and chuckled when he spied her trews hidden underneath. He picked her up and carried her to the bed, laying her down. He pulled off her leather boots, untied the cord holding her trews in place, and pulled them off, throwing them onto the floor to the growing pile of clothing.

Kenzie watched as he untied his sporran and kilt, those, too, falling to the floor with a swish. She sat up, pulling off her shirt and the light shift beneath, exposing herself to him. The breath in her lungs expelled when he did the same, the corded muscles on his abdomen flexing with each movement. He was so strong, a magnificent Highland warrior, and he was all hers.

Ben crawled up the bed and came to lay over her, hoisting her legs to sit about his waist. "I canna wait to have ye lass. Say you'll let me have ye now."

She nodded, heat pooling at her core as he undulated and teased her flesh. She wouldn't deny him a thing.

Kenzie moaned as he slid into her, deep and sure. He filled her, made love to her with sweet, endless strokes that drove her to distraction. A perfect combination of pleasure and torture—much like their relationship.

Kenzie woke the following morning warm and snuggled under a multitude of animal furs, less the man she wanted to be beside. Somehow, she'd also managed to get back to her room. A small smile lifted her lips at the thought of Ben carrying her, trying not to be seen at the break of dawn.

The sound of wood being thrown onto the fire had her looking toward the mantle where she spied her maid, busy preparing the room for her. Kenzie sat up and stretched. "May I have a bath sent up this morning?"

The maid dipped into a curtsy. "Of course, m'lady. I'll have one prepared straight away."

Kenzie watched her go, not for the first time wondering what would happen to the people who lived here. Where did they go when Castle Ross came under siege from the unknown assailant? Were they killed, driven off without the protection of a laird? Enslaved?

A little while later, the maid returned along with some male servants who set about pouring her bath with a multitude of buckets. Kenzie sat before the fire and asked one of the female servants to sit with her. The poor girl worked her hands in her lap, and Kenzie smiled, trying to calm her nerves.

"May I ask your name?"

"Of course, my name's Beth, m'lady."

"And Beth, do you like working here?" The woman's eyes widened before she nodded.

"Aye, I do m'lady. I was the late mistress' lady's maid prior to her death, may she rest in peace. I'm a Ross myself, although many times removed from the laird. But this is my home, and I feel safe here." The woman paused. "Am I in trouble, m'lady?"

"No," Kenzie said, not wanting to scare the girl. "Not at all, but there is something that I need you to do over the next week, if possible."

"Of course. Anything."

Kenzie took a deep breath. "I need you to give me a list of all the families with children that reside under the care of Castle Ross. And I need to meet with them, not at the same time, but in groups, if possible."

"Are they in trouble miss?"

"No, they're not, and that's exactly how I want it to stay."

~

*K*enzie was up to something. Ben stood at the battlements and for the fourth time that week he'd watched the woman, whom he'd die to protect, who he adored as much as his son, stride from the castle walls toward the small fishing village beyond his gates, her maid Beth, religiously in tow.

He shook his head, smiling a little at their business as Bruce came to stand beside him. "So, yer lass if off again on her mission."

"Aye, and before ye ask me what she's about, I do not know. I'd hoped she'd tell me when she was ready, but she has not."

"Yer being very trusting. Are ye not the least bit curious what her and Beth are up to each day?"

Ben was more curious than he'd ever thought possible, but he wanted her to tell him when she was ready. But now, after four days, it was time he found out just what his lass was up to.

"Did ye know that she's been visiting not just the villages, but the people that live just outside the walls? Talking to them about hygiene and food preparation. What in the name of all things holy is hygiene anyways?"

Ben grinned. "Nay, I have no idea." But the thought that Kenzie was trying to make the people who lived at

Castle Ross better left him prouder than he'd ever thought possible.

How he loved her. She was such a capable, independent woman. There was much to admire.

"I'm sure she's just trying to help, and mayhap if ye listened to her you may learn a thing or two."

Bruce scoffed. "I know all there is to know about life. I dinna need any lessons from a woman."

Ben turned at the sound of the laird of Clan Grant and his son Evan arguing in the keep below. He leaned against the battlement and watched. The lad Evan was hot-headed and too quick to wield a sword. The laird, although no more trustworthy, at least thought on matters before acting on half-truths or slurs.

"Did ye know that Evan Grant asked Kenzie to be his wife? Confronted the lass on the way back from ye planting the other day."

A cold, thundering rage stormed through him. Evan Grant had asked her to be his wife? He would kill the man for acting so presumptuously. Kenzie was his and no one else's. He should never have left her alone that day. Anything could've happened to her. She could've been killed, raped, kidnapped. The list was endless. He ought to be horse-whipped for allowing his temper to get the better of him.

"Ye aren't allowed to kill the Grant lad, Laird. 'Twould start a war that we're little prepared for."

Which was another thing that lay at Ben's feet. Had he not gone off whoring, drinking himself into a stupor for the months after Aline's death, his clansmen would be better prepared for any attack they may come up against. And most importantly, the one that was to take place in May.

He frowned, wondering if Kenzie's frenzied discussions with his people had anything to do with what history had coming for him. Was she trying to save them all?

"I have no intention of starting trouble with the Grant clan. They are my son's family, after all, but I will not allow Evan Grant to think he can even touch one hair on Kenzie's body. She's mine and no others."

Bruce turned to him, clapping him on his shoulder. "I like Kenzie and I think she'll do well as ye lady. When are ye going to ask her to be ye bride?"

That he couldn't marry the lass left Ben empty inside. He'd promised himself that he would never marry again. Never put another at risk by having his children. The past weeks he'd been sleeping with Kenzie they had been careful, and he'd had the town healer send up a portion of wild carrot to mix with her tea to stop any unnecessary complications, but still… The image of Kenzie heavy with his child, Alasdair on her hip, was a picture he'd kill to see. The realization struck him like a blow, and he fisted his hands, leaning over the battlements to regain his mind.

She was too young to die. He wouldn't ask her to marry him, no matter how much he longed to spend the rest of his life with the lass. Kenzie had made her plans perfectly clear from the start. She would return home, but if they were able to enjoy each other's company in the meantime, so be it.

"Kenzie is not like other women and dinna wish to marry just as I dinna want another wife. We're enjoying each other and nothing else. But I still do not appreciate Evan Grant pressing his desire for the lass onto her. I'll not have it."

"Ye must speak to him, for I do believe he's quite determined."

Ben frowned. "Tonight, after the evening meal, I wish to discuss a matter with ye, but in private."

"Should I be on guard? What is it about?"

Bruce threw him a concerned glance and Ben shook his head to dispel the clansman's worry. "Nay, not yet, at least, but bring with ye an open mind, for what you're about to hear may be a little unbelievable."

"Aye, of course, my Laird."

~

*B*en knocked on Kenzie's door and hearing no reply opened it, finding the room empty. He went in and shut the door, sitting on the end of her bed to wait her return. The room smelled of roses. Seeing the fire starting to wane, he threw a couple of logs and a peat block onto it.

The door swung open, and Kenzie breezed into the room like a wave of fresh, springtime air. A grin quirked his lips at seeing her before she shut the door, bolting it.

"What a delightful surprise. Have you come to sweep me up in your arms and make reckless love to me?"

If only he could, but that would have to wait. "Nay, not yet, but come here. I need ye."

She went willingly into his arms, and he breathed deep her scent. He sat his chin on top of her head, pulling her close. "What have ye been doing all day, lass? The last time I saw ye you were heading into the village."

Kenzie pulled out of his arms and he missed her immediately. Untying her cloak, she wouldn't meet his eyes as she laid the garment over the one chair that sat before the now roaring fire.

"I wasn't up to anything bad if that's what you are asking. I just went for a walk. With my maid."

"*Hmm*," he said, wondering why she didn't want to tell him what she was really up to? Did she think he would stop her from continuing her plan that she was on? "Kenzie, look at me." Reluctantly, she did. "What are ye doing, love?"

She sighed. "I've been trying to prepare the village, your people, should anything happen to you. Not that I've been coming out and saying their laird is under threat and could possibly be hurt in the next month, but just a little bit on how they can go to Gwen and Braxton, or even Laird Macleod for help. To think about where they ought to go should the town come under attack or where they could hide in the house. Building a cellar or something similar, to keep the children safe."

Ben rubbed his jaw. "When the castle goes under attack, not that I think any such thing will happen in the foreseeable future, the women and children are always sent for the hills to hide within the forest. They know to wait for it to be safe before returning. The men help fight. The town—this castle and Clan Ross will stand for many years to come. There has been no sign of threat from anywhere and I've increased the guards and lookouts. If there are any coming, we'll be ready for them."

"What if they're already here, Ben?" She kneeled before him.

"'Tis not Clan Grant."

"But what if it is? What if they want all of this for your son, but not you. If they remove you, they have all of this until Alasdair comes of age." She paused, biting her lip, and he clasped her cheek, making her look at him.

"What are ye thinking now in that brilliant mind of yers?"

"I hope, I do—with all my heart—that I'm wrong and no threat knocks on your door. I hope that my arrival here has skewed history in some way, stopped what happened to you. But if not, you need to be ready and willing to see that perhaps the threat is already close and that's why you've not heard anything from your guards."

Ben watched the flame lick the wood. Could Kenzie be right? Could Clan Grant want Castle Ross for themselves, or at least the fertile land and his cattle? But why... "It makes no sense for Clan Grant to want me dead. I'm an ally, related by my son and have done nothing to them to raise their ire. If they're in trouble I would help, and I would expect the same help in return. We are family."

"You seduced the laird's daughter, ran off with her, and married her without so much as a care toward her father to see if it was okay. Maybe the laird has calmed down after all these years, but Evan Grant seems pissed off with you most of the time. That's not normal, surely."

What Kenzie said was true and could be a reason to prepare for an attack from within the walls. Kenzie had told him that Castle Ross was burned to the ground after the attack. He would be a simpleton should he ignore anything that she suggested. The lass was educated, certainly a very smart woman, and with her help, mayhap he could outsmart the villain. "Nay, 'tis not normal, but Even Grant has never cared for others, so to take offense over anything that he says would be of no help. But I shall speak to Bruce, tell him of my concerns and put in place the appropriate measures to keep those within the castle walls safe."

Kenzie's shoulders slumped in relief, and she leaned

between his legs and cuddled him. "Thank you for listening to me. I hope what I'm worried about never comes to pass, but I think we need to do all we can to help the people under your care, your son, and yourself safe, should history prove to be true."

Ben rubbed her back and they clutched each other for a short time, the crackling of the fire the only sound in the room. "Ye didn't tell me that Evan Grant asked ye to be his wife."

$\sim$

Kenzie smiled against Ben's chest and pulled back a little to look up at him. "You weren't talking to me at the time, so no, I did not."

He cringed. "Again, lass, I'm sorry for my temper. 'Twas just what ye said was not what I expected to hear."

The thought of marrying the too-proud-arrogant-ass that was Even Grant made her stomach roil. "He asked me, and I said no. I'm not going to be his brood mare." But of late Kenzie had been wondering what it would be like to be Ben's lover forever, to marry him and possibly have his children, a little brother or sister for Alasdair.

"I think ye should leave before the allocated time that ye say the castle falls. To be certain that no matter what happens, whatever the future has set in stone for me dinna affect you, threaten yer safety and life."

Kenzie started at his words. "I can't go back before that time. I won't do it, Ben. If I can be of any help here, even if it's to protect little Alasdair, I will. Should I return home and the battle does take place and I did not stay until the end—to try and stop whatever happened to you, I would never forgive myself." Pain clawed at her stomach, and she fought for breath. To leave Ben and never see him again hurt more than she'd ever thought possible.

"I can't go, Ben."

"Ye have to go," he said, sitting up, pinning her with a hard gaze. "I will summon Gwendolyn if ye do not go back of your own volition. This time is not safe, and if what ye say is true, if what is going to happen here in under a sennight, then ye must leave."

"I can't," she repeated, shaking her head.

"Why not?"

Kenzie swallowed. "I've fallen in love with you, and to lose you not to just time but death itself, to know you didn't go on and have a long and fruitful life would be too hard to bear. Please don't make me leave."

She straddled Ben's lap. "Somehow, in my madcap adventure to see medieval Scotland and the famous Black Ben, I've found my soulmate. I never meant for any of this to happen. In my time, I'm a successful business woman. I'm not looking for a long-term relationship. But for you, I'd give up all of that, even if it's only to ensure you stay safe and alive in this time."

Ben clasped her cheeks, shaking her a little. "Ye cannot stay, no matter how much I love ye in return. You deserve to live in freedom and enjoy the wonders of yer time. Not here, where every day is a gift, or any day someone could come storming the keep and threaten all that you hold dear."

"And yet, it changes nothing, because I'm staying. And should you summon Gwen I will simply tell her what you've told me, and she'll not make me go back."

"But ye family, lass. Yer mother will be devastated, should ye not return."

Kenzie had thought about that, and maybe she could

return home just to let her mama know. To say her good-byes and leave all her properties to the current Laird MacLeod. "As much as I love my mama, and will miss her, she's not my future. You're my future. I want to stay here with you. Marry you, if you'll have me."

His silence was deafening, and Kenzie had the awful thought that his feelings were not as strong as her own. Love came in many forms. Maybe he saw her only as a little fun between the sheets? Heat infused her face, and she scuttled off his lap when he refused to answer her.

"I do not wish to marry again, lass. I know ye have ye own protection against increasing with a babe, and had ye not had such security, I would never have touched ye. I dinna need another heir. I have Alasdair. And I canna watch another woman I care about die simply to give me heirs. I will not do it."

Kenzie pulled a woolen shawl about her shoulders, the chill from the stone floor making her feet sting. "We don't have to have children, Ben." As much as she loved children, she'd be fine should she not have any. Alasdair was a sweet little boy and would soothe any pain she might have of not having her own children. You didn't have to be a biological parent to a child to be its mother. To care and love it with all that you are.

"Mistakes happen and with such, your life could be put at risk."

"My life is at risk, anyway. Every day you could die. Nothing is fail proof. You cannot wrap everyone in cotton wool to keep them from living. You did not kill Aline. She died in childbirth. An unfortunate and sad fact of life women are very aware of when they wish for a child. But we do it anyway, because, of course you do. There is no other choice."

Ben rose from the bed and joined her before the hearth. Taking her hands, he stared at her and nothing in his features gave away what he was thinking.

What is he thinking? "I'm sorry, lass. I canna marry you."

He dropped her hands and walked to the door and Kenzie stared after him, unable to comprehend what had just happened. "Pushing me away will not keep me safe, Ben."

His stride never faulted as he ripped open the door and continued down the hall. Kenzie shut the door behind him and frowned. This would never do and if he thought he could be rid of her so easily he had another thing coming. Love was worth fighting for, and no matter his dislike of the marriage act, in her heart, Kenzie was secure in what he felt for her.

She was not wrong.

CHAPTER 14

*B*en sat at the dais, breaking his fast and staring
out over his clansmen eating the morning meal
before him. The Laird of Grant sat beside him, the sound
of his chewing louder than his heifers chewing the grass in
the fields.

He took a calming breath, wanting to tell the old man
to shut his mouth but did not. Hitting out at others never
solved anything, and the Grants had nothing to do with the
fact Kenzie Macleod had asked him to marry her and he'd
cut her down with his words just as fast as he could with his
sword.

Taking a sip of mead, he sighed. He'd hurt her. Out of
his own fear he'd pushed her away, possibly bringing forth
her own departure due to his careless, fear-driven words.

"I've been meaning to ask ye, Ben, if ye are interested
in marrying my lass Athol. We've been here some weeks
now, enough time for ye to get to know the girl and see her
potential as ye wife."

Ben choked on his drink and covered his surprise with

a cough. "As much as I cared for Aline, I'm not looking to marry her sister. No matter how bonny the lass is, 'tis not what I want. Nor do I believe Athol would be pleased by such an event."

Laird Grant nodded, rubbing a hand over his graying beard. "I see yer point, and yet the lass would do well under yer care. She's bonny to be sure, but she'd also be a good mama to my wee grandson. Think on the possibility, dinna dismiss it so quickly before ye've had a chance to see all the positives such a union would bring both our families."

Ben spied Kenzie walking through the great hall toward the outer door. A thick woolen cloak sat about her shoulders and partially covered her head. No maid accompanied her. He stood, determined to ensure her safety wherever she was headed.

"The Macleod lass is not for ye, Laird. She's pretty, too, I grant ye, but she doesn't know the way of our lands, our people. 'Tis best if ye marry the family that is closest to ye outside of ye own. That being us."

Ben frowned. "Ye didn't approve of my marriage to yer daughter, Aline, so I'm curious as to why ye seem so determined that I marry her sister." Laird Grant shifted in his seat and threw a glance at his son Evan who stood by the fire.

"I know we dinna have the best of starts. I did wish for Aline to marry Laird Macleod, and yet she was happy with you. Her letters certainly seemed to show that she'd come to care for ye a great deal, and so my hatred of ye has ceased. Ye made my lass happy during the time she was here and that is enough for me."

Had Ben not been sitting, the laird's words would've

knocked him on his ass. "I cared for Aline a great deal, and I always will. She's the mother of my boy, and for that I'm forever grateful. But I'm not looking to marry again, and I do apologize for giving ye any further cause to disapprove of me, but I cannot marry Athol. No matter how much of a suitable woman she may be as my wife and mother to my boy."

The laird clapped him on the back. "'Tis what I thought ye would say, but Athol was determined to have ye as her husband, and so it was a father's duty to ask." He paused. "I must ask ye why it is ye're so determined not to marry again and give some brothers and sisters to the wee Alasdair. The lad would do well to have some siblings to love and combat with."

Guilt roared within him that he was living and his wife no longer was, due solely to the fact he needed an heir. To think of losing Kenzie in such a way tore his soul in two. "I canna ask another to risk her life by having more of my bairns. 'Twas the ultimate sacrifice from Aline, and had she not fallen pregnant, she would be alive today."

"Aye, she would've," Aline's father said, pulling a roll of bread apart and throwing some into his mouth. "And yet, had she survived or only now be trying for a child, she would change nothing of her course. The lass, no matter how prickly she may have been toward some, was a good girl and wished for children of her own. Ye would not have changed her outcome. 'Tis God's will, my boy."

Ben stood. "If ye will excuse me, Grant." He strode from the room, the words from Aline's father going around in his mind like a wheel. Mayhap, the old man was right and so, too, was Kenzie. Was he being too hard on himself in regard to his wife's death? Once married, he'd actually enjoyed the state. The marriage bed was one he'd enjoyed, and during his time with Aline, he'd been faithful. Could he do it again? Could he risk allowing himself to care for another with the knowledge that he could lose her, as well?

Ben spied Kenzie at the well, talking to three young children. Whatever she was telling the small boys, they were enthralled with her tale. What was it that she was telling them? He walked over to her and wrapped his arms about her waist, pulling her hard against his chest.

The three boy's eyes widened at the sight of their laird showing such affection in public, and they scuttled off, laughing.

"What do you think you're doing?" she asked him, her voice hard and distant. The opposite of her pliant, warm body against his own.

"I love ye, Kenzie, lass, and I want to be yours. Always."

She spun about in his arms, staring up at him, the smile on her lips bringing forth his own. "Are you serious?"

"Aye," he said, nodding. "I'm serious."

"So, you're not going to make me go home, if I want to stay here with you? Fight alongside you and stop anyone who dares to hurt the Laird of Ross?"

Ben took a calming breath, not wanting her anywhere near the skirmish that she'd predicted. Not that he would tell Kenzie so. "'Tis what I wish. I know we dinna have the best of starts, by God you've seen the very worst of me. Black Ben at his darkest, most vile, and yet, here you stand, loving me as much as I love ye, and if my fate is to die, then let it be that I die married to the beautiful, clever, vexing Kenzie Jacobs of Clan MacLeod."

Kenzie smiled, wrapping her arms about his neck

before leaning up and kissing him quickly. "So, we're to be married soon then?"

"The priest in the local village will perform the ceremony as soon as ye are willing. I am hoping though, lass, that it will be within a day or so. I dinna want ye in a different room to my own. I want ye with me. Always."

"You're sounding awfully romantic Ben. Nothing like the hardened, sword-wielding warrior history has painted you as."

He laughed. "Ye should not believe everything that ye read, lass." And never had he hoped this was the case—especially with his impending demise. Was history wrong? Had he really died, or did they just not know what became of his clan? Either way, he was going to marry the woman before him, the one and only lass he'd ever truly loved.

"True," she said, leaning up to kiss him again. This time a little less sweetly.

❧

*O*ver the next two days, Kenzie, with the help of her maid, made-over a gown she'd deemed suitable for a wedding dress. The priest, just as Ben had said, was prepared to marry them in haste and to make the celebration even more joyful, Kenzie had put out an invitation to all the villagers and clansmen of Castle Ross to attend.

On the morning of her wedding day, the castle kitchen staff had laid out an assortment of food on the tables within the great hall and all those in attendance would be free to eat and drink to the early hours of the next morning.

A little extravagant, and yet Ben had thought it a wonderful idea, and so the plan had been set. Kenzie had written to Gwen and Braxton, inviting them, too, but due to the short notice, she doubted they would get here quick enough.

A light knock on her door sounded, and Kenzie bade them enter. She turned to see Athol at the threshold, her face hardened with unrestrained hate.

"Come in, Athol. What can I do for you?" she asked, dismissing her maid who left and shut the door behind her. Kenzie went and sat before the fire, gesturing for Athol to join her there.

Athol sat and folded her hands in her lap. "I've come to ask ye to leave off this marriage plan with Laird Ross."

Kenzie had known this was coming. The lass was determined to have Ben for herself, but there was no way in hell Kenzie was letting Ben go. "I'm sorry, Athol, but that's not possible. I love the laird and want him to be my husband, and he wishes for me to be his wife. Nothing will change that."

"I am Aline's sister, and would suit the role of mother and wife much more than you. The boy is my blood."

"Alasdair, you mean. He does have a name."

Athol narrowed her eyes. "Ye are not suitable nor of high birth. Ye bring nothing to this marriage other than your ability to lay on your back and act the tramp."

Kenzie smiled, not willing to let this woman know how her words hurt her soul. She would not stoop to the woman's level, no matter how much she may wish to. "You don't know me. I fail to see how it's my fault the laird prefers me over you. Everyone has a choice and his has been made. While I'm sorry you're hurt by that choice, it is something you'll have to live with. Now," she said, standing, "I have a wedding to attend and you have a door to walk through. Good day to you, Athol."

"You'll regret this," Aline's sister said, spitting the words like little arrows.

Kenzie watched her leave. No, she would never regret marrying Ben, when one married her soulmate, regret was an emotion that could never raise its ugly head.

CHAPTER 15

They were married in a small stone church that sat at the edge of the forest beyond Castle Ross. A harpist played a tune that was unknown to Kenzie, but it was as magical as the man who stood beside her. His best kilt and whitest shirt with the Ross tartan across his shoulders and chest gave him an air of authority, a tall, strong laird beloved by all his people.

He was the best of men and from this day forward, he was hers. Which Kenzie admitted meant that the seventeenth century Scotland would be her home forever, too. Maybe after she spoke to Gwen there was a possibility that she could return home and tell her mother of her choice and say goodbye to both her and her cousin, the current Laird Macleod. She hoped.

Kenzie stood beside Ben and watched as the castle children ran about the keep. Everyone seemed in high spirits that their laird had found a woman he cared for enough to marry. The Nurse exited the castle and brought over Alasdair. Kenzie reached out and took Ben's boy. He fussed a little in her arms. When she placed her finger inside his little mouth, he settled again.

"Ye have a way with him." Ben smiled. "I'm glad."

"I'm not sure where it comes from, because I've never been a mother. But I intend to be the very best that I can be." It was a declaration Kenzie was determined to keep. And maybe they, too, would have a child together. Loving Ben as much as she did, nothing more would please her than to give him a daughter to complete their set.

Ben leaned down and kissed his son's head before kissing her. Shouts and heckling sounded from the keep and Kenzie laughed, smiling when Ben yelled out for them all to get on with their own celebrations and let him kiss his wife.

"I'm sorry that Gwen and Braxton are not here. I know ye were hoping they would attend."

"You heard from them?" Kenzie met Ben's gaze. "They weren't mad that I've decided to stay and marry Black Ben of Castle Ross.?" She laughed when he frowned.

"Nay, they weren't mad. In fact, they sent their congratulations and well wishes for the day, but with a warning."

"What warning?" Kenzie didn't like the sound of that, and with Gwen's abilities it could mean anything.

"A warning to me to be true and kind to ye or they'll bring war down on my head."

Kenzie laughed, relieved to hear it was only familial concern and nothing sinister. "I have complete faith in my choice and in you."

He kissed her again, deeper this time, and Kenzie pulled back at the sound of shouts outside the castle walls. "What is that?"

Ben pushed her toward the castle doors, and she stumbled. "Get inside, lass. I dinna know what that is."

"Ben," she said, going back to him and clasping his arm. "Don't do anything rash. This isn't late May, but it's not far off. It could be those outside the gates mean to do you harm."

Ben yelled out for his men to arm themselves, and Kenzie watched as the women and children stood about as the men transformed from clansmen enjoying their laird's wedding day to men about to defend their home and families.

The yelling for Laird Ross to come out and face the foe outside the gates increased and dread pooled in Kenzie's stomach. She watched as he strode to the stairs to look out over the gates and see who stood outside. The tensing of his body and the quick speech to Bruce, commanding him, no doubt, told Kenzie all she needed to know about how her wedding day would end.

With Ben dead and possibly her, too, since she was still here. She yelled out to the families standing about, their faces drawn and pale with worry. "Everyone, go to the safe places we've talked about. Use the exits that will give you best passage and do not, under any circumstances, come back, until you know it's secure."

The women within the walls rushed to do as Kenzie bade them, and she, too, did what Ben asked her to. She went into Castle Ross and shut the door on the keep, bolting it closed.

～

a small flicker of relief pumped through Ben, seeing the castle door close behind Kenzie and his boy. Looking down on his keep he saw his clansmen, all of them mayhap a little drunk from the earlier celebrations, but it was nothing that they'd not been before in battle.

Ben stood at the top of the battlements and watched Clan Grant, in particular Evan, the eldest boy and heir who was holding the hilt of his sword like he knew what to do with it. Which Ben had to concede, he probably did. "Are ye looking for a fight, Evan?" Ben yelled down, receiving a glare in return.

"Ye are a disgrace to the Highlands, and ye should not be laird of Castle Ross any longer. We're here to make sure our nephew is raised away from yer softness toward the fairer sex and yer weak ways with ye clansmen. Yer wife," Evan said, spitting beside his horse, "is not fit to be the future laird's mother, and we'll no stand for it."

Anger thrummed through Ben at the insult to Kenzie. She was more than fit to fill Aline's position and was certainly a much better choice than the other Grant daughter, who was nowhere to be seen.

"And I suppose that ye think that your sister Athol makes a better wife for me?" Ben laughed. "I dinna think Aline would have been too happy should I marry her sister and I'll be choosing my own wife, thank ye very much. I'll certainly not have a pompous ass like yerself telling me what to do. These are my lands, this is my castle, and I'll do whatever the hell I like within them. If I wish to be a caring, thoughtful laird toward my people and clansmen, I shall. If ye had any brains in that wee head of yours, ye'd do the same."

"After today, no one here will be left living nor will the

castle be standing. So ye can give us yer bride so we can be rid of her. That is yer only choice, if ye want ye home and people to remain as they are."

Ben laughed, throwing his head back, wondering where the poor wee man-child got his ideas. He could never let the castle fall to such a fool. Even with the knowledge of what Kenzie had told him, there was no way it could happen. Certainly not in his time. And never to Evan Grant, whom he'd never liked nor considered a threat.

"If ye want a fight today, Evan Grant, let it be between me and yerself. Whoever wins may do what he wishes with the castle and lands. But none of my people are to be hurt, should I fall."

Evan turned to his father and they conversed for a moment before Evan raised his chin. "Shall I win the bout I can promise ye the people will be unharmed, but I shall rid the world of ye wife, and yerself. Are ye in agreement?"

Ben nodded. "We're in agreement." Ben walked from the battlement and beckoned his clansman Bruce over to him. "Have Kenzie and my child pack a small bag and send them to Clan MacLeod. The Grants would never try and take that castle. Send them now, before I head out of the gates, because if there's one thing Aline taught me about her family, was that they were untrustworthy. I know Kenzie has sent the women and children away from the castle. Make sure no one is left here except the men who are willing and able to fight for their home. Ye understand?"

Bruce nodded. "Aye, of course, Laird, although I think my place is here with ye." He ran off to do his bidding, and Ben viewed his clansmen, armed and eager to take down Clan Grant. "My good clansmen, it seems the Clan

Grant want to ruin my wedding day. The future laird wants to take my son, kill my wife and me because I refused to marry one of their choosing. I will not," he yelled, raising his sword. His men roared, and Ben smirked. "The mighty Evan Grant wishes to fight one-on-one with me, and I ask ye all to come stand behind me and ensure the fight remains fair. They're wont to do what they please, should they start to lose, which he will. I need you, my good men, to guarantee that he remains true to his word."

Ben went and stood at the gates, nodding to his clansmen to open them. With his men behind him, he waited for the wooden doors to open so Evan Grant would, once and for all, be silenced forever.

~

Kenzie watched from one of the upper windows as Ben stood at the gates, his men lifting the heavy wooden pole that kept it locked. He looked formidable, strong, and capable but the underlying knowledge that Ben would die in the fight about to occur left her cold. It was too inconsequential that the Grants had turned against Clan Ross. The fight that was about to begin was written in the history books, and dread lumped in her stomach like lead.

"Wrap up Alasdair and make up some sort of carrying device so I can have my hands free. We need to leave." Her maid Beth nodded and quickly did as Kenzie asked. Kenzie went about the room and found a little woolen hat for the baby. The air this high up in Scotland was cold, and she didn't want him becoming ill.

The door burst open and in the threshold stood Ben's

clansman Bruce, his closest confidant, which only meant one thing. Ben was worried that today would not turn out to his advantage. "The laird wishes ye to leave, and I've come to make sure that happens. If ye will follow me, Kenzie."

"I'm just organizing Alasdair. I shan't be long." The maid carried the boy over to Kenzie and placed him into a hammock-like structure that hung about her neck and was held in place by another piece of cloth that tied about her stomach. The child wasn't visible unless you looked into the little hammock. Kenzie checked that Alasdair seemed comfortable and slid the little woolen hat over his head. "You should go, too, Beth. The castle could fall to Clan Grant, and I cannot promise ye safety."

"My mother is alone in the village, mistress. I should like to be with her, if you're happy with me leaving ye."

"Go," Kenzie said, ushering her to the door. She watched as the lass ran down the hall before she headed to her own room, picking up a thick shawl and placing a little dagger into her pocket.

"Are ye ready, Kenzie?"

"Yes," she said, following Bruce down the hall and toward the stairs. Roars and shouts sounded outside, and tears pricked her eyes. She placed a hand around the baby to try and protect him as much as she could, although if anyone attacked them there would be little she could do with her small dagger.

"This way, Kenzie." Bruce gestured her toward the bailey wall that had a large green vine growing over it. Pushing a part of it back, a small hidden door was revealed. "Through here."

The battle spilled into the bailey just as Kenzie went through the door, but leaving didn't take her view away from what was going on. There were many Grants, far more than she'd realized when Ben had gone out to fight Evan Grant."

Just as Ben had said, the fight was no longer just between the two of them, but clan against clan. The front door of the castle was kicked in, and as Kenzie slid down the steep hill leading away from the castle, the distinct smell of smoke met her senses. They had lit the castle on fire. So where was Ben?

At the bottom of the hill she turned to look and saw Ben and Evan. Sword clanged against sword, the sounds only broken when one would slip or stumble.

"You must leave, Kenzie, lass. There are horses in the trees just beyond. The laird wants ye at Laird MacLeod's where he will, God willing," he said, making a sign of the cross over his chest, "meet ye in a few days."

An arrow shot out from the trees near where Ben fought with Evan, and like a slow-motion horror movie Kenzie watched as the weapon distracted Ben from the threat directly in front of him.

Evan sliced and then used the sword in a dagger-like fashion, and Ben was struck. He dropped to his knees, clasping his side and the breath in Kenzie's lungs froze. She heard a woman scream and realized as she ran toward him that it was her.

"Ben," she said again, skidding to a stop beside him. Evan Grant was walking toward the castle, having completed what he set out to do. To kill the laird of Ross.

"Is it bad? Let me see," she said.

He lifted his hand to clasp her cheek before dropping to touch his son. "Get to MacLeod land, lass. Ye must leave. Now. Before it's too late.

"I cannot leave you here." Out of her peripheral vision

she saw Bruce lead two horses from the trees, gesturing her to join him.

"Ye must, lass. Save my boy and yourself." He paused, meeting her gaze. "I love ye, Kenzie. So much. I'm sorry."

Kenzie swiped at her tears, leaning down and kissing him quickly. "You're not going to die here, Ben. I can't let that happen."

He chuckled a little, but even Kenzie could tell he was losing a lot of blood. She grabbed her shawl and pressed it against his wound. Hard. "It is I who should be apologizing for what I'm about to do."

Evan Grant yelled, and Kenzie looked toward the castle to see both him and his father cantering toward her on horses. Never in her life had she ever seen anyone with such determination to exterminate someone. In this case, her, Ben, and Alasdair. Surely, they wouldn't kill their own grandchild?

"Please, Kenzie. Go. I can't see ye killed in front of me."

Kenzie sat Ben up a little, getting behind him and wrapping herself about him as much as she could without squashing Alasdair "I'm sorry Ben, but I won't leave you." And with the image of Clan Grant barreling toward them Kenzie started to speak the words that would pull her from this time into her own. The thundering of the horse's hooves made her words faster, and clasping Ben tighter, the seventeenth century started to dissolve before them. The last thing Kenzie saw was the shocked visages of Evan and the Laird of Grant as they disappeared. As if they never were and never would be again.

$\backsim$

*T*hey landed inside Druiminn Castle. Since Kenzie had the ability to pick where and when she wanted to land. So to speak. And at Druiminn Castle, her cousin and current laird of the clan would help her with Ben.

With Ben bleeding badly, she ran down the stairs, yelling out for Richard whom she hoped would be home. He met her in the Great Hall. "Kenzie, what is it, lass? You're as white as a ghost. And…" he said, stepping back and looking at her as if for the first time. "You have a baby strapped to your front."

"Please, hold off your questions about what I've done, and who I'm carrying, and please help me. I have a man upstairs, and he's bleeding badly."

Richard frowned, looking up toward the stairs. "Show me."

They ran up together, the action and all the yelling waking up Alasdair, and yet he seemed happy to lay in her arms while they tended Ben.

Richard helped Ben off the floor in the upstairs room and hoisted him onto the bed. Together they stripped him of his kilt and shirt. The clothing was soaked with blood, and Ben was pale and lethargic. Not a good sign.

"Ring down to the kitchen and have Mrs. Bell phone Dr. Thompson. Tell him to bring his doctor's bag and that we need discretion, above all else."

Kenzie ran to the phone, dialed down to the kitchens, and told Mrs. Bell all that her cousin demanded. She then ran into the adjoining bathroom and grabbed some towels and wet a face washer to clean the wound so they could see, without all the blood, how bad it actually was.

By the time she got back to the bed, Ben had slipped

into unconsciousness. "Is he going to die?" she asked Richard, fear threatening to cripple her and make her completely useless. She wiped around the wound, which had, thankfully, stopped bleeding and merely oozed a little.

"I'm not sure, lass. He may need to go to a hospital, but since I'm assuming this man would not have any identification, I'm not certain how to get around that."

It seemed to take hours for the doctor to come, but eventually he arrived. The older man came into the room, accompanied by one of the laird's employees who shut the door behind them when they left.

"What seems to be the problem?" Dr. Thompson asked, heading toward the bed. He checked Ben's temperature, frowning a little when he removed the blood-soaked bandage and seeing the gash on his abdomen. "Never mind, I see what the problem is."

"Thanks for coming out, doctor. We really appreciate it. We'd also appreciate absolute secrecy in regard to your attendance here tonight. Whatever you require in payment for your services, send it directly to me, if you will," Richard said.

"Well, let me have a look first at this wound. He may not be able to stay here." He paused, feeling about the wound. "What exactly happened?"

Kenzie met Richard's eye and receiving a nod from him, she told the doctor the details. She did tweak the story a little bit to exclude that they were actually in the seventeenth century and that it was a clan war that had erupted and ended with Ben being injured. She merely mentioned that they had been at a reenactment battle and the sword was not supposed to be real, but it was.

The look of disbelief from the doctor told Kenzie that her story hadn't fooled the man one little bit.

"Help me roll him over, so I can check if the sword went right through." Kenzie and Richard rushed to do as the doctor bade, and she was relieved to see that the sword hadn't come out the other side. Not that that meant there wasn't some serious damage done to Ben's body. He lay as still as death, his skin covered with grime and blood. Not to mention, he cringed in pain whenever they prodded him.

"While I don't believe any major organs have been injured, I will not know for sure unless you bring him into the hospital to have a CT scan. His pulse is accelerated, and he's tender across the abdomen. This could all be due to internal bleeding, but until I see the CT scans, I can't diagnose further." The doctor threw them both a pointed stare. "What is your decision?"

Kenzie frowned, having not thought of the legalities of helping Ben in her time. To have pulled him from his century had been a knee-jerk reaction when she'd thought she was going to lose him. "Call an ambulance, Richard. Ben must go to the hospital."

Within a few minutes, the ambulance had arrived and standing out in front of Druiminn castle, Kenzie watched Ben be stretchered into the vehicle before it roared out of the yard and toward Druiminn township.

"Come, I'll drive you," Richard said, wrapping his arm about her shoulder. Kenzie welcomed the support and went with him. "Bring the car around, and I'll meet you here. I just want to check that Alasdair is going to be all right with the staff."

"Of course," he said, heading off toward the car garage that had once housed carriages.

Alasdair was asleep in the nursery, a room that was kept clean and tidy at all times since it was shown off to the paying public who came through the estate to see where the current laird, and all those before him, had spent a great deal of their childhood. Seeing the boy asleep and safe in the small cot removed some of the tension haunting her these past hours.

"Thank you for looking after him so well Mrs. Bell. You've given him a bath, I see."

"I did, Kenzie. He was a little dirty and had a minor nappy rash, so I've put some cream on his bum that should relieve that until I can get to the store tomorrow."

"Thank you for doing this. I know you're not employed here to do this type of work. I really appreciate it."

"'Tis no problem at all. Ye looked very distressed upon ye arrival, so I'm happy to help."

"Would it be alright if ye stayed in the castle tonight? I'm going to the hospital with Richard, and we're unsure what time we'll be back. If I know you're here and looking after Alasdair, I'll be forever grateful."

"Nay, no thanks needed. I have nothing at home, I can stay here for one night. In fact, 'twould be the first time I've ever done such a thing. Quite a privilege."

Kenzie went up to the older woman and hugged her. "Thank you, again. I'll call with any updates, but I'm sure Richard, at least, will be back tomorrow to fill you in on what happens."

"Good luck to ye, lass, and ye man. I do wish him well and good health."

Kenzie left, biting her lip to try and hold off the tears. She hoped so, but there wasn't anything more terrifying than seeing a person you love ride off in the back of an ambulance with no idea if he would survive the night.

CHAPTER 16

*B*en remained in surgery the rest of that evening. The sword had nicked his kidney and his internal bleeding was life threatening. Kenzie paced the corridor just beside the waiting area, hating the fact she'd not acted sooner. Because of her fear of having a man with no ID, no record, nothing, she had not sought help for him as soon as they'd arrived.

She should have acted immediately, and because they'd called for a doctor first, she may have killed the man she loved.

Her heart ached at the thought of Ben not recovering. She couldn't live without him, didn't want to. For the rest of her life, she wanted him beside her.

A doctor pushed through two double swinging doors and smiled a little when he spotted her. Kenzie braced for what he had to say.

"The man has pulled through, though I did not think we could control the internal bleeding. But he's a tough one. Very fortunate."

Kenzie doubled over, relief washing through her like a balm. "Thank you so much, Dr. Thompson. I don't know how I'll ever repay you."

"As for that, I understand that the man is not a citizen. Does he have medical insurance in his own country or holiday insurance?"

Panic overtook Kenzie's relief. "He hasn't any of that. Can I make arrangements to pay the bill? I will admit, I don't know how the medical world works, but I'm willing to work with the hospital so you're reimbursed for your expertise tonight."

"Is the gentleman your husband, by chance?"

How could Kenzie forget! "Yes! Yes, he is." Although technically, not in this time, as she'd married Ben in the seventeenth century. But the priest at the family's church could surely tweak the registry to show they'd been married a week or so. She would talk to Richard about it when the doctor wasn't around.

"Then we'll put the paperwork through under your name and insurance and hope for the best. If you would give your details at the desk in A&E, they'll take care of the rest."

Kenzie took the doctor's hands, clasping them tight. "I can't ever thank you enough. Truly, Ben is everything to me. I would be lost without him."

The doctor seemed humble. "You're welcome, and 'tis my job to keep people alive if I can. I'm glad I was able to accomplish that today. Ye husband is in an induced coma, not for long, mind ye. We'll start pulling him out of it in a day or so. Putting him in this state enables the body to relax and heal. Less stress on his system. But ye may sit and visit with him later today, once he's moved up to ICU."

Kenzie nodded, understanding but wanting to go to Ben now. "Thank you, doctor." She watched him go back through the doors he'd come through, and she turned toward the administration counter, silently making another little prayer that her insurance company would approve Ben's treatment.

～

*T*he bed in which Ben lay in was beyond the softest thing he'd ever experienced, and he'd had his fair share of feathers, straw, and abundant fur skins to make his sleep most comfortable. But this bed, he shifted a little, and it seemed to hug him, and he sighed. How odd…

A cool hand touched his brow, and he fought to open his eyes, his lids resembling little, heavy stones that refused to open much more than a slit. "Kenzie," he croaked, his voice hoarse. Hell, he was glad to see the lass, which meant only one thing. They'd survived the attack from Clan Grant.

He frowned, not remembering much of what happened, but one thing he did remember was Evan and his father thundering toward him and his family, determined to slice him in two and finish him for good.

"Where am I, lass?" The room was white as a cloud, with perfect walls, and an odd, little box on the wall that had hundreds of moving people on it. The window was a massive, perfectly clear pane of glass, and he'd never seen one so big in his life.

He tried to sit up a little, but Kenzie pushed on his shoulder and bade him lay back.

"You're in a hospital, Ben. People are treated here

242

when they're sick or hurt. You've had an operation on your abdomen, which will be a little sore and tender, but you're going to be okay. You were fixed up, in short. Nothing more to worry about."

"And Clan Grant? Where is Alasdair? Did Castle Ross survive?"

Kenzie shook her head and the room spun at the thought of his son having been killed. No. Not his boy.

"The castle is gone, Ben, and so, too, is Clan Grant, but Alasdair is perfectly fine and safe. He's with my cousin back at Castle Druiminn.

"Aedan has him?" Ben sighed in relief. "Good, the boy will be safe with Aedan and Abigail."

The pain and fear etched on Kenzie's face gave Ben pause. "What is it, lass? What are ye not telling me?"

"Alasdair isn't with Aedan and Abagail. He's with Richard, the current MacLeod laird in the twenty-first century, not seventeenth. I...I..."

"Ye what?" he asked, looking about the room again. It dawned on him like a blow to the skull. "What have you done, lass?"

Tears blurred Kenzie's gaze, and she bit her lip. Never a good sign. "The day of the attack at Castle Ross, the Grants were coming toward you on their horses, and you were injured yet struggling to get back up. I couldn't run away with Alasdair and leave you to die. I couldn't allow that to happen. I wouldn't."

Ben swallowed and fought for calm as a terrible realization started to take shape in his mind. "Kenzie, tell me."

"I held the two most important people in the world in my arms—you and Alasdair—and brought you back... back to my time."

If being stabbed wasn't bad enough, Ben didn't think the severing pain slicing through his body could get any worse. But it could. The thought of never seeing Castle Ross, his clansman, not to mention Aedan, Abigail, Gwen, and Braxton... He shook his head to clear it. "Ye sent Abby back to Aedan, so ye can send me home, yes? I must return. My time isn't here."

She swiped at the tears streaming down her face, and he hated himself for hurting her. But this time wasn't his own. He didn't belong here. Kenzie may, but he would never suit. Ever.

"I can send you back, but you'll be going back to nothing. I love you too much to see you hurt so, Ben. Not to mention I don't want to live the rest of my life without you."

"They could've killed ye and Alasdair. Cut ye down as well. Ye promised me you would take care of my boy and keep him safe and yet ye put him directly into harm's way."

"Ben, calm down, I did what you would've done in my situation. When I saw them coming toward you I decided that if you were to fall, then we would fall with you."

"Ye should've headed to castle Druiminn, as I instructed ye. Had ye done so, my boy would still be in his rightful time and have Castle Ross to come home to." He struggled to sit up, and she stepped back. "It matters little. Once I'm healed, you'll send us all back to our rightful time, and I'll take back my home and lands."

"You need to understand that there is no home for you to go back to, Ben. Clan Grant burned it to the ground. It was already alight when I pulled you through time. Had you stayed, both you and Alasdair would've died. I came back in time to find out what happened to you, and your home, and I did. I now know why there is no reference of you in the tomes of history. I know why you disappeared like a ghost."

"Ye do. Then tell me, lass, because I'm most interested to hear." His voice was hard and cold, and yet he could not help but feel betrayed by Kenzie. He'd long reconciled, with his life and the time, that dying was an everyday threat.

But to think of Kenzie and Alasdair rotting in some forgotten land was too much to bear and his temper increased.

"It's because of me, Ben. It's because somehow in this magical world we live in, it was me who took you away from your time. It was me, all along, who pulled you from the seventeenth century and into the twenty-first where you can live out your days—with me. Safe from any clans who wish to battle or do you harm. Safe from Clan Grant who never forgave you for seducing their precious Aline—removing her from the MacLeod Clan who were much more powerful than your own."

"I dinna think the MacLeod's are more powerful as such, mayhap the castle is larger."

"Ben, you're changing the subject. You were never destined to stay in your time, and you didn't. The history books say as much, and I realized this when I pulled you through time. You're my soulmate. We're supposed to be together. Here and now."

"We will be?" Ben ground his teeth, not yet ready to forgive the lass for what she'd done. To lose one's home forever wasn't something that was easy to stomach. And what kind of life was there for him here? He was educated, yes, but nothing like those he'd come to believe this century boasted. He was a warrior and laird, not the type of man who lived in Kenzie's century.

Kenzie slumped in her chair, hurt clouding her eyes at his words. "You don't want to be together?"

Of course, he did, just not in this time. This was not his home. "Are ye able to send me back, should I wish it?"

"Yes, if that's what you want, but the Grants saw you disappear before their eyes. The shock on both their faces told me they'd seen something that wasn't explainable. Should you return, you'll have to explain what they saw. How it was possible for you to just disappear into thin air."

"I'll not have to explain anything, as they'll be dead. And dead men tell no lies, nor do they ask any questions."

Kenzie stood and unhooked her coat from a hook on the closed door. "I'll be back tomorrow."

"You're leaving." Well, of course she was, he'd all but said he didn't want to stay here with her. Why would she want to do the same for him?

"I need to go back to Druiminn and check on Alasdair, and I need to think."

"About?" he asked, watching her closely, and yet with Kenzie's guard well in place, she was hard to read.

"Us and what it will mean, if you go back to the seventeenth century. I need to choose whether it's something that I want, even though I love you more than life itself. But your time is hard, dangerous, and after the battle, hearing the screams of men and seeing the deadly determination on men's faces, men I'd dined with… I don't know if I can go back. I'm not sure I can handle that."

Ben nodded. What he really wanted to do was get out of this cushioned bed and take Kenzie in his arms. Wrap her up where she'd never be able to leave. He didn't want to go back, if she stayed. But what would he do here?

Other than her, there was nothing for him here. "I will see ye on the morn."

She turned and left the room without another word and the gnawing ache of indecision left him tired and weak and unsure of what the next or right move for his family would be.

CHAPTER 17

The following morning Kenzie received a call from the hospital stating that Ben had discharged himself, meaning the man had literally dressed in whatever clothing he could find and walked out of the hospital.

With Dr. Thompson's help, they were able to allow Ben's discharge under the guidance of the doctor, as long as a trained nurse would attend his wound daily until he was fully recovered.

It took Kenzie an hour or so before she found him walking through a parkland, heading toward Castle Druiminn. Without a word, he got into the vehicle, although his silence and white knuckled hands betrayed his nervousness.

They pulled up before Druiminn, and Kenzie watched Ben closely as he took in what once was his closest friend's home. The new laird, Kenzie's cousin, stepped from the front doors and smiled at Ben in welcome.

"I'm Laird MacLeod, or Richard, which is what I prefer. I'm honored to meet ye." Richard held out his hand to shake Ben's in welcome and Ben stared at it with an expression of confusion.

"In greeting someone in our time, Ben, it's customary to shake the other person's hand." Kenzie demonstrated, and Ben followed suit, relaxing a little once he understood.

"I'm Ben Ross, Laird of Castle Ross. Black Ben to those who cross me."

Richard smiled. "I consider myself warned. Now come," he said, gesturing them into the castle. "The wind is biting today, and it's much warmer before the hearth."

They followed Richard inside, and Kenzie helped Ben settle in the great hall before a roaring fire. Of course, in this time, the house had central heating, and some floors were heated, but there was nothing better than a fire to chase the chill away.

"I will go and fetch us some tea. I'll not be long."

Ben watched the laird go with a critical eye and met her stare. "You serve yourself in this time?"

Kenzie sat beside him and tried to take his hand. He pulled it away and folded it in his lap. *Will he ever forgive me?* Of course, she could send him back, but in truth, she didn't want to. She wanted to be selfish and keep him here. Where it was safe from any threats of not only the human kind, but those you couldn't see, such as disease.

"There are servants here, but the majority of the time we pour our own drinks and fetch tea. The cook does prepare the meals, though. Richard was never very good in the kitchen."

"Ye know this man well, then?"

The scathing tone gave Kenzie pause. "Are you jealous of him?" She laughed, unable to hold it back. "Unlike in your time, Ben, we don't marry our cousins. Of course, I know him. He's my family, but no, not in that way."

Ben made a non-committal sound and stared at the flames. He was angry with her, and she couldn't blame him. Not really. Had she been in his position, she would've been pissed off, as well.

"I'll go get Alasdair from the nursery and bring him down. I think he's missed you."

At the mention of his son, Ben's demeanor changed to one of happiness. Kenzie went upstairs and asked Irene to take the boy down to visit his father. She didn't return to be with them. It was probably best she let them have some alone time. Little Alasdair adored his father and would enjoy having him to himself for a little while.

At least that's what Kenzie said to herself as she plodded back to the room that Richard had allocated her when she'd returned. She was feeling all kinds of awful for ruining Ben's life. She sat on the end of her bed and stared out the window, not focusing on anything really at all.

If Ben wouldn't stay, could she?

She couldn't imagine not having him in her life, but could she give up all that she loved here for him? Leave her mother, her family, and home? There was no denying she lived a comfortable life, having inherited the family estate, something her mother no longer wanted anything to do with. And when she was back in the seventeenth century things were different. She'd thought to stay, and would have been happy there, but now, now that she was back, Kenzie wasn't so sure that decision was right for her.

Just as Ben had people in the past relying on him, she had people relying on her now. The estate, the very one Gwen and Braxton had been given by Gwen's brother, Laird MacLeod, was hers now. There was a small tenant village situated upon the lands that rented from her, some of whom worked her farmlands. She had a successful B&B

business and with the restoration of Castle Ross, that too would be a source of income for her in the years to come.

It was a lot to leave to go back to what? Ben's home had been burning when they left, and it remained a blackened shell to this very day.

Unless…

Kenzie stood and smiled. Oh yes, there was a way to keep him here, and maybe happily so. She just needed to get him better, and then she could put her plan into place.

CHAPTER 18

*B*en pushed the little black stick that Kenzie called a remote and fought to remember how to turn the blaring black box on the wall off. It was just one of many of the annoyances Ben had to deal with now that he was in the twenty-first century.

No longer was there quiet, the sounds of the sea or the tweeting of birds in the trees or his clansmen busy with their chores or maids gossiping in the halls. Now there were cars that ran past a road up behind the estate. The town lights that shone bright in the night and stole the view of the stars.

The absence of his friends: Aedan and Abby, Gwen and Braxton whom he missed more than he thought possible. Living in this time brought with it the cold, hard truth that they were all gone now. Long buried in the Scottish soil and no longer around to visit, to drink with. To reminisce old stories and sing clan songs. All of that gone.

A maid walked past the room Kenzie termed the lounge and threw him an odd glance. He supposed he was an oddity. He didn't know how most things worked. That the candles had been replaced with electricity, a magic he'd never understand.

That castles such as this one were restored, made comfortable and draft proof. Well, a lot less drafty than he was used to. That kitchen stoves were replaced with electric and gas ovens. That horses were ridden for pleasure not as a means for transportation and warfare.

Ben lay back in the chair, staring at the black box on the wall. Stupid, loud thing that it was. The only saving grace of this time were the running water and hot showers. Should he return to the seventeenth century, he would study this more and try and work out a way to have such luxuries in his home. That one invention was a marvel.

~

*K*enzie walked into the room and despaired at the boredom that she could read on Ben's face. "Get up. I want to take you somewhere."

"I'm comfortable here," he said, not moving.

She came over to him and pulled him to stand, glad that he didn't fight her considering he looked less than pleased to be moved. "We're going for a drive. I want to show you something." Now that Ben was well enough for Kenzie to take him in a car it was time to pull out her trump card. The drive wouldn't be too long, but for a man who loathed vehicles, it would be an interesting trip, to say the least.

"I know we haven't spoken of it much since you came back to Druiminn from the hospital, but before I send you back, I wanted to show you something." Something she hoped would convince him to stay.

They drove into a valley and before them lay a dense

forest of trees. It was lush and beautifully green, and Kenzie wondered if he'd even recognize the place. The trees were larger; there were more of them; and there was a road leading to his old home, yet, it was also eerily familiar.

"I know this place."

She smiled at him and continued on. Within minutes, they passed the small village that sat by the bay and Kenzie smiled when she saw Castle Ross looming on the cliff above it all, as grand and foreboding as it ever was.

"You brought me home?" His tone didn't give much away. Kenzie put the car in park before the gates and turned to him. "Come, I want you to see what I know as Castle Ross."

❧

*B*en could feel the ghosts of his clansmen, of the centuries that had passed since he'd been here. Since any laird had occupied Ross land, and a shiver stole down his back. To see his home in such disrepair, broken and burned, covered by plants and trees alike, left a gaping wound in his heart.

He should have been better prepared. Fought harder against Clan Grant. That he hadn't, and he'd allowed his people to be killed, and chased away without any support, shamed him. Ben ground his teeth and walked into what used to be the great hall.

"'Tis odd to be here. The place is the same, and yet so different."

Kenzie came and stood before him, taking his hands. "The moment I saw Castle Ross I decided I must know the man behind the name. Who was Black Ben and what

254

happened to him? And while I know all that, and I love you beyond anything in this world, you're not happy, and I want to change that."

"How?" he asked, not liking the way his lass was speaking. A sense of impending dread hovered above his head.

"If you wish, I can send you back, and I will; you just have to say when, but I need you to know that in my time, my estate, too, is a working farm. I, too, have tenants to look after, and while the system has changed since the seventeenth century, there are still people relying on me here. The home that Gwen and Braxton lived in is now mine and is where people come to stay, to visit and learn about our family and its history. I'm what people call a business woman, someone who earns money and is her own boss, her own master, in a sense."

His gut clenched, and he frowned. "Ye're not going to return with me, are ye? Is that what you're trying to tell me, lass?"

Kenzie nodded. "I'm so sorry, Ben, but I can't go back. My life is here, and I'm going to be selfish and say I want your life to be here, too. I don't want you to go back."

'Twas an impossible choice. How was one supposed to choose between one's home, land, and all the responsibilities that came with that, for the other side of their soul? Without doubt, he could not live without the woman before him, but could he live without his home? He wasna sure.

"I dinna want to leave ye either, lass, but 'tis an impossible choice you've given me. This is your time and mine is in the past. Alasdair is supposed to be the next Laird of Ross. By staying, I take his birthright away from him. All that I am, that we are, would be gone."

"Clan Grant took Alasdair's birth right away from him,

and you don't know what type of trouble you'll be walking into, should I send you back to your time. The castle is in ruins, your people scattered. How will you stay? Rebuild? Is that even possible?"

Ben ran a hand through his hair, looking up at what once was a high, wooden ceiling and now showed nothing but crystal clear blue skies. There were funds for rebuilding, for their future, but the castle had been attacked prior to being set alight, and there was a good chance Clan Grant had stolen all that he had, taken anything of value for their own keeps.

"I dinna know, lass."

"Before you decide, there is one last thing that I have to offer." Kenzie's hands were clenched before her, and she looked on the verge of tears.

"What is it?"

She stepped away from him and went to stand in the middle of the great hall. "If you stay, I can give you all this. I can help you rebuild your home in this time and have all that you want, but in my time. With me."

He frowned. "How is that possible?"

"Before I traveled back to your century, I bought this estate. I always intended to restore it to its original state. Have it as an inn, of sorts, that people could come and stay in, make it reliant on itself again."

"And now?" Ben waited for what Kenzie said next, hoping that it was what he wanted to hear.

"Now I want it for us. My ancestral home from Gwen and Braxton can be opened up to the public full time, but we'll keep Castle Ross for ourselves. Work on it together and make it a home for you, me, and Alasdair. What do you think?"

Relief poured through him like wine and striding toward Kenzie he picked her up, clasping her tight against him. "To know that I'm home, living in the castle, in the place where I grew up, was part of—to be back here with you and my boy would be a perfect consolation prize. I will not deny that I shall miss my friends, my clansmen, but I'm willing to say goodbye to that life, if this is to be our home."

"You'll stay then?" Kenzie sounded shocked, and he chuckled, keeping her against him and not letting her go.

"Did ye think that I would leave ye with such an offer as this? One that I dinna think was even possible."

"I did believe you'd leave, yes. As much as me showing you Castle Ross and what I wanted to do with it, it still isn't your time, and I know better than anyone how hard it can be when living in a place and situation that is foreign to them. But I love this place as much as you, and I had to give it one last chance, to bribe you, in a sense, to maybe change your mind. I'm not sure I can live without you."

"I know I canna live without you, and if I had gone back, I would've made ye come with me. I love ye, Kenzie, so much so that 'tis maddening."

She grinned up at him and he lifted her chin and kissed her, lingering over her lips before meeting her gaze. "When can we move in?"

"The building work is to commence next month. There is a lot to do, cleaning out the debris, rebuilding the walls, and roof, and then, the internals. But that's months away. It's a big job, Ben, are you sure you wish to take it on? It may be less work for you if you did return to seventeenth century Scotland."

"Aye," he said, laughing and looking around the dilapidated great hall, seeing only what it could be once again. "I'm ready, lass. Let's make Castle Ross our home."

She nodded, coming to hug him again. "Sounds perfect, my liege."

"That it does."

EPILOGUE

Three Years Later

"*K*eep ye eyes closed, lass. No peeking."

Kenzie allowed Ben to lead her through the second-floor halls and the area of the castle that had been restored to bedrooms. She had an inkling where he was taking her, and she smiled, enjoying the little game he was playing.

A door creaked open and he guided her into a room that was decidedly warmer than the hall. "Can I open my eyes now?"

"Ye are so impatient." His breath whispered against her ear, and she shivered. Finally, after three years of hard work, determination, tears—on her behalf—and sleepless nights, the castle was finally ready to be moved into.

"Three years of renovations will do that. Show me your surprise." She wanted to see and see now.

Ben untied the blindfold and let it drop to the floor, revealing their room, the very same as she'd had when she went back in time. Right down to the animal skin rugs to the peat by the fire, everything was as she remembered.

"Please tell me there isn't a straw mattress on the bed?"

"Och, ye wound me. 'Tis nothing wrong with a straw mattress."

She went to the bed and checked what it was they were going to be sleeping on, happy to feel a very padded mattress. Tears pricked her eyes, and she swiped them away. How was it that anyone could be so happy? She was truly the luckiest woman on earth.

The past three years hadn't been easy for Ben, but the strong, willful Highlander that he was, he'd conquered all the weird and wonderful twenty-first-century peculiarities that he'd come across and was now better than her when it came to finding something on TV to watch.

The castle was a true testament to his era, not a stone replaced was cut by a machine, the castle rebuilt by hands of clansmen who were still loyal to clan Ross, even after all these centuries. Having the men around Ben had eased him into this life, and although he still hated cars, he was at least willing to travel in them when the need arose.

"I dinna have the room made up for ye to upset ye, lass. I wanted a little piece of our past to be a part of our future. We fell in love in this very room, these walls. I want ye to remember always how much ye mean to me. How much I love ye."

"I know how much you love me." Kenzie slipped past Ben and locked the door. Turning about, she watched him as she kicked off her flip-flops and started to undo her blouse button.

"What are ye doing? There are workmen about!"

She shrugged, kicking off her jeans. "So, we'll imagine

they're clansmen going about their duties while I seduce the Laird of Ross."

A devilish light lit within Ben's eyes before he strolled over and picked her up, flinging her on to his shoulder and walking back toward the bed. Kenzie squealed and laughed as he dumped her in the middle of the mattress, coming down over her.

She bit her lip as he slid between her legs. He was still fully clothed, and the naughtiness of their behavior, the spontaneity, made her ache. She flipped open his jeans and pushed them down just enough so he could finish what they'd started.

"Eager, lass?"

"For you? Always." He kissed her hard, and she moaned as he slid into her, filling her up just the way she liked it.

It was so good, this sizzling desire that coursed between them. Ben fit her perfectly, and she lifted her legs to sit about his hips as he thrust within her, pushing her toward climax. Never before or with anyone else had she enjoyed sex so much. He made her complete in so many ways, and this was just one of them.

He kissed her hard, nibbling on her bottom lip, teasing and tantalizing her at the same time. But it wasn't enough, his slow, torturous lovemaking wasn't what she wanted right now. She needed more.

With all her might she pushed at his shoulders. Understanding dawned in his eyes and he rolled onto his back, bringing her with him. Atop him, in this position, Kenzie leaned on his chest, his heart beating fast beneath her palms even with him still fully clothed. His strong hands clasped her hips and he guided her onto him, hard and fast, allowing her to take what she wanted, almost selfishly.

"Ye're so beautiful, lass. I will never get tired of this view."

She was so close, and the deep, seductive timbre of his voice only made her want him more. His hand slid across her thigh and pressed against her sex, two fingers finding her bud and stroking her as she fucked him.

Pleasure built throughout her body, and her whole focus was on where they were joined, and what Ben was making her feel. She would never get tired of loving him, being with him, and having him whenever she wished.

Kenzie moaned Ben's name as she climaxed. Ben sat up, holding her as his own orgasm rocked through him. She watched as his eyes darkened, a loss of control before he kissed her and it was gone.

She laughed as he flopped back on the bed, pulling her with him. "I dinna intend on us doing that when I brought ye up to the room. But now that we did, I may have to sneak ye away more often. 'Tis a pleasurable pastime."

Kenzie snuggled into his side, idly running her hand across his jaw before she let it drop onto his chest. "I love you so much and I know our life is going to be filled with adventure, travel, children, and happiness. Thank you for staying. Thank you for choosing me."

Had Ben returned to the seventeenth century, Kenzie would've followed. There wouldn't have been any other choice. Even when they were only separated a day she longed to see him again, to be near him and hear his voice. There wouldn't have been any chance in hell she would've lasted the rest of her life without this man. As he'd said himself, they were two halves of the same soul. Joined forever, no matter how much time had once separated them.

"'Twas not a hard choice. As much as I wanted to

return to my time, claim my home and lands once again, I was living in a state of denial. History threw me out of that time for a reason, and a very good reason at that. When ye said you would stay, my own fate was sealed, no matter my words spoken to dissuade ye at the time. I couldn't have lived without ye, lass. Just as I never want to live without ye now. This time, although different and new, is good for me and Alasdair. My boy will grow up in a world where he isn't threatened by who he is or how much land he owns. We're free to enjoy it, and ye gave me that gift and I'll be forever grateful."

Kenzie leaned up on her elbow and gave him a long and lingering kiss. "So, either way, we were destined to be together."

"Aye, ye saved ye savage Scot, and I thank ye for it. Now come back here, and kiss me again."

"Of course, my liege. 'Twould be my pleasure." And it was, of course. Always.

Thank you for taking the time to read *To Save a Savage Scot*! I hope you enjoyed the second book in my Time-Traveler's Highland Love series.

I adore my readers, and I'm so thankful for your support with my books. If you're able, I would appreciate an honest review of *To Save a Savage Scot*. As they say, feed an author, leave a review!

And, great news, 2021 will see the release of book three in the series, *To Win a Highland Scot*. You can pre-order your copy here!

Alternatively, you can keep in contact with me by visiting my website or following me online. You can contact me at www.tamaragill.com or email me at tamaragillauthor@gmail.com.

Tamara Gill

TO WIN A HIGHLAND SCOT

A TIME-TRAVELER'S HIGHLAND LOVE, BOOK 3

Coming 2021
Pre-order your copy today!

LORDS OF LONDON SERIES
AVAILABLE NOW!

Dive into these charming historical romances! In this six-book series, Darcy seduces a virginal duke, Cecilia's world collides with a roguish marquess, Katherine strikes a deal with an unlucky earl and Lizzy sets out to conquer a very wicked Viscount. These stories plus more adventures in the Lords of London series! Available now through Amazon or read free with KindleUnlimited.

KISS THE WALLFLOWER SERIES
AVAILABLE NOW!

If the roguish Lords of London are not for you and wall-flowers are more your cup of tea, this is the series for you. My Kiss the Wallflower series, are linked through friendship and family in this four-book series. You can grab a copy on Amazon or read free through KindleUnlimited.

LEAGUE OF UNWEDDABLE GENTLEMEN SERIES AVAILABLE NOW!

Fall into my latest series, where the heroines have to fight for what they want, both regarding their life and love. And where the heroes may be unweddable to begin with, that is until they meet the women who'll change their fate. The League of Unweddable Gentlemen series is available now!

LEAGUE OF UNWEDDABLE GENTLEMEN

ALSO BY TAMARA GILL

Wicked Widows Series

TO DREAM OF YOU

League of Unweddable Gentlemen Series

TEMPT ME, YOUR GRACE

HELLION AT HEART

DARE TO BE SCANDALOUS

TO BE WICKED WITH YOU

KISS ME DUKE

Kiss the Wallflower series

A MIDSUMMER KISS

A KISS AT MISTLETOE

A KISS IN SPRING

TO FALL FOR A KISS

KISS THE WALLFLOWER - BOOKS 1-3 BUNDLE

Lords of London Series

TO BEDEVIL A DUKE

TO MADDEN A MARQUESS

TO TEMPT AN EARL

TO VEX A VISCOUNT

TO DARE A DUCHESS

TO MARRY A MARCHIONESS

LORDS OF LONDON - BOOKS 1-3 BUNDLE

LORDS OF LONDON - BOOKS 4-6 BUNDLE

To Marry a Rogue Series

ONLY AN EARL WILL DO

ONLY A DUKE WILL DO

ONLY A VISCOUNT WILL DO

ONLY A MARQUESS WILL DO

ONLY A LADY WILL DO

A Time Traveler's Highland Love Series

TO CONQUER A SCOT

TO SAVE A SAVAGE SCOT

TO WIN A HIGHLAND SCOT

Time Travel Romance

DEFIANT SURRENDER

A STOLEN SEASON

Scandalous London Series

A GENTLEMAN'S PROMISE

A CAPTAIN'S ORDER

A MARRIAGE MADE IN MAYFAIR

SCANDALOUS LONDON - BOOKS 1-3 BUNDLE

High Seas & High Stakes Series

HIS LADY SMUGGLER

HER GENTLEMAN PIRATE

HIGH SEAS & HIGH STAKES - BOOKS 1-2 BUNDLE

Daughters Of The Gods Series

BANISHED-GUARDIAN-FALLEN

DAUGHTERS OF THE GODS - BOOKS 1-3 BUNDLE

Stand Alone Books

TO SIN WITH SCANDAL

OUTLAWS

ABOUT THE AUTHOR

Tamara is an Australian author who grew up in an old mining town in country South Australia, where her love of history was founded. So much so, she made her darling husband travel to the UK for their honeymoon, where she dragged him from one historical monument and castle to another.

A mother of three, her two little gentlemen in the making, a future lady (she hopes) and a part-time job keep her busy in the real world, but whenever she gets a moment's peace she loves to write romance novels in an array of genres, including regency, medieval and time travel.

www.tamaragill.com
tamaragillauthor@gmail.com

Made in the USA
Coppell, TX
15 March 2021